A Celebration Of
FREEDOM

j. kelly wright

For Mom & Dad ... for always believing in me.

For Travis ... without whose love and support I would've never had the courage to begin writing novels.

Acknowledgments

I want to personally thank everyone who played a role in helping to make this dream a reality.

Thank you Bob & Elizabeth Collins and everyone at Gardenia Press for your expert guidance and personal attention.

Thank you Mom, Dad, Travis, Cheryl, Gretchen, Crystal, Holly, Jen V. and everyone else who helped to promote my book with as much enthusiasm as I have.

Thank you Randy Thompson, VistaGraphics, Inc., for the incredible marketing support and for believing in my professional capabilities to perform simultaneously on multiple levels.

Thank you Gerry Jordan for an outstanding cover design.

Thank you to everyone who has offered me kind words of encouragement throughout this endeavor. You may never know how vital you were in helping me to maintain the level of confidence necessary to make this happen.

Prologue

President Shane A. McAlister remembered the birth of the idea as if it had come to fruition just days ago. His eagerness to be involved was driven by a combination of his genuine desire to defeat those who threatened the free world and his longing to be accepted as a true leader of the United States.

Elected when the public longed for a fresh young face, President McAlister was the John F. Kennedy of his time. His boyish looks and youthful personality had won the hearts and minds of his followers. Born in the mountains of South Carolina, he had a genuine small town – and somewhat sheltered – upbringing that had groomed him well for the scrutiny of the public eye; life experience as a lawyer had opened the doors to his career as top public servant.

McAlister believed that he could make a difference if he were only given a chance. His party leaders confided in him their belief that he was what the country was searching for. Even if their support was built on a shallow foundation, Shane was determined to prove himself worthy in their eyes by the end of his term. Did they really believe that his small town, Southern characteristics were the only values he brought to the office?

This cooperative organization was his first attempt at an aggressive program designed to improve the State of the Union. He was determined to show his colleagues what he was made of.

Shane longed for success in this endeavor with such heated desire that he found himself distracted from efforts to complete his speech. Breaking from his drudgery, he shuffled the written notes aside and peered through the window, catching a glimpse of a family walking by in the distance. He could sense their excitement, the result of their visit to the nation's capitol, the White House ... his office. These people were the reason he chose this path in life. Their gleaming smiles infused him with the motivation to get back to work.

The Special Services of a United Free World was formed as *Homeland Security* teams were put together in the United States and abroad. The leaders of the countries involved in the *War on Terrorism* quickly realized that in order for combined resources to produce efficient results in this encounter, the effort had to involve more than just a united front on the battlefield.

As a prerequisite for success, the organizations had to train together, fight together, and provide equal support in this war. Shane requested a guarantee of support from other countries: a commitment to train men, share intelligence, and most importantly, a mutual obligation to provide soldiers for the physical and mental battles that lay ahead. Thus, the Special Services of a United Free World was born.

The temporary coalition had been put together solely to realize one goal – the defeat of the terrorist cells in the world. The group's objective was to complete the task in a period of five years. Given all factors involved, theory held that *Operation Freedom Ensure* would move to completion with speed and efficiency.

Initial concerns about trust and the unavoidable power struggle were overcome because of the true desire to defeat terror once and for all. Shane was appointed as the chairman of the powerful, but temporary, organization.

A bond of trust was forming between the countries despite a history of mistrust and deceit. The coalition could restore the faith of the citizens of the free world, confirming that freedom would survive the battle against terrorism. Involved parties couldn't ignore the possibility that this faith could result in the development of a confidence that could be misinterpreted as arrogance by those watching from a distance. Believing that the well-organized terrorist cells could be rendered extinct by putting forth minimal effort could be dangerous.

This concern occupied Shane's mind as he continued to prepare his address, a formal introduction of the coalition, to the nation. Could the countries involved in this task force truly come together as a united front? No longer just promising support, but to deliver troops to fight and intelligence to prepare an offensive strategy, this group of world leaders had a road of discovery paved in the path that lay before them.

Shane could feel the concern weighing on the minds of his colleagues around the world. Undeniable problems lingered on the horizon, but it was a necessary risk. Sacrifices were essential for a peaceful, or at least safer, world.

Weakened knees reminded Shane of the seriousness in the moment. Popularity could carry him only so far in his career. The time had come for him to exhibit the mastery of command he'd worked so hard to achieve. Under his supervision, the free world could flourish. An attempt to clear his throat caused his tongue to stick to the roof of his dry mouth. With closed eyes, he struggled to swallow before taking his place on the stage.

"Good evening, afternoon, or morning to all corners of this united world. I stand before you today, proud to be the first to witness the dawn of a new era. With the concept of a free world intimidated by cowardly acts of terrorism forced upon our shoulders, we've proven that freedom will overcome, no matter what." Applause shook the stadium-like structure, instilling a strong pride within President McAlister that had been halted on the day of the last terrorist attack.

A moment slipped by in silence as McAlister looked from one side of the stage to the other. Appointees from the Russian Federation, United Kingdom, Germany and Canada stood and applauded their new chairman.

With a raise of his hand, Shane motioned for silence. He waited for an opportunity to continuing speaking.

"It is not yet over. We all know that we have a long road ahead.

But, we will not lose sight of our main objective, Operation Freedom Ensure."

The applause started again, and the crowd began to stir with energy. Thrilled over promise of a safe and prosperous future, the attendants roared. A standing ovation signified their confidence in the team standing before them. Yelps of joy and whimsical screeches rocked the house like that of a sports arena in the midst of a Michael Jordan-led championship game. Imaginary pom-poms shook with positive aggression from the fists of the physically charged spectators. Anxious to hear what President McAlister had to say next, the fans returned to their seats, giving the press secretary the opportunity to open the floor for questions.

Securing her nod of approval, the senior white house correspondent was the first to take advantage of the moment.

"Mr. President, what will be your first plan of action?"

Other questions arose, as if a floodgate had been opened.

"How many soldiers will each country supply to this united front? Who has the most effective intelligence, and who'll be the judge of which intelligence to take most seriously?" asked the second white house correspondent in line.

Questions fired away. Seconds and minutes blended together, creating a vacuum of time. President McAlister waited with patience for the press secretary to quiet the press pool.

"We have many questions to work through. The members have written codes of conduct and have taken oaths of honesty, integrity and loyalty. This is a qualified group of world leaders who are working together toward a common goal. Do we have details to sort out? Of course we do, but we're well ahead of schedule. Most important, though, we're right on track to meet our objectives. Trust in your leaders and in the Special Services of a United Free World, for these alliances are *yours*. We will succeed. Without doubt, our objective will be met.

"Look around at the coalition before you. We pledge ourselves, as well as the citizens we represent, to be the strongest display of unity this world has ever seen. Ladies and gentlemen, I present to you the United Free World."

Applause rang out, blanketed with strength and pride. The wave of energy among the crowd gained momentum as it bounded from person to person. Cheers of confidence echoed across the horizon.

As the president walked across the stage, he executed a strong handshake with each member of his new *cabinet*. Shane took three steps down to ground level, when a quick right turn placed him in the midst of four Secret Service agents. Brisk movements carried them through an underground hallway into his car. After three years in office, Shane had made it his personal goal to end his term as president on a positive note. He sat with his head in his hands. Could this ambitious plan ever work in reality?

"Was supposed to rain today," Shane said to his driver. "But the sun's coming out. Maybe the storm will pass us by."

"Maybe, Sir."

Lifting his chin in the direction of the sunshine, Shane welcomed the warmth of the rays on his cheeks. Hidden from his view, dark clouds rolled in.

***

The tapping of computer keys echoed throughout the world in response to the speech. Electronic lines of communication moved with such force that the blue waves of electricity were almost made visible to the human eye. Surges of power from the incoming messages culminated in one central location, a terrorist-sponsored website that was known only to those who'd trained in one of their camps. Questions reflecting concerns about the stability and security of their organization were posted one after another onto the site's guest book.

Should we break from our work for a while?

Nervous that his Middle Eastern ethnicity would make him a natural target of the new alliance, the invisible voice reached out for answers from his leader. Another desperate plea appeared.

If they all cooperate, do you think they will have an easier time uncovering what we are doing?

The reader prepared his return message in upper case letters to accentuate the passion of his words. The panic of his cell made him all too aware of their emotions, a weakness he had to attempt to quell. This state of chaos wouldn't bode well for his organization. Strength, faith, and confidence were necessary if they were to achieve their goals. His words posted on the message board, leading all future inquiries.

DO NOT CARRY CONCERNS. THIS NEW ORGANIZATION FOR THE HONOR OF FREEDOM GIVES US EVEN MORE OPPORTUNITIES TO FURTHER OUR CAUSE. IN FAITH, WE WILL SUCCEED.

Wavering pangs of electronic nerves calmed themselves within minutes of the message posting. The chatter on the Web page quieted, and the men went back to work.

Monday, August 14th, Present Day

- 1 -

Shane secured the laces of his running shoes and lunged twice for a quick stretch. Stepping away from his office door, he peeked in the direction of his security team. Hearing them absorbed with talk about an upcoming pre-season football game, he knew he was in the clear. An incognito presence sometimes helped him to slip by without being noticed. But not this time. He could feel their resistance before anyone spoke.

"Sir, where are you headed?" The Secret Service agent trotted to catch up with his boss.

"I'm going out for a run. Thanks for asking." Shane formed a devilish grin.

"But, sir, you know we need to be with you at all times." The agent sounded awkward as he disciplined the president.

"Okay, well if you can keep up, come on." Shane shot off toward the door. "You might have a hard time in those shoes, though."

"But, sir—" The agent looked helpless. "We can be ready in five minutes."

"Okay, okay. Meet me at the door. But if you're not there in five minutes, I'm going without you." Shane peered back over his shoulder at the agents. They shook their heads. He knew he kept them on their toes.

Last minute plans were frustrating to them for sure. But spontaneity was necessary for him to stay grounded. Shane liked to feel like he was part of the community. The reactions he received from other joggers were fun to see. Today in particular this would do him good. He had heavy news to review, and this was the perfect way for him to unwind before settling into the business of the day.

With some surprise, Shane viewed the reports in front of him. To date, the UFW, or United Free World, had managed to find, kill, or capture an impressive quantity of known world terrorist leaders. The locations of the remaining targets were being narrowed to a short list of possibilities, and the objective of the operation was in sight. The diverse countries that comprised the United Free World had managed to work together toward their goal. Ideological differences were less important than the stability of their existence ... until the day when that threat seemed to come to an end.

The news of the death of Mohammed Atif exploded across worldwide wires, overcast by question and doubt. Although his body had been found by a special services operative and identified by the top officials of the UFW forensics team, an unsettling sense of paranoia lingered.

In his mind, Shane went over the facts in the documents multiple times. He reflected on the news, attempting once again to allow this reality to sink in. With as much doubt as confidence in truth of the report, he read the words until they were etched in his brain. Was it possible that Mohammed Atif and his top men had been found and captured? Even though this was the result of years of work, the tracking of these men appeared too simple. Almost too good to be true. Shane read the reports a final time.

The phone rang just as he finished his reading. "McAlister. Hi there, Alan, I was just planning to call you."

General Alan Jackson was the committee chairman of the *Joint Terrorism Task Force* of the United States Government. He'd developed into Shane's right-hand man in his efforts with the War on Terror and, in doing so, had also become a friend.

"Do you have a few minutes to come to my office?" Shane glanced at his wrist to see how much time he had before the announcement.

"I'll be there in a bit."

The documents held Shane's attention until his friend opened the office door.

"Hey, Alan, have a seat."

"So, Shane, what's on your mind?"

The news of Atif's assassination was hard to believe. Shane was a mastermind at logical thinking, and Alan expected to be handed a list of questions and uncertainties to clarify. Couldn't blame him for wanting answers.

"I'm pleased, of course, with our latest accomplishments as a coalition. But, Alan, I've gotta say, I'm cautiously optimistic about how easy this was to pull together. What's your take on what happened?"

"I'll explain the events with as much detail as I can. Jump in when you want."

Alan made himself comfortable in the chair facing Shane. His ten years as a general in the Marine Corps had given him the opportunity to work alongside some impressive world leaders, both domestic and international. Shane McAlister, despite his younger age, had already made his mark on Alan Jackson. He enjoyed the one-on-one interaction he had with his president, not only as a superior, but as a partner in the endeavor. While speaking, he twirled his wedding ring with his thumb.

"We'd been watching for signs of a possible link between suspected terrorists to a leader or leadership group of some sort. When we came up with nothing, we went at them from another angle. Wealthy they may be, but this organization didn't have an unlimited supply of funding. They would have to reach out for monetary support at some moment, and it was in this process that we hoped to catch them off guard."

"I remember that change in direction, Alan." Shane nodded. "Based on some information from our partners, we found signs of their activity supporting a direct link to drug traffic."

"That's right, Shane. Once we were able to trace the movement of funds to suspected terrorists, our plan was to seize one suspect in the hopes of him leading us to a larger group. That's when we located a Turkish guy, Arvidis DaKish, in Germany, who'd been shipping large quantities of opium to a variety of locations around the world. Our overseas partners were able to find him. But when our men surprised him, he shot himself to avoid any exchange of information with our team—typical, huh?"

"Right. It would've been great if we had this guy to confirm evidence."

"I know. Yet, we moved along without him, sir. When we were able to take a deeper look into his surroundings, we exposed a computer that DaKish used daily. Our operatives uncovered a world of information by exploring old emails as well as other files from his hard drive. We retrieved messages sent to recurrent addresses as well as records of many different shipping methods and destinations, showing how and where he'd been sending the drugs."

Expressing agreement, Shane's mannerisms offered evidence that he comprehended what had happened.

"A gold mine."

"You bet," Alan agreed. "Once we found that, we were confident that these contacts represented a role call of international terrorist cells. We gave our theories a test-drive by sending emails from his computer to some of the addresses that appeared most often on his mail list. By sending fake information about drug deliveries, we were able to trace the return messages, leading us directly to other terrorist cells. By doing this, we were also able to identify an address that appeared to be that of a leader."

Shane sent a questionable look in Alan's direction. "How did you know that?"

"Well, one guy replied with a vague answer to the message we'd sent. We traced the address, finding it matched the one related to several known suspicious web sites. Our men abroad took aggressive action and attacked his location, against my better judgment. I would've preferred a capture, but the popular belief was that he wouldn't be taken alive."

Shane sat in silence, hoping for a sense of relief from the news he'd been given.

"Thank you, again, Alan."

His heart pounded in an irregular beat. Butterflies in his stomach fluttered out of control as if dancing to the rhythm of a classic rock-n-roll song. Shane's nerves didn't often affect him prior to a speech, but today was different.

**

Straining to hear over the voices surrounding him, George Lonitesci moved closer to his office. Was that the phone? Another ring prompted his quick entrance through the door and, somewhat short of breath, he answered.

"Good afternoon, First Family of Fireworks, to what celebration can we add a blast for you?"

George carried his jovial persona with him through work and play. A graduate of a prestigious university in Pittsburgh, Pennsylvania, and a unique love of sciences, coupled with innate business skills, had delivered him to the leadership of his family business. Appropriate to his fun-loving style, the business was pyrotechnics, or fireworks. His personality allowed him a way to relive fond memories of his childhood each day he was on the job.

The short moment of silence from the other end of the phone encouraged George to hang up, but then he heard a voice.

"Mr. Lonitesci?"

"Yes, speaking."

"Please hold for General Alan Jackson," responded a soft voice.

Surely this must be a joke. Who was it this time? His sister? Acting as the class clown came with a price. People were always trying to get one over on him. Taking a sip from the mug on his desk, George's sour expression confirmed that the coffee had been sitting for too long. This was a bad time for joking around. He wanted to work in a few more hours of experimenting with that ocean green or turquoise color he'd always wanted to achieve.

"Mr. Lonitesci?" questioned a male voice.

"Yes, speaking. Let me guess, this must be the general?"

George's reply reeked of sarcasm.

"Actually, Mr. Lonitesci, I realize this must seem a bit odd, but this *is* General Jackson. Do you have a minute?"

"Oh, umm ... well, of course. What can I do for you?"

"I don't usually make calls like this myself, but, in this situation, I feel it's only fitting, considering the delicacy of this matter." Alan paused. "Mr. Lonitesci, before I go on, I must ask that this conversation remain confidential. Some news will be presented to the world in forty-five minutes, and the president wishes for it to be heard for the first time in his words."

"No problem, sir." George's brow wrinkled in confusion. "Well, Mr. Lonitesci—"

"Please, sir, call me George."

"Of course, George. I'm proud to say that our efforts to overcome the threat of terrorism have finally paid off. We've accomplished our goals, and we've ensured the protection of a free world. George, you're the first citizen to hear the news. How does that feel?"

"Wow, obviously that feels pretty darn great! This is unbelievable. I'm shocked – pleasantly shocked. Not that I didn't think we would succeed—" George trailed off, but he returned to the conversation after a moment. "But why are you calling *me*? I just can't see how a phone call to me would fit into your day at the moment. I mean, I know I might be a pleasure to chat with and all—" George laughed, stumbling over his words in excitement.

"Well, George, I thought my phone call might surprise you. Allow me to explain. Once we'd confirmed the results of the latest attack on an undisclosed terrorist location, the UFW coalition leaders agreed on one fact. We must celebrate. Our organization wishes to openly proclaim the victory of freedom over terrorism. So, we decided to structure an international celebration of freedom. A worldwide *Independence Day*, if you will ... complete with all the bells and whistles. That's where you come in, George."

"You want us to put together a show, sir? That hardly seems a reason to call me with this news first, does it?" A nervous laugh slipped from George's mouth.

"No, I wouldn't think so, George. But we don't want you to put together *a* show." Alan stressed the singular article. "We want you to put together *twenty-five* shows. We're looking to have the same exact show go off in all of the twenty-five major cities located in our prominent UFW member countries, simultaneously, wherever time zones cooperate, of course. We're looking for a memorable show with fireworks to be shown all over the free world. And who would be better for me to call for this job than the First Family of Fireworks? I have to say, I was proud to be able to tell the committee that this *first family* was based right here in the States. So, George, what do you say? Can you help us?"

After taking a long, deep breath, George looked at his production calendar. He had a list of jobs a mile long waiting to be put together, not to mention the family vacation planned for the following month. But there was no chance he would pass up this opportunity. This was history in the making, and the Lonitesci's were the First Family of Fireworks.

"General Jackson, my family and I would be honored. When do you expect to hold the celebration?"

"Well, that explains the direct phone call to you. The president would like to announce the date of the ceremony today. We've chosen September eleventh. We hope to bring some positive reflection to Patriot Day. Anyway, that date is one month from now. As we thought about it, we realized we'd better be sure it's even possible to get our party together by then before this was announced. Therefore, I wanted to confirm with you first. What do you think?"

"With all due respect, this is an awful lot to ask in such a short time. I'm not quite sure where I'd find the trained manpower to ignite the fireworks safely. Any suggestions?" George's hand stroked the rough stubble on his chin as he waited for an answer.

"George, we'll do all what we can to help. We can offer men from the armed services to help in the detonation of the fireworks. I understand they'd require some basic training."

"General, I couldn't be more honored. I think with a cooperative effort we can put on quite a show, or shows, around the world. Just tell me what you're looking for, and we'll get started."

George felt nervous, but elated. This was the biggest job in his family's history. He knew his father would've been proud.

"Okay, George, I'm looking forward to this. I'm certain your family is the right choice for this job. I'll be in touch again soon to discuss the details. Keep this under wraps for another half hour or so."

"My lips are sealed. I must say, this has been an honor." George spoke through a wide smile.

"The pleasure is all mine, Mr. Lonitesci ... I mean, George. Talk to you soon."

George stared at the phone in amazement as he lowered the handset to its charger, still wondering if he hadn't been the victim of the most convincing practical joke ever played. His doubt vanished when he turned on the television.

The news broadcasts were serious in tone. Each major network buzzed with the broadcast of an unexpected speech from the president. Speculation on the content of his speech varied widely, since no one knew why he was making this announcement on such short notice.

The thrill of being one of the few in the know about the matter intoxicated George. His desire to tell someone, anyone, what he knew drove him to sit alone in his office until after the president spoke.

* * *

"You're on in five, Shane," reminded the vice president. "Is there anything you need from me?"

"No, I think I have everything I need. I've been preparing to make this speech for years." Shane's voice trailed off in thought as he hooked the tiny microphone to his shirt collar.

A flashback of three years earlier reminded Shane of his occasional nervousness before speaking. The calmness in his stomach reminded him of the changed times ahead.

-2-

Long strides moved Shane over the loose planks of the makeshift halls. Accompanied by his security team, he rushed through the back stairwell to the temporary stage that had been constructed at Manhattan Memorial Park, NY. Shane was energized by the support he received from his international colleagues. This choice of setting was the unanimous decision of the UFW council. To Shane, this represented an obvious token of appreciation to the United States for the prominent role they'd played in their recent triumph. Convincing the Secret Service that this venue was the best choice wasn't so easy, though. They'd get over it. Signaling for his escorts to pause, Shane waited for Alexei Gousev, the Assistant Chairman of the UFW, to catch up.

Alexei worked with President McAlister in the coalition. Like Shane, he'd been elected to his role by a unanimous vote of the coalition members. He possessed a strong will to defeat the world's terrorist network, and he carried with him the complete support and resources of his home country, the Russian Federation.

Born the son of a Soviet military officer, Alexei learned at an early age to respect the goals of his country. In his teen years, Soviet Russia dissolved. He witnessed firsthand the turmoil and economic devastation associated with a fallen regime. Alexei's hard work in school brought him to a position within the ranks of the new Russian hierarchy, where he'd hoped to find a different world than that which had taken his father from him. He was still searching.

Alexei felt confident that he'd proven himself a valuable player in his leadership role within the UFW. Relentless in his drive, he'd often given President McAlister the necessary encouragement to take blind steps into unknown terrorist *battlegrounds* around the world. When doubt seeped into the offices of the UFW, he was the one to remind everyone of the coalition's mission, handing out his share of encouragement to the members of the council. His positive attitude was a role model.

As his friend approached, Shane watched with a grateful heart. Without Alexei's support throughout this battle, he knew he would've had a difficult time continuing forward with focus and drive. Under Alexei's direction, key intelligence had been obtained, and under his command, UFW military initiatives were executed. Shane wondered if he would've ever made it to this day without the help of this man.

In private, he scolded himself for all of the times he'd questioned the true interests and motivations of his Russian colleague. A smile crept its way into place along the lines of Shane's lips. The man walking his way radiated comfort, like an unexpected visit from an old friend. In the end, everything had been handled with honesty, integrity and determination. Shane's paranoia was unwarranted after all.

"Come on, Alexei, let's not keep the world waiting," joked McAlister. He couldn't remember a day so bright in years.

With smiling faces, Shane and Alexei walked stride for stride in the direction of the stage. Their glowing facial expressions were enough to ignite the spectators into a cheer.

***

In the midst of a Pennsylvania summer thunderstorm, George Lonitesci worked to create the largest set of pyrotechnic shows ever put together. Still not having perfected the formula for turquoise fireworks, he'd decided to forego this project in favor of designing the Celebrate Freedom shows.

Time didn't permit for experimentation of additional colors. In less than thirty days, formulas had to be set, shows designed and fireworks manufactured. Company efforts would be exhausted in the creation of the show designs and the training of the help alone.

Preoccupied while rounding the corner from his office, George neglected to see his nephew, Tony, galloping toward him. Loose-leaf papers exploded into the air and fell to the ground like large pieces of confetti. George grabbed Tony's arm, hoping to keep himself from toppling over. The final sheet of airborne paper floated to rest on the elder Lontesci's forearm.

"Geez, George, I haven't seen you in this much of a frenzy since you set the state capital building on fire during a show," said Tony Lonitesci, joking. He snatched the floating document. "I wish you could tell me what this big shebang is all about. That might help to get my creative juices flowing with the design of these shows, if you know what I mean." Admiration of his uncle shone in his devilish grin.

George bent over to retrieve his scattered paperwork. "You'll know soon enough. In fact, let's head to the television. I think it might be just about time. Besides, I'm already working on the designs for this show, and they're coming along nicely, if I dare say so myself. You just get started on the orders for that list of sup-plies that I gave you. And put rush orders in wherever possible. I'm not kidding when I say that this show is huge."

George nudged Tony in the direction of his office.

"Here we go, I think they're ready to start." Taking a seat in an armchair, he focused on the old nineteen inch TV that sat in the corner. "Turn it up, will you please?"

"What? I can't hear ya, old man." Stretching from his position at George's desk, Tony turned up the volume. He winked as he caught his uncle's eye.

* * *

With pride, Shane McAlister approached the podium to stand before an anxious audience in Memorial Park. Behind him sat the council members of the UFW and Shane's crew: the Vice President of the United States; General Alan Jackson, the U.S. Anti-Terrorism Task Force Director; and several additional members of his cabinet. Warm blood ran through his veins as he charged himself up to begin speaking. Exhilaration pumped his heart with the strength of a jackhammer.

"Ladies and gentlemen of this proud United Free World, I stand before you today prepared to make a most satisfying announcement. Through intense forensic studies, a number of intelligence missions, and information from undisclosed sources in the Middle East, we've come to the conclusion that the whereabouts of Mohammed Atif have been accurately identified and approached. A strategic initiative of the Special Forces of the United Free World has proven successful in containing Atif, along with others we believe to be five of his main cell leaders. An attack in the middle of the night killed these individuals."

A contagious expression of welcomed shock moved from face to face among the listeners. An explosion of chatter instigated the shuffling of notebooks, clicking of voice recorders and mumbling into cell phones. Shane observed the immediate action of his press secretary in his attempt to quiet the crowd. Once he felt confident that he'd regained their full attention, the president continued.

"Verification of their identities has been confirmed by the UFW Forensics Team. Ladies and gentlemen, Mohammed Atif is dead." The roaring applause reminded Shane of earlier announcements he'd made. How fabulous it felt to be delivering the news that they'd succeeded.

"Through our research, we've also been successful in identifying a number of terrorist cells throughout the world. Our forces have detected, located, and killed or captured a number of suspects."

Shane waited as the crowd absorbed the news. He observed pencils hanging frozen in mid-air and voice recorders capturing the awkward silence. This is for real, people.

In a delayed reaction, the audience cheered as the long awaited news was celebrated. Shane and his colleagues knew the press would have many questions, and they were prepared to answer. Joined by his partners on the Manhattan stage, he welcomed this festivity. The time had come to celebrate freedom.

***

With Tony by his side, George stared at the television in disbelief. Based on the work order from the general, he'd imagined a large celebration. This was far better than his wildest dreams. It's over. The fear of terror that surrounded everyday life was now believed to have passed. The United States had survived longer wars, but this one had been a new type of battle. Most free world citizens wondered if this war would ever be won.

George knew he had to get his team started right away. He had his work cut out for him.

***

If computers could recognize humor, they were laughing. The messages came with less frequency, but their direction remained the same.

This is what we have been waiting for.

The first voice sang through the electronic lines. The message posted at 1:58 p.m., five minutes after President McAlister delivered his closing words.

-3-

"Hey, Tony." George strained to peer into the next room. The position of George's desk made it difficult for him to see. A sharp pain darted from the base of his neck to the top of his shoulder. Darn pinched nerve. "You still out there?"

"Right here. I'm working on these orders. What's up?"

"I just want to make sure we have enough supplies. With such short notice, potassium perchlorate might be hard to come by in these quantities. But we do need every bit of what we've allocated for this. I can't think of another oxidizing agent that'll be as effective, at least not with the complexity of these shows. And, they all have to be exactly the same." George stressed the importance of the symmetry.

"George, relax." Tony's tone carried a mild sense of annoyance. "I just mentioned that I was working on the orders ... potassium perchlorate to be exact. I know it'll be difficult to find in large quantities, for a rush order at that, but I've got it under control. There's a chemical plant in China that makes this specifically for the manufacturing of fireworks. We can place our order on-line and receive shipment in three days. We'll be just fine. I've sent an email inquiry to confirm that they have enough product. They're checking on it."

"Have we dealt with this company before?" inquired George.

Tony annunciated each word with crisp clarity. "The truth is that we have an aggressive deadline to meet. I've used them before. In fact, if you ever reviewed your invoices, you would see that recently they've been the *only* supplier I've used."

"I'm sorry, Tony. You're right. I should leave the ordering to you. You've demonstrated time and time again to be more efficient in this end of the business than anyone, including me. I'll go back to the design of the show, since that's where I shine. Keep up the good work."

"Nice word choice. Now get goin' on the most awesome *shining* you've ever achieved. If we can pull this off, we'll be more than just the First Family of Fireworks ... we'll be the only family in fireworks." A proud smile spread across Tony's face as he winked at his uncle.

Years ago, a pre-fabbed desk in the corner of the shop had become the youngest Lonitesci's workspace. Even though it was old and cluttered, it still felt comfortable to Tony. He rolled his chair over to face the computer and waited for his emails to download. The first of three new messages was from the Chinese chemical supplier.

He read the confirmation of inventory. Anxious to start the work for the fireworks, he scrolled to the supplier's website in his list of bookmarks. Several clicks of the mouse took Tony to the home page. In seconds, he'd entered the quantity of product he needed. After checking his work, he pressed the button to send his order.

Electronic waves traveled the mysterious roadways of the World Wide Web. Tony waited as the computer screen in front of him flashed from the yellow background of the site's home page to a blank white template. Jargon at the top of the page indicated a redirect of paths. Before he could read the message, a white security warning box popped up in his view. He clicked the *ignore* button and waited for his order to process. All systems go!

The page took some time to load, so Tony read through the list of his remaining inventories. Was potassium perchlorate all that he needed from this supplier? After reviewing his notes, he looked up to find a confirmation page awaiting his approval. He clicked his agreement to the order and proceeded to confirm his billing and shipping information.

* * *

The typing began again.

Our wait is almost over.

The echoes of the keys could be heard around the world, if only the average person was aware of what to listen for. The wheels were set into motion.

-4-

Shane could hardly wait for the crowd to quiet to announce the plans for International Celebrate Freedom. He was sure this would be recorded as a profound display of unity among countries, as well as a celebration to top all others.

"Ladies and gentlemen, I share in your excitement and relief." Shane tried to speak above the noise of the crowd. He waited until the audience stopped to listen. Years in politics had taught him how to effectively silence a group. When idle chatter replaced roaring, loud voices, he spoke.

"I'd like to continue with the announcement at hand, but I feel it's only fitting to turn the podium over to my assistant chairman, colleague, and friend, Alexei Gousev. I know he's anxious to discuss our plans." Shane moved aside to welcome Alexei to the podium. The celebration was Gousev's idea.

Alexei had come to Shane with the thought of a celebration within a short time after reading the intelligence and forensics report confirming the death of Atif. He suggested this event to demonstrate what true dedication and unity could accomplish for humanity. He was also behind the idea to set the date of the celebration for September eleventh, Patriot Day. Shane was nervous about the concern from the rest of the committee, but, in the end, Alexei's persistence had won everyone over.

Shane felt guilty for questioning Alexei's motives. His colleague's actions had proven his desire to support the mission of the UFW. Shane had made a pact with himself to stop doubting Alexei's motives months ago. This was the dawn of a new era. The cold war was history. The time had come to take steps in a new direction, for a new world of freedom and unity. That felt refreshing.

"Welcome, welcome." Extending his right hand, palm up, Alexei stood straight and addressed the crowd with pride. He was a bit surprised that Chairman McAlister had turned this segment of the assembly over to him. He hadn't formally prepared, but he was ready to talk about the celebration.

"I am proud of collaboration displayed by Special Services of United Free World. I am also proud of patience and support by citizens of member countries. Without all these, our efforts would have been weak and our objective not reached. In honor of our thanks and pride, we, the Committee of the UFW, announce the first ever International Celebration of United Free World, we call Celebrate Freedom!"

In American fashion, the gatherers raised their arms and yelled out praise for the plan.

"Right on, brother," yelled one onlooker, intoxicated with enthusiasm.

Alexei waited for the applause to quiet. "With this, we celebrate unity, freedom, and dedication to our cause. We celebrate a victory, and you are all invited." His mouth opened wide to offer a smile.

Shane observed Alexei's slightly crooked teeth. This characteristic made the Russian's face appear distorted in the sunlight.

"This celebration is planned for September eleven with fireworks displays in many cities."

Alexei looked to Shane to continue. While waiting for his colleague to speak, he wiped his clammy palms on his pants.

"This fireworks display is symbolic of freedom from the battle against terror. The consistency of the shows is symbolic of unity, and the bright colors represent the outcome of a chemical reaction. When chemicals are put together and given necessary elements to produce results, many times, scientific progress is achieved. Likewise, through our combined efforts, we accomplished great achievements in the battle against terror. Now, that's impressive.

"Following the fireworks, the real party begins. Each participating country will host its own celebration. Our lives will be getting back to normal, if anyone can define that term anymore. Once again, I say thank you. I'm honored to have played this role in history and to have been able to bring us all to this new beginning. Thank you."

"Mr. President?" The senior white house correspondent stepped up, ready with her first question. "How can we be certain that this war is over? Do you believe the chance exists that we're celebrating too early?"

"It's over," Shane assured her. "It might be hard to believe, but it's true. Mr. Gousev led the forensics team himself in confirming the evidence. Next question."

"Mr. President, this question is for both you and Mr. Gousev," called the second white house correspondent upon his signal from the Press Secretary. "Would you say that the two of you and the other members of the committee are in agreement about this celebration? Do you think the date of September eleventh is appropriate, and if so, how was our country chosen to be the first to launch this celebration?"

"I will take this, if you allow it, Mr. Chairman," Alexei requested.

Shane nodded and stepped back to open the floor to Alexei.

"When I started in discussions about this organization, I had questions. From an eastern nation, I had doubt that any other country would watch my back ... as you say."

Alexei's crooked grin followed his words. He welcomed return smiles from Shane and the members of the audience.

"I listened to them, and I knew we all shared same concerns. We fear future terrorist attacks, and we feel desperate fighting them alone. Forming a united front made sense. This was the only way. Every man hesitated. But when our committee met in private, we realized we all play on the same team. To survive in this war, we need to work together. I tell you this now, and I ask you to listen: this organization would not have success or power without this man beside me."

While grasping the microphone, Alexei used his free hand to motion toward Shane. The concentration of the committee members behind him held his attention.

The cast of the UFW crew initiated another round of applause. Alexei waited for a more quiet moment to finish speaking.

"Any celebration of victory should be first in the United States. There is no better day than September eleven. Of this, we all agree."

A short but intense round of applause echoed from the crowd.

Shane stepped forward to the podium. "We need to wrap this up. We have other stops to make and we're eager to get moving. I thank you all for coming, and I ask you to stay informed of the activities of September eleventh. They thought Woodstock was a big deal –" The president flashed his playful, boyish smile in the direction of the press pool.

Shane watched as the crowd responded in their usual favorable manner. With limited time left in his term, he hoped for an easy ride to the finish line. A final but brief gesture toward his committee members marked the close of the press conference.

***

The plans were under way. The date in September had given them an aggressive goal to meet, but their targets were broad. The confirmation of the chemical order set the plan in motion, and they remained on course. One message sent a clear picture to all who read it.

The shipment has been set. We have succeeded.

The bragging voice reflected a strong ego. Internet chatter sparked through the wires. Now all that was left to do was to wait.

-5-

The delivery van carried Chuck along the New Hope, Pennsylvania highway to the Lonitesci Fireworks plant. Something about a truck full of boxes marked "Careful, Highly Explosive Material - Handle With Care" made him a bit more nervous than usual. His boss had assured him that the warnings were nothing more than precautionary, and he confirmed that the contents of the boxes would only be dangerous if they were mixed with other chemicals. None of that information mattered at the moment. This was his fourth twelve-hour workday in a row, and he was anxious for his well-deserved vacation to begin.

The overtime Chuck Lyons had been working had helped him to save a handsome vacation fund for a two-week trip with his wife, Robin. They planned to spend the first week with her family and they were off to Jamaica for the second.

He was actually leaving the country. Having never been out of the country before, Chuck was excited, and he knew Robin was, too. He could already see himself on the beach, a lager in his hand. Maybe one of those reggae bands would be playing in the background. He'd never been a big fan of that music, but anything was better than the crackling of his dispatch radio.

The trip to the Lonitesci plant marked his last delivery of the day. Once the order had been accepted, he'd be on his way home to begin his vacation. He jumped down from the van, still thinking about his approaching time off. The creaking of the metal door to the plant's delivery entrance jolted Chuck from his daydreaming.

"You must be as happy to see us as we are you. I'll be taking quite a load off your hands," Tony said, welcoming Chuck inside. "How many boxes do we have? I know it should be quite a few. If it's more than fifteen or so, I'll have you drive around back to the loading dock."

"Well, sir, we have a fair amount." Chuck flipped through the pages of the shipping manifest. "I'd say eighteen to twenty. Sorry, I lost count while loading up. Got distracted by all the warning signs posted on them boxes. What exactly is that stuff? I'm kinda surprised it was shipped standard air delivery. Don't they make special arrangements for stuff like this? I mean, don't guys who work with chemicals wear special suits or something?" Chuck's facial expression implied an element of genuine, if uninformed, concern.

"You don't have to worry, my man." Tony released a friendly chuckle. "Alone, this stuff can't do any harm. It needs to be triggered by something else. In other words, until it's put together with the other ingredients, it's just a boring old chemical. Hey, what happened to this box?" Tony gestured to the corner of the pile, where he noticed a box that had been taped up along the seams.

"Oh, yeah, sorry. That box got a little damaged. It didn't seem to have any effect on the merchandise, even with all of the warnings. So my boss told me just to tape it up. You know, since you all were in such a hurry. You can refuse delivery if you want. I don't mind. I'll be on vacation after today."

"Don't worry about it. I *am* in a hurry, and I need every bit of this delivery in order to meet our ship date. Shouldn't be anything wrong with it. Potassium perchlorate is about as harmless by itself as a common cleaning product. Ha, it's probably even safer than some of the cleaning products out today. Let's get it loaded in."

As they stacked the boxes in the stock room, Tony noticed that the packaging was different than other shipments he'd received from this company. In the past, the orders came packaged in iron drums. In this case, all of the containers were wooden boxes. At least they were sturdy. He opened the top box and observed that everything seemed to be in order.

After signing for his delivery, Tony sent Chuck on his way, wishing him a grand vacation. He thought about asking where Chuck was going, but a glance at his watch reminded him that he'd better get back to work if he ever hoped to take another vacation himself.

A push of the button closed the large door that separated the manufacturing plant from the loading dock. The vibration of the door blended with the background noise, the sounds of machinery echoing from the tall warehouse ceilings. All systems were on track for the most impressive display of fireworks ever. Tony was certain that the celebration would be one for the history books.

Strolling through the plant, he remembered exactly what it was about this business that made him so proud. It was the way that his products impacted the lives of everyone who saw their shows. Tony wasn't only in charge of ordering the supplies, although lately he sure felt that way. He was also the Sales Manager of the company. He took pride in every show, and the results were always the same —smiling, happy people. Witnessing adults as excited as children while viewing the fireworks shows made him proud to be able to spread this feeling around.

Tony felt somewhat responsible for the royalty status of the Lonitescis in the world of fireworks. He was aware that their reputation had rewarded them with this job. As he let himself into his uncle's office, he heard George on the phone.

"But, sir, with all due respect, I'm not sure this is such a good idea. Have these men ever worked with pyrotechnic detonation before? I'm not confident that a simple instruction manual is sufficient to ensure the safety of these men and of our staff. Can't we at least send a video? I can have something prepared in a week or two, and then my staff could follow up by phone." George stopped talking. The look of disgust on his face signaled that he may have been interrupted.

Tony watched as a faxed document fluttered in the grip of his uncle's hand. He recognized an official government insignia at the top of the paper. His efforts to read the rest of the fax were thwarted as George rolled the paper into a cylinder and bounced it up and down on his desk in an irritated fashion.

"Yes, sir," continued George. "We'll do our best."

George placed the phone on the receiver, and slumped back in his chair. He held the cylindrical fax behind his head with both hands as he let out an audible sigh.

"This might be tougher than we thought, Tony. I'm questioning whether we can succeed in this venture while maintaining our safety standards." His eyelids drooped, and he was weary with concern.

"Uncle George, of course we can do it. The supplies have all made it to us right on time, and the production team is working around the clock to meet our deadlines. You know as well as I do that nearly anyone can set off modern day fireworks. They're as idiot proof as they could be. Plus, I thought the people who were going to help us were military personnel. You couldn't ask for a more disciplined group to work with." Tony spoke with confidence, and he meant every word that he said.

"Tony, what would I do without you?" A smile returned to George's face as he gave his youngest nephew a pat on the back. "Are you hungry? I told your Aunt Marian I'd come home for lunch. You feel like tagging along? She's got a plate full of her famous homemade perogies waiting for me. As great as they taste, I sometimes find it hard to get up and come back to work after a lunch like that." George rubbed his round belly.

"Sounds good. Just let me take care of a few quick things, and I'll meet you at the car." Tony respected his uncle. He knew his father would have, too, if he were alive to see what his brother had accomplished with the business. "Hey, George, you don't expect me to be able to entice you back to work after Aunt Marian's lunch, do you? I mean, I'm good, but no one's that good."

"Of course not. I don't expect miracles. I just thought that if you decided to take a nap after lunch, then I won't have to feel so guilty about resting myself." George tilted his head in playful question. Revived from his earlier stress, his eyes sparkled with new energy.

* * *

Shane looked over the list of Celebrate Freedom cities. Even after multiple readings, the information didn't change. The list needed to be cut by nearly half, because in order to keep a consistent display for the fireworks, he had to limit the number of venues for the show. The other cities can still celebrate at the same time, they'll just have to supply their own fireworks. No big deal.

A chuckle escaped from Shane's mouth. He realized how trivial this matter was compared to what he'd been dealing with for the past three years. The quiet giggle evolved into unmistakable laughter.

On a yellow sticky note, he wrote a message to General Jackson.

Please edit and revise. Cut number of sites by fifty percent, and get back to me.

He spoke aloud as he wrote. An afterthought provoked an extension to the note.

Please be sure to include a broad sampling of cities both in U.S. and abroad. Domestic cites should equal approximately twenty-five percent.

Again, Shane recited his written words. When he finished writing, he looked up to find his secretary at the door.

"Is that what you wanted to have delivered to General Jackson?" asked Cheryl Williams. "There's a package going to the Pentagon now."

Cheryl had been the executive secretary to the president for the past six years. Born and raised in Kentucky, she'd been intimidated by living in D.C., to say the least. With open arms she'd accepted the opportunity to expand her horizons by meeting the elite crowd. Cheryl enrolled in secretarial school after having followed her high school sweetheart to the city. Her then fiancé, Robert, was in the armed forces, and he traveled often.

Elated by the news of her pregnancy a short time after her marriage, she was still nervous to share the information with her husband. She knew that working and raising a child with an absentee father would be difficult, but she felt up to the challenge.

Following her business school graduation, Cheryl was introduced to the working world. She landed a job as an office manager in a retail store where she met her first official business contact in Washington, D.C.

Hard work on her resume, combined with some good old-fashioned motivation, landed her an interview for a secretarial position at an area law firm. She charmed Shane McAlister with her southern personality, which she knew he would relate to. When she accepted her first position with Shane, she never imagined that one day she would be working alongside the President of the United States.

Times had been tense in this office, but the air was so much lighter these days. Cheryl watched as even Mrs. McAlister moved about as if a heavy weight had been lifted from her shoulders. These days, being at work was a walk in the park.

"That's right. Still time to get this in the package?" Shane asked, reminding Cheryl of the memo to Alan.

Cheryl blinked her eyes and returned to the moment.

"No problem. But he's not in right now. His assistant called to say he'd stepped out, in case you asked."

"Okay, just make sure she gets this in front of him as soon as he gets back. Thanks, Cheryl."

***

Examining the list in his hands, Alexei paced from the media center to his office. He spoke aloud to the empty room.

"This is quite a list."

His staff wouldn't arrive for three more hours. He'd gotten used to working late at night. With his U.S. partner, this seemed to be the only way he could stay involved with day-to-day activities. Funny though, because he was eight hours ahead of Washington. Shane McAlister should be the one to have to work in the off hours if he wanted to stay on track. Trying to rationalize this argument was pointless. McAlister ran this show, not Russia, and certainly not Alexei.

Without question, he felt that the Russian Federation was viewed as the redheaded stepchild in this coalition. He was halfway surprised that his country had even been invited to join the group. Oh well, this was life. The bottom line was that Russia and the United States were allies now. Fighting to accomplish common goals had made them cordial partners. But this partner had to be at work in the middle of the night to make sure he was included in any UFW business that went on throughout the workday of President McAlister. Paranoid? Alexei didn't think so. He was just eager to be involved.

Alexei feared that the one time he would leave work before one o'clock in the morning, Shane would make a big decision without him, right at the end of his workday in Washington. He didn't want to take any chances. Not even now, when the only mutual business left was to plan a celebration. But this wasn't just a celebration. This was a turning point for the world, and Alexei wanted to make sure that he was prepared.

* * *

Shane reviewed the revised list of participating cities for Celebrate Freedom. "This is much better, and obtainable," he mumbled. "Twenty-five cities worldwide, celebrating independence from the fear of terror. Now that's something to be proud of."

"Hey, Cheryl, you mind faxing this over to the Lonitesci office? Put it to the attention of George Lonitesci. I know he's been waiting for this."

"No problem. And, if it's okay with you, I'd like to remind you I'll be on vacation in September."

Licking his finger, Shane separated the pages of his calendar. "September tenth through the fifteenth, right? In Orlando? That sounds like fun. And you'll still get to see the Celebrate Freedom show. The proposal that Disney submitted to be included in our participating cities was impossible to overlook. Is this a family trip?" She was a single parent, and he knew she could use some time away. Shane was sure this would do her good.

"Yes, sir. My daughter, Hannah, was given the trip by the Make-A-Wish Foundation. She's always wanted to go to Disney World. Gosh, my daughter's so excited she can hardly sleep, and I'm looking forward to some time away from this city myself."

"Do me a favor and remind me about a week before you go. You know how my memory can be."

In all of the craziness over the years, Shane had never lost sight of Cheryl's situation. Her daughter had AIDS. A blood transfusion at birth had left the child stricken with the disease. She was only ten years old.

It was shocking that as recently as ten years ago people were still contracting HIV through blood transfusions. It didn't happen often back then, but one occurrence was one too many.

Hannah's condition had been upgraded from HIV positive to AIDS six months ago. Her father chose to exercise his skill of poor timing and took the opportunity to ask Cheryl for a divorce. A rough few months followed for them.

Thrilled that Cheryl and Hannah had this opportunity, Shane was pleased that he'd written the letter to the Make-A-Wish Foundation. Everyone at the White House had signed it. Just because he was the president didn't make him too good to do something nice for a friend. He was confident that no other mother-daughter pair deserved this trip more.

*　*　*

George carried the fax into the conference room where Tony

waited for him. Both men, still full from lunch, looked tired.

"Well, here it is, Tony. We kick off simultaneously in New York, Washington, D.C., Atlanta, and Orlando. Now, we have to decide who will travel to Great Britain, Canada, France, Italy, Germany, the Russian Federation and all of these other countries. Oh well, we have a few weeks for that. Check with our crew and see who is available. I don't want to ruin anybody's vacation plans."

"No problem, Uncle George. Hey, we should've opted for that nap after lunch. I'm exhausted, and it's your fault. I wish you'd never put that idea in my head!" Tony spread his lips wide apart and engaged in a yawn. The corners of his jaw cracked.

With concurrent movements, the two men looked at their watches, realizing the day was only half over. In less than a month, everyone could partake in a well-deserved rest. For now, it was back to work. One behind the other, they exited the conference room.

Friday, August 25th

-6-

The sun had barely broken the horizon of the western Pennsylvania sky. Morning humidity lingered with a final push of summer weather. Tony Lonitesci had kicked off his blankets hours earlier, in an attempt to get comfortable. He could hear the birds singing outside the bedroom window. In what seemed to be ten or fifteen minutes time, the sounds had been transformed from chirping crickets and the distant hooting of owls.

Tony had slept little the night before. The thoughts of work responsibilities had kept him lying awake for what seemed like most of the night. Now, in the early hours of morning, he realized it was time to get up and start his day. Closing his eyes, he made a last desperate attempt to salvage a few more minutes of sleep. A ray of sunshine filtered through the mini blinds as if it were aimed at his eyelids. He squinted as he reached over and smacked the alarm clock. It was set to go off in three minutes anyway. No use fighting it. Coaxing his feet over the side of the bed, he stood.

Exhaustion was painted on his face. The dark half moons below his eyes accented his heavy lids. Even splashing cold water in his face didn't help. If he wasn't under such a crunch with the Celebrate Freedom show, he may have considered taking a sick day, or at least going in late. But there was no time for self-pity. This show had to go on in less than three weeks, and so much work was left to be done. There would be plenty of time to rest after September eleventh.

While in the shower, Tony made a mental list of things to do that day. To date, his crew was a few steps behind on the production of the fireworks, but all they required was some reorganization to guarantee delivery on time. For his plan to work, he needed to get back on the line and help with the labor. Years ago, he'd graduated into management, an easier job, which bore a lot more responsibility, but very little hands on manufacturing work. However, this was his only choice if he was to meet his deadline, and he refused to risk disappointing his uncle. Anyway, it would be fun getting his hands dirty again.

Tony questioned whether the anxiety building deep down inside his gut was the result of excitement about the show or nervousness about going back on the line. Either way, in a few short weeks, the work would be over. He just wished he had a little more energy. This wasn't the time to be getting sick. He convinced himself that his fatigued state was the result of too little sleep. He wasn't getting any younger.

The sticky, heavy air outside enhanced Tony's sluggishness. He dragged himself into the garage and plopped into his Pathfinder. As the electronic garage door opened, he found himself feeling thankful that he didn't have to get out and manually open the door.

Motivated by the reminder that his vacation was planned for right after the celebration, he plowed forward. The time off would be necessary. He backed out of his garage and into the street. No one in his cul-de-sac was up this early, so he owned the road. Chalk one up to rising with the sun. In sync with his character, he found a positive to leaving early in the morning. Smiling, he headed on to work.

At the plant, George greeted Tony in the parking lot. Draping his hand over his nephew's shoulder, he escorted Tony toward the door.

"Hey there, early riser. I thought you were gonna get an extra hour or so of sleep this morning. I meant it when I said you were no good to me, or this project, sick. Plus, your Aunt Marian would never forgive me if I worked you until you dropped."

"I know, Uncle George. I feel okay. Plus, I couldn't sleep any-way. I kept thinking of things I wanted to get done once I got here, so I thought I'd just come in. I can always go home early."

"All right, son. I do appreciate your dedication to this com-pany. Your father would be proud. But, promise me, if you start to feel any worse, you'll take some of that cold medicine your aunt swears by and head on home. We'll get this done. Don't you worry." George flashed his nephew the look of a concerned father.

"Okay. I'll come knockin' if I need the miracle cure, Uncle George. You know we had three men out sick yesterday. Maybe they've got a touch of this flu that you think I have."

As he spoke, Tony wiped the sweat that dripped from his fore-head. "Or, maybe they just can't handle this humidity. What a sticky day. This thick air alone can beat a person down. I'm gonna crank up the air in the plant, if that's okay with you."

"No problem. Do what you have to, son. I'll be in my office if you need me."

Tony nodded and walked ahead to the plant entrance, as he watched his uncle move to the right, toward the office door. He hadn't entered through the plant in quite a long time, not since he had taken over as sales manager. He was looking forward to the change of pace.

Having few reasons to worry about the daily operations of the manufacturing side of the business, George rarely visited the industrial division of his company. For his own design work, he'd created a private tech lab. Closing the office door behind him, he watched Tony disappear through the plant entrance.

George knew that Tony was a gem of an employee. Everyone on his staff was excellent. He was a lucky business owner. He made a mental note to host a barbecue for his employees after the Celebrate Freedom job was behind them. They all deserved a cel-ebration of their own. George plopped down at his desk and scrib-bled a reminder on his desk calendar: *BBQ for staff.*

The words filled the block designated for September twelfth.

Now, all he had to do was to remember to tell his wife. That's the real challenge. Enough fun old man. Back to work.

George looked at the list of the scheduled shows, starting first in the United States, on the East Coast: Washington, D.C., New York, Atlanta, Boston, Orlando and Pittsburgh. The East housed the majority of the participating domestic cities. For a moment, George wondered which show the president was planning to attend for the kick off of the celebration. Would it be D.C. or New York? Deep down, his boyish side wanted to be present at the show President McAlister attended. That would be something.

"At 9:15 p.m. on September eleventh, the world will begin a long awaited celebration," announced the anchorwoman of the popular New York morning news show. The sound blared from the television in George's office. "An exhibition of brilliance, supplied by the well-known First Family of Fireworks will be the kick-off to a series of celebratory activities around the world. This day will be the most widely demonstrated gesture of gratitude, support, and appreciation of a combined military effort that our free world has ever seen. New York has been named a host city for this commemoration of freedom—"

The voice on the television trailed off in the background as George made a call over the plant's PA system.

"Hey, men, this is yours truly, George. I just wanted you to know that the announcement of our upcoming fireworks show, or should I say large group of shows, is all over the news. Since this seems to be the topic of conversation on the morning shows, I want to remind you that there's no pressure here. We have the whole world waiting for our creativity and talent to light up their skies in the opening minutes of this great celebration. That's all. No big thing. Carry on." He loved it when he cracked himself up like that.

After seconds, his fingers found the button to the microphone once again. "Oh yeah, on September twelfth, we have a celebration of our own. It's a Marian Lonitesci special barbecue, complete with all the trimmin's. You and all of your families are cordially invited, as a token of our appreciation for all of your hard work on this project. Thank you. Now, I better call my wife and tell her about this. For some reason, she hates to hear about these things through the grapevine. All right, back to work," George muttered. He put down the microphone and went about his business.

In the plant, the men completed a mock champagne toast in the air in honor of their boss. George was known for taking great care of his employees, and his cookouts were always a good time.

From inside the manufacturing plant, Tony listened to the announcement. Uncle George was quite a guy. He had a way of adding confidence to what seemed like impossible jobs. Tony knew that his uncle's carefree attitude was one reason why the Lonitesci's were the First Family of Fireworks. Lowering his eye protection, he took a closer look at the chemicals he'd been mixing together. He set up the potassium perchlorate to be the oxidizer and added some pine root as the fuel.

"Add the emitters for color, and, bam — there's a pyrotechnic," he sang. Just like riding a bike. This was going to be a piece of cake.

***

More messages posted to the hidden site. They waited for the responses to their inquiries, which took some time to appear live on-line. Sometimes days would pass before they'd be certain that their questions had been received.

No worries. We'll just wait for the show.

Their leader responded with assumed calmness.

The colors shall be brighter than anyone has ever witnessed before. Just as we planned.

***

Cheryl couldn't wait to leave work. In preparation for their trip to Disney, she and her sister had planned an afternoon of shopping. Kendra was meeting her at the Pentagon City Metro Center to begin their day. They had until nine o'clock that evening, when Hannah's nanny, Abigail, was scheduled to leave.

Cheryl never understood why Abigail was different than other caretakers, and she never asked. She assumed that somewhere along the line, somebody close to her nanny had been inflicted by this disease, which had made her both driven to fight it as well as strong enough to deal with it. Cheryl knew that children with AIDS were typically the most difficult patients for people to work with. These innocent children had been written unfortunate tickets in life and emotions ran high when caring for them. Cheryl was impressed that this never crushed Abigail's spirits. She was a jewel.

Abbie accompanied Hannah to school, when she was up to attending classes. She played with Hannah when the little girl's energy level permitted, and Abbie read to her when she felt tired. Abigail was the first person offered the third ticket for the Disney trip, but she'd politely declined. She had other responsibilities at home.

Cheryl understood that Abigail could use the well-deserved break herself. Today was going to be just that for Cheryl. A break. She couldn't wait for noon to come.

The plan was for the ladies to head to The Shops at Georgetown Park after making it through all of their planned stops at the Fashion Center. Just a few subway stops from Pentagon City in Arlington, The Shops at Georgetown Park marked Cheryl's personal favorite shopping destination. She was amazed by the fact that this shopping center sat right behind a crowded Georgetown street. The welcoming iron gate entrance masked the mall as if it were nothing but an office building. Distracted by her anticipation of the afternoon, Cheryl thumbed through the forms on her desk. She failed to absorb even one word from the paperwork.

Smiling, she realized her mind had been drifting all day. Who would ever think that a day of shopping could generate such excitement? Her daughter's illness had taught her to savor life's simple pleasures. Despite having been dealt her share of sad times, she'd maintained a positive attitude.

Cheryl was confident that this positive attitude had played a role in Hannah being awarded the trip to Disney World. Good karma had its own way of coming back around. She glanced at the illuminated clock on the corner of her desk. Glowing green numbers read 11:22. In thirty-eight minutes, she could officially start her time off. A mental stopwatch began the official countdown. Her knees bounced in a quick rhythm. Fidgeting from side to side, she forced her excitement inside and focused on work. She wouldn't have fun shopping if she felt guilty for having ignored her duties at the office. She could hear her sister offering a lecture.

"Don't get me wrong," Kendra would say. "I respect how hard you work. But, Lord, Cheryl, you work all the time. You have two full-time jobs between the White House and taking care of Hannah. They're both worth it, but sometimes you need to make time for *you*."

Cheryl loved her sister, but she was different.

***

Kendra gave her husband, Gerry, a firm good-bye kiss on the mouth.

"Thanks for lunch. I'll be home later this evening. Call me on my cell phone after the dinner rush. If I don't answer in five rings, send a search party after me. I might be buried in swimsuits and Capri pants! Love you."

Swinging around, she smacked herself on the cheek with her auburn ponytail. Her playful laughing echoed through the restaurant's foyer as she made her exit.

Giggling, she pulled into the Metro parking lot and turned off the ignition to her convertible. One thing she'd learned about the D.C. metro area was that there wasn't much demand for driving. The Metro system was the answer to travel throughout the city. Inexpensive, reliable, and safe, it was the best choice. Kendra took her Metro card, swiped it through the gate and entered the boarding area. In a just a few minutes time, she and Cheryl would be doing what girls love best — shopping!

* * *

Cheryl checked to see if Shane needed anything before she left for the day. With his approval, she went on her way. Fumbling for her Metro card, she found it in her wallet. Juggling her purse and card in one hand, she turned her wrist to check the time. She realized she'd better get moving if she was going to make the 12:15 train.

In an effort to be on time, she accelerated her pace from quick steps to a light trot. She was almost to her stop when she realized she'd left Shane's latest memo from General Jackson on her desk. Darn! After toying with the idea of going back, she decided to take care of it in the morning. After all, she was off duty, and the memo wasn't urgent. It was just a forward of something from the fireworks company. Cheryl moved toward the train station. What store would she go to first?

-7-

Robin, Chuck's wife, walked through the door of their beach-front chalet and poked her head around the corner to peer at the motionless lump in the bed. Watching him stir, she felt comfort in the confirmation that he was still alive.

"Chuck, I really think you should go to a medical center. You've already slept through our entire first day of vacation, and you don't seem to be getting any better. I knew I should've pressed you harder to go to the doctor while we were at my brother's house last week, but I thought you just didn't feel like socializing with my family so much ... not that I can blame you. They can be a bit high maintenance. Come on my darling, come out to da beach wit me. After a few vodka drinks, you'll be feeling just fine." In a poor attempt at a Jamaican accent, Robin sang her words. She walked over to the bed and yanked down the covers. There he lay, shivering and curled up, in a compact fetal position.

"Come on, Rob," whined Chuck. "That's not funny." He grabbed the blankets and pulled them back up around his neck. "I feel awful. I wish we would've planned to take our first week of vacation here and then finished up with your family. Leave it to me to get the flu. Maybe if I take some medicine, I'll feel better by dinner. Do you have any?"

"Honey, when do I ever travel without medication of some kind? Let me check my mobile pharmacy." She opened her shoulder bag to expose a baggie full of over-the-counter remedies. "Decongestant, acetaminophen ... oh, here we go ... Coldtrax. If your condition hasn't improved after you've taken all of this, you will go to the medical center. Deal?" Just out of Chuck's reach,

Robin held the foil-encased tablets in her hand, awaiting agreement to her plan.

"Okay, Rob, okay. I promise. But I don't think it'll come to that. I think this is just the result of too many long hours. You know how hard I worked to pay for this trip. I still say we should've spent the first week down here."

Robin rolled her eyes and tossed the medicine on her husband's chest. From the refrigerator, she removed a cold bottle of spring water.

"Whatever you say, my love. I refuse to respond, because we both know it was you that planned this deal. If my memory serves me right—and it always does—you didn't want to conclude your valuable time off by hanging out with my brother and his *bratty kids.* Just take your medicine and get some more sleep. If you feel up to it, join me on the beach. I'll be getting some sun and reading my book. I can't wait to tell everyone in my family about this trip. I'll bet they won't imagine a beach this beautiful."

She handed the water to her husband, fluffed the sweaty hair from his forehead with her cool hand and gathered up her beach bag. Slipping on her shoes, she strolled back out toward her chaise lounge. From her experience, Coldtrax usually took about an hour to start working. The way she saw things, she had sixty minutes to read in peace.

Robin and Chuck Lyons had been married for fifteen years. Having been together since high school, they were wed at the young ages of nineteen and twenty, respectively. In their hometown in Pennsylvania, getting married young was normal. Together they'd managed to build a good life for themselves. But at times, Robin still felt incomplete.

She had always wanted children, but Chuck was against the idea. He'd grown up in a large family, and Robin knew he'd experienced years of financial struggling. She tried to convince him that it would be different for them, but he hadn't been ready to listen. Recently, he'd started to change his tune. Elated, she tried to conceal her excitement for fear that it may be premature. She couldn't help but to think that this trip could be just what they needed to get started on the family she wanted. Well, it *could* be the start ... if Chuck would get better. Dropping her book in the sand to her right side, she calculated what the date would be in nine months. Closing her eyes, she dozed off in a relaxed slumber.

The soft reggae music woke her from what she guessed had been a quick nap. She saw the sun going down in the Negril sky, and she realized she must've been on the beach longer than she'd planned. Sliding the top strap of her bathing suit to one side, she exposed a line of white pigment beside her sunburned skin. Shaking the contents of her beach bag, she found her aloe lotion.

Squinting into the setting sun, Robin strained to see who was playing the music. In front of her stood three young boys, all equipped with old instruments. Out of tune chords from a standup string bass played to the raspy beat of a single snare drum. She thought she recognized the song the boys were singing, but the Jamaican twists they inserted into the music kept her from identifying the title. Realizing she was one member of an audience of three, she felt obligated to wait until the song was done. Why hadn't Chuck come out to join her? He had to be up by now.

When the song ended, the audience applauded. Robin tossed a few Jamaican dollars into their cardboard box. She made her way to the courtyard, down the cobblestone path, and to the chalet.

***

As if they were teenagers in the mall on a Friday night, Cheryl and Kendra pranced around the shops. After trying on hats in the accessory store, playing with all the latest toys in toy store and reading their horoscopes in the book shop, they settled down for a quick bite to eat in the food court.

Cheryl chose a garden burger for her dinner, and witnessed Kendra taking a chance on the sushi at the far end of the court. While waiting at their predetermined meeting place in the center of the restaurants, she pondered the question of where people ate before the introduction of food courts. As her sister approached, Cheryl wrinkled her nose at the sushi rolls on Kendra's tray.

"Hey, Gerry gave me his credit card and told me to treat all three of us to some fun stuff for vacation," Kendra said, avoiding the subject of food. "He won't take no for an answer. So, where should we go next? To get some cute outfits for Hannah?" Kendra continued to talk in spite of her sister's objections.

"Kendra, you and Gerry do so much for us already. Let's compromise. You can pick up a few things for Hannah. I want her to remember this trip as the happiest time she's ever had." Cheryl spoke with a fading voice. The tears she struggled to hold back were difficult to hide from her sister. She knew that Kendra could see through her.

Kendra was aware of the pain that her sister felt. She believed in the strength that Cheryl possessed, but the last year had taken its toll. Hannah's disease had escalated from HIV positive to AIDS. The prognosis wasn't good.

"Come on Cheryl." Kendra tried to interrupt the thoughts she knew were racing through her sister's head. "Let's get going. I have some shopping to do for my niece."

Kendra slid her arm through Cheryl's, and directed her toward a popular children's clothing store. She escorted her sister through the entrance to the first Sales Associate.

"What cute outfits do you have in a girl's size eight?"

* * *

Robin twisted her key in the lock. The opening of the door invited what little light was left in the sky into the dark room. Feeling her way around, she found the table lamp on the nightstand. She slid her hand up to the bulb, where she touched the switch. One turn offered a dim, artificial light. After the second click, the sheets on the bed began to move.

"Hey, Rob. Wow, that's bright." Chuck whined from under the blankets.

"I bet it seems bright, sleepy head. You haven't moved since I left you here hours ago. How are you feeling?"

"I took Coldtrax twice, but I still feel like crap. Maybe I need some more sleep. What time is it?"

"It's eight twenty-five." Robin announced the time in Chuck's direction. "Chuck, did you hear me? It's time for dinner. Why don't you take a shower? I bet that would make you feel better."

Stepping toward the bed, she tugged on the blankets to expose her husband's face, only to realize that he'd already fallen back to sleep. This was one heck of a twenty-four hour bug. She gave him a gentle shake and slid into the bed next to him.

Along her arm, Robin could feel the heat that escaped from Chuck's feverish body. For a moment she wasn't sure if it was coming from him or from her own sunburned skin. She felt a more serious concern, as she observed the beads of perspiration on the pale skin of his neck and forehead. She shook him again until he opened his eyes.

"Hey Robin. What's up? How was the beach?" Chuck was out of it. "Are you hungry, baby?"

Robin leaned over so her husband could see her face. "Chuck, honey, I'm worried about you. You need to see a doctor. I'm sure he'll give you something to make you better. Then you can enjoy the rest of our vacation. I'll call the front desk. They can tell us where to go."

Holding the handset of the phone in her left hand, she used her right hand to flip through the hotel directory and dial the front desk. No one answered. She hung up and tried again. The phone rang twelve times, and still, Robin received no answer. She dropped the phone back into the cradle and stroked Chuck's head.

"Baby, you promise you took the Coldtrax?"

"Yeah, yeah, honey. I took two packs of that stuff. I have one more for later. Let's go eat, sweetie. Okay? I'm gonna get in the shower, and you find us a place to eat. Just something light and casual sounds good for tonight. Don't you think?" Chuck hoped for agreement. "And let's stick close by our hotel. I think if we make this an easy night, and I get some more sleep, I'll be a new

man in the morning. I'll take you somewhere fancy for dinner
tomorrow. Promise." Chuck's dangling hand executed a poorly
formed sign of scout's honor.

"That sounds good, honey. While you shower, I'll take a walk
around the resort and see what they have. Be back in a few minutes." Robin's lips brushed her husband's salty forehead as she
slid from the side of the bed. She walked into her shoes and headed
out the door.

Chirping and croaking of crickets and frogs resonated through
the cool evening air. The sweet smell of night jasmine playfully
chased Robin down the cobblestone path. She'd never forget this
trip. In an effort to inhale her surroundings, she took a deep
breath.

Upon returning to the room, she wasn't surprised to find
Chuck still in the bed, once again fast asleep. There was no sense
in waking him now. After such a long day, she was tired herself.
A phone call solved the dinner dilemma.

Friday, September 1st

-8-

The alarm clock buzzed for twelve minutes before Tony could find the strength to turn it off. His lack of sleep had started to take its toll. With an effort, he lifted his arm and hit the snooze button. He was convinced that nine more minutes would give him the energy he needed to spring out of bed and start his day. Only ten days left. This celebration had been a long time coming, but he couldn't wait for that day to be over. His negative attitude troubled him. However, it didn't bother him enough to keep him from enjoying the extra sleep.

*　*　*

George paced in his office. Mumbling, he recited from the list in his hand all twenty-five participating cities. As he named each city, he identified the crew that would be there, the service men assigned to that location, and the number of the show.

The shows were numbered in the order of their detonation. They were grouped into time zones or countries in the order that they'd be launched. The east coast cities made up the first group, and George focused the majority of his concern on them. He hadn't heard back from General Jackson yet with a response to his memo. He'd expressed his concern about his sick crew members. He'd begun to feel ignored when the general called to reassure him that he'd have as much help as necessary.

"This is a promise," the general had told him.

George wanted the shows to go off without flaws. Although this was his goal for every Lonitesci show, these performances were unique in design. In the rare instance that a Lonitesci show was flawed, the audience never knew the difference. All twenty-five of these shows had to be exactly the same, so an error in one show couldn't be passed off as part of the plan. Only through television coverage would someone be able to compare the shows, anyway. George knew he was worrying without reason, but he wanted everything to be perfect.

He studied the clock on the wall and wondered, again, where Tony was. His nephew was reliable, and it wasn't like him to be late without calling. Tony was more like a son to him than a nephew, and George worried as any father would. Just as he was about to pick up the phone, he saw Tony's SUV pull up outside.

"Hey, George." Tony greeted his uncle with forced enthusiasm. "Sorry I'm late, but I have a plan. I'd like to have everything shipped by next Friday, September eighth. That gives us one week. Likewise, we need to activate our crews in each city on Saturday, the ninth, to make sure we have all of the equipment that we need. How does that sound for a schedule?" Tony searched for approval.

"That sounds fine. Please, promise me that you'll take a vacation after this is all over. Okay?"

"I *will* take a vacation. I could use some rest and relaxation." He smiled at his uncle and started out toward the plant entrance.

A week seemed like an eternity to Tony. However, seven days were barely enough time to finish the work that needed to be done. He sat down at a workbench with his clipboard and plotted out a plan for the week. Lucky for Tony, he was going to oversee the New York show, so he had only a short distance to travel.

The next morning, Tony planned to pick up his son from his ex-wife's house at nine o'clock. For Tony, spending the weekend with Jake was better than having a day off. Although he loved every day he was able to spend with his five year old, he wondered if he could muster up the energy to show him a good time. Maybe Jake's mom would be interested in switching weekends. That way, Tony could invite Jake to the big show in New York. At least then he'd be more relaxed, and the trip was sure to be fun.

Tony scrolled through the phone listings on his cell phone until the highlighted area rested on his ex-wife's name.

"Hello?" Karen's light voice answered on the other end.

"Hey, Karen, it's Tony. What's up?" He walked to a quieter corner of the shop.

"Tony, hi. How's everything goin'? How's the big show coming together? You must be excited about that."

"Oh, everything's going okay. Just been a lot going on at work. This is the biggest job we've ever seen, and the most important ... which is kinda why I'm calling," explained Tony. "Is there any chance you'd be interested in switching weekends with me? I know it's short notice, but this job has been super exhausting. Friday crept up before I knew it. I could use the weekend to finish up some important work." He mildly embellished the situation. "Plus, I thought if I had Jake next week, then he could come with me to New York for the big show. You know he would love that."

"That sounds fine, Tony. I'm sure Jake will be disappointed not to see you tomorrow, but that won't outweigh his excitement about next weekend. So, you'll pick him up Friday evening? What time?"

"Six o'clock. I'll be there with bells on," Tony confirmed. "Thanks Karen."

In one fluid motion, Tony flipped his phone closed and attached it to the clip on his belt. He walked to his workstation, preparing himself for another long day.

***

Alexei moved swiftly past the line of his colleagues to take his place at the front. He expected his impatience to be excused, because he had so much work to do in preparation of Celebrate

Freedom. His glance shifted from side to side, as he identified the men in line. The top heads of the Russian Federation had voted to make this inoculation mandatory for government officials.

As with many governmental actions in his country, news of this decision was not made public. Alexei questioned why this had been mandated, but his queries had been left unanswered. He was only certain that his participation was expected. He knew better than to press the issue. Unsolicited questioning of government business could be viewed as espionage activity and was punishable by death.

He slipped his arm from his shirt and turned to expose his shoulder. He waited while the nurse administered the inoculation. He read the after care thoroughly and returned the flyer to the technician. On his way back to his office, he put his arm back into the warmth of his shirtsleeve.

***

Robin sat with Chuck as they waited for the airport shuttle. Where had this week gone? The long awaited vacation had come and gone in record time. Saving money for three years, time spent on-line searching for affordable airline tickets, securing adequate hotel accommodations and finding a kennel for their dog had delivered less than satisfying results. She was sure that this would be one of the dreariest moments of her life. Hanging her head, she focused her view on the sand below. Using her toes, she pushed the granules around in a circle. Would they ever get the chance to take a vacation like this again?

The approaching shuttle caught her eye. She smiled while watching the van come barreling around the corner and screech to a stop. The craziness of the Jamaican drivers made her laugh. She stood and tapped Chuck on the back.

A large bottle of water in hand, Chuck made his best attempt at lifting his suitcase. Before he could get the bag off the ground, the shuttle driver stepped over to help.

"Hey, mon. I get that for you. You still on vacation, ya know."

The local man lifted the suitcases with ease and tossed them into the back of the van.

Chuck nudged Robin into an empty seat at the front. He allowed his body to fall down beside her. His condition hadn't improved during their stay. He'd found enough strength to venture out to the beach for a few hours each day, and he'd forced down his share of jerk chicken and rice. However, the exotic nightlife and romantic moonlit walks on the beach Robin had hoped for had never become a reality.

After days of Chuck's stubborn refusals to visit a medical center, Robin gave up trying to convince him to go. She understood his obstinate attitude, because she knew it wasn't unsubstantiated. She accepted his claim that he didn't trust Jamaican doctors. Horror stories of people who were sick on vacation and only got worse when they went to the doctor had tainted his perception of island medical practices. As much as Robin wanted to argue the point, she had to admit that she felt the same way. They agreed to make the best of their vacation with the aid of over-the-counter American medicines. In return, Chuck had promised to go to the doctor as soon as they returned to the States.

So, they sat on the shuttle awaiting their return trip. Despite the heat of the island, Chuck carried a hooded sweatshirt on his lap, with every intention of wearing it on the flight, if not sooner.

From her window seat, Robin took one last look at the resort. The beauty of the island had been worth the trip, but she was still disappointed. The possibility of returning home with *additional baggage* had swirled down the drain.

The shuttle driver hopped into his seat and ground the ignition to start. "Here we go folks. To de airport." He took the first curve in the road with such sharpness that Chuck slid over onto Robin's lap.

An hour and a half later, Robin found herself standing in line next to Chuck at the Montego Bay Airport. The end of vacation blues had taken over her thoughts altogether. She was so absorbed in feeling down that she didn't even notice the red splotches on

Chuck's neck.

They walked to the front of the ticket line and checked in. After receiving their seat assignments, they were pointed in the direction of U.S. Customs. Another long line awaited them, and Chuck wondered if he could remain standing for that long.

"Hey Rob, let's sit down on that bench over there and wait for the customs line to go down. I can't take another long line right now."

"Hon, we can't sit now. We don't have much time before our flight boards. Let's just get through customs and get settled near our gate. Then we can sit down while we wait. Okay? Come on, I'll help you with your bag." Robin made an attempt to compromise.

Chuck grabbed his own bag, despite his wife's offer to help. He took his spot in the line for customs and plopped down on his suitcase. He rested his face in his palms, exposing the red dots on the back of his neck.

"Hey, I think you have a bug bite or something on the back of your neck." Robin reached out to feel the red bump. "Does this itch?"

"A little," Chuck answered. "Could have been anything that bit me with all of the bugs in the room."

"Come on, babe." Robin spoke in a more compassionate tone than she had earlier. "Let's go. The line's moving."

Little by little, they inched forward. Robin helped her husband along, and by the time they reached the front, she was acting as his crutch.

Hood and all, Chuck wore his sweatshirt in an attempt to combat the chilling effects of his fever. As he approached the front of the line, he reached for his bag using every bit of energy he had to swing his suitcase to the waist high table. With a thud, his bag landed on the aluminum top, causing a loud clanging sound. His body jolted from the force of having heaved it from the ground. The hood of his sweatshirt fell limp, as he jerked his head back. He looked with apologetic eyes at the female customs officer for having thrown his bag with so little control. Through his blurred vision, he could see the shocked expression in her eyes.

Without hesitation, a second airport employee raised a radio to his mouth and made an urgent call. A nearby officer asked Robin and Chuck to step to the side, while the people behind them were allowed to pass through the line. For a split second, Robin felt anger creeping up through her body as she wondered if her husband would be stupid enough to smuggle home some Jamaican grown marijuana. Her anger turned to fear when she caught a glimpse of him staring back at her. She fought to maintain her composure as she examined the pustules that covered his face and his neck.

"My God, Chuck," Robin gasped. "You must have the measles or something."

Before Chuck could answer, the man with the radio corralled them to an emergency exit. He scooted them into a van that was waiting outside. Mumbling something to the driver, he slid the door closed. Before she could find out what was going on, Robin watched as the driver flipped a switch and a siren began to wail.

Minutes later, she and Chuck were settled in a room at the Montego Bay Hospital. A small crew of doctors and nurses stood outside, waiting to enter. Each member of the group wore a mask over his nose and gloves on his hands. She knew she shared Chuck's feelings— a mixture of fear and frustration. She hoped for some answers when the first doctor entered their room.

Keeping a safe distance from his patients, he introduced himself.

"Hello, I am Dr. Trilas, Chief Resident of the Montego Bay Emergency Services."

"Why are we here?" Robin asked, now becoming nervous. "Is he gonna be okay? You can treat measles, right? Do you want the name of our doctor at home, in the States?" She continued to speak until the doctor held up his hands to signal silence.

Dr. Trilas removed a small flashlight from his pocket and began to examine Chuck. "Mr. and Mrs. Lyons? How long have you been sick?"

"My husband has had the flu for about a week, right honey?" Robin answered the doctor and looked at Chuck at the same time. She noted an expression of comprehension from Dr. Trilas as Chuck shrugged his left shoulder in an attempt at a nod of agreement. "But I feel fine. I mean, I'm not sick ..." Robin proclaimed.

Dr. Trilas continued the examination. He focused his attention on the rash that had formed on Chuck's face. After asking Chuck to lift his shirt, he checked his back and his arms. As he expected, the rash was only present on his face and neck. Before excusing himself from the room, the doctor motioned for Chuck to lower his shirt.

Robin leaned over and put her arm around her husband. She tucked his balmy head between her cheek and her shoulder and stroked his forehead. "It's gonna be okay, babe. We just need to get you feeling better, so we can go home to our doctor. I'm sure this was just a precautionary measure. You know they can't let you fly on a plane full of people if there's a chance you could have the measles or something. I wish they would tell us what's going on, though. I mean, why don't they give you a shot?" She realized that she was talking to herself now, because Chuck had fallen fast asleep.

* * *

Tony finished his work for the day. He felt positive about the progress. Everything was on schedule, and he was free to catch up on sleep. After saying goodbye to his few remaining co-workers, he followed an evening ritual and headed to George's office to say good night. The dark interior offered evidence that his uncle was already gone. As unusual as this seemed, Tony felt relieved. Now he could head home and get some rest.

The walk to the parking lot seemed longer than usual. Tony counted his steps, hoping to make the trip more bearable. The step up into his SUV took more energy than he had. Tilting his head back, he closed his eyes for just a second. Several moments passed, and Tony realized that if he didn't start driving home he'd sleep the night right there in his car.

Tony preferred to drive in silence. He liked to do a lot of his thinking while in the car. But, tonight was different. He turned on his radio, and the music worked as an effective aid to keep him awake during his short drive home. He pressed the scan button and felt satisfied to listen to the first station that came in tune. Within minutes, the radio DJ was talking about the upcoming celebration of freedom.

"This is supposed to be the biggest celebration in the world," the talk radio host announced to his listeners. "I mean it, in the world ... people are gonna be partying all over the place. I think it's great. Okay, it's time for a contest. Give us a call and tell us what you'd like to be doing on September eleventh during this celebration. We're looking for originality here, people. We're talking *fantasy*. The winner gets a free trip to Washington, D.C. for the kickoff of Celebrate Freedom. VIP tickets. Whatever that means. 888-555-3333 What? We have a caller already? That was fast. Hello—"

Tony smacked the button to cut the sound. For some reason, he wasn't in the mood to hear any more about the celebration. Over the past few days he'd developed a less than enthusiastic attitude about the upcoming party. He was certain the feeling stemmed from the amount of overtime he'd been putting in. Whatever the reason, he was looking forward to a weekend without hearing the words "celebrate freedom."

Monday, September 4th

-9-

Monday mornings always seemed to come so fast. But for Cheryl Williams, this Monday was different. This Labor Day marked the beginning of the last week before she left for her trip to Disney World. She'd opted to work the holiday in exchange for an extra day of vacation. With the added work of the upcoming celebration, her schedule change was welcomed.

Still surprised by the good fortune of this trip, Cheryl counted her blessings once again. First of all, this getaway couldn't have come at a better time for Hannah. In the last year, her condition had progressively worsened. After confirmation that Hannah had advanced from HIV positive to AIDS, Cheryl witnessed her daughter's physical and spiritual health begin a slow deterioration. However, she knew Hannah was strong enough to enjoy this trip. If this opportunity had come along later, they may have had to decline the offer.

Over time, she had come to terms with the prognosis. Having been blessed by ten years with her daughter so far, she felt grateful. Every day with Hannah was a gift, and she had faith that things in the world happened for a reason. Taking the time to bow her head, she said her morning prayers. This daily ritual kept her strong. No God would make a child suffer through a disease like AIDS without a good reason. There's a master plan for everything. She knew that Hannah, and every person on earth, was part of a bigger picture that one day would be clear. As hard as this was to bear at times, her faith remained strong. She felt that good things came her way because of that. This trip was one of those good things.

With a quick sign of the cross, she started to get ready. Bending over and aiming the blow dryer at the underside of her hair, she wondered once again who the kind person was who'd written the letter to the Make-A-Wish Foundation.

Hannah had always wanted to go to Disney World. As much as Cheryl dreamed of taking her, she never had the money to do so. Whoever wrote that letter had made one ten-year-old happy.

Cheryl grabbed her purse and peeked into Hannah's room. The blinds were drawn, and her daughter was still sleeping. She stepped to the side of the bed and planted a delicate kiss on Hannah's forehead. She waved goodbye to Abbie, who stood in the corner of the room preparing the child's morning meds.

Cheryl was no doctor, but she knew this trip would be good medicine for her daughter. Hannah had been drawing pictures of Disney characters ever since she'd been notified by the foundation. By now, the walls of her room were lined with her artwork.

* * *

This particular Monday morning acted as a heavy weight on the shoulders of Tony Lonitesci, and working on Labor Day added to his sluggishness. He had a rough time getting out of bed. Even after a refreshing shower, he felt clammy and feverish. After swallowing three pain tablets, he tossed the bottle with the rest of the pills in his messenger bag. The light bag contained only paperwork and the bottle, but it felt heavy. By the time he made it to his car, he was dragging his bag behind him. For a fleeting moment, he considered a trip to the doctor's office. No time for that today ... or this week, for that matter. He'd have plenty of time to get better after his work was done. Medicine and rest would make him well. It would have to. He'd been telling himself this for a week now.

As he pulled into the parking lot, he stopped his car in its normal space. He stepped out and wrapped his arms around himself, shaking. In the last hour, the air had cooled. Was rain on the way?

Soon after entering the plant, he was sweating again. He walked to the thermostat to check the air conditioning. A voice from behind halted his progress, and he turned to see his uncle.

"What's up Tony? Too cool in here for ya? Don't worry, we can afford to crank the AC. We've got plenty of money coming in to pay the bills," George teased.

Tony cocked his head and gave George a confused look. "Is the AC cranked? I was checking to make sure it was working at all. I'm sweating bullets. I think it's cooler outside than it is in here." Tony looked around for a chair, a box, or anything where he could sit for just a second.

George showed immediate concern. "Tony, come on now, you're sick. You have the flu. Look at you. You're dripping with sweat, and it's only sixty-five degrees in here. You thought it was cool outside, and it's one of the hottest, muggiest days we've had all summer. You have to go home and get some rest. Stop by Dr. Peterson's office on your way. I think you need a shot of something."

"Uncle George, I didn't think doctors gave shots anymore. Besides, I'm okay." Tony tried to sound convincing. "I know I probably have a touch of the flu coming on, but I have my trusty sidekick with me." He shook his bag so George could hear the rattle of the pills in the bottle inside. "I need to get everything in order for this show. After that, I'll take some time off to rest and get better. In fact, if you'll let me get to work, I hope to finish up early today."

"Okay Tony, but, remember, you aren't Superman. Get done today what you feel you must and get outta here. And that's an order." George did his best to carry out a parental scolding.

Tony mustered enough strength to raise his hand and salute

his uncle. He pivoted, and with a click of his heels, he walked toward the plant entrance.

***

Shaking his head in frustration, Alexei paced in his office. His preparations for the following week's celebration in Moscow were more overwhelming than he'd expected. As he reviewed the plans in his mind, he noticed some of the other government officials locking their offices and leaving for the day. They had all agreed to meet early the next morning to go over the last minute details.

Concerned that his colleagues might be working with a hidden agenda, he spent a few moments observing the obvious preoccupation they'd developed regarding their plans for the days following the celebration. Or was this worry a product of his overactive imagination? He returned his focus to the business at hand.

The detonation crews were in place for all three cities within the Russian Federation. Alexei was to oversee the Moscow celebration, which would start fifteen hours after the launches along the East Coast of the United States. He was also in charge of addressing his entire country prior to the launch. He was honored to be making the local kickoff speech and pleased to be stationed close to home for the event.

Noticing the time was nearing five o'clock, he paused from his work, amazed at where the day had gone. The hours had been whisked away during his diligent preparation. He turned off the light in his office, locked the door and started home.

While on his way, an annoying distraction occupied his mind. Alexei often wondered how he ever came to be part of the committee of a United Free World in the first place. When the United States made its initial declaration of war on terrorism, the leaders of the Russian Federation had taken a cautious approach to supporting their efforts. Soon, the heads of the federation unanimously agreed that they needed to join forces with the United States in this war, at least on a public front.

Alexei felt guilty for questioning the motives of his government, but he couldn't help to wonder what had fueled their change of heart. Was this a poor attempt to expunge their own negative record by masking mistakes that they'd made in the past? If so, present good deeds wouldn't erase old errors. They should know this. Alexei was certain that his colleagues worried that the actions of their predecessors could one day come back to haunt them. So maybe their support of UFW was simply a cover up ... an attempt to look good. Were they really that shallow?

The officials of the Russian Federation had been successful in convincing Alexei that their country needed representation on the board of the UFW. Not only did they want him to be that token person, but they wanted him to be selected to assist President McAlister in chairing the board. Alexei shuddered. Doubt about their true motivations still clouded his pride in the achievement of being elected.

On most occasions, Alexei refused to give in to the paranoia of his country's leaders. But his officials did a fine job of convincing him that everyone and every country in the world was out for itself.

"It is fine to work together as allies in a war against something bad, but in the end we all must look out for ourselves first," his military advisor had told him. He spoke to Alexei about World War II, where Russia and the United States had been allies. But he'd also reminded him that, a short time later, the United States did not care at all about what happened to Russia.

"They are friends now, but once this war is over, they will not care what happens to us." The Russian president had spoken his words with conviction.

Alexei had been raised not to question the methods by which his superiors conducted their business. For this reason, he'd listened and refrained from expressing his doubts.

After four years of working side-by-side with President McAlister, Alexei began to see things from a different view. McAlister's country was looking out for itself, as it should. But he felt that the leaders of the United States were genuine in their desire to achieve universal freedom. Alexei knew that this war on terror had been waged in the defense of the freedom of the world, not just for the United States.

No one wanted to hear his opinion on this matter now. He knew they'd make a public mockery of him for showing concern and crucify him in private. How dare he create a scare before such a grand celebration? He knew they would portray him as the questionable one. Too much time had gone by, and too many plans were already in the works. All he could do was wait and see what would happen next. Celebrate Freedom was going to kick off a new era ... this, he knew for certain.

He drove straight to his house, a humble home by the standards of the Russian government.

Sharona greeted him at the door. Reaching for her, he scooped up her small frame and squeezed his arms tight around her waist. He felt her feet lift from the ground. He hoped she knew how much he loved her.

"Did you go to the doctor today?"

"Yes, Alexei, I went. But they said no shots for women."

"Did you show them the letter? The letter from my office will override that rule. Did you show the letter?" As he repeated his question, he raised his voice.

Sharona guided her anxious husband to the sitting room. She encouraged him to relax in his favorite chair, even though she knew he preferred to remain on his feet. Her Turkish background had taught her to be submissive to the men in her life, so disobeying Alexei's wishes was not an option for her. She took his jacket and left him standing as she went to hang it in the closet.

"I tried, Alexei, but they wouldn't have it," she said from the hall. "I do not know why you are so worried about this anyway. Why all of the fuss?"

"Never mind, dear. I will straighten this out. You are right. There is no reason to worry." He sat down, trying to appear unalarmed. Dear, sweet, naive Sharona. If only she knew how important that shot could be.

Sharona stepped around her husband, lifting his feet as she moved. When she was convinced he was comfortable, she entered the kitchen to fetch his drink.

Alexei watched her graceful movements. He wished he could function with as much ease as his wife. How refreshing it would be to not worry about anything. Not to care about what tragedy the next few days could bring. In quiet meditation, he expressed thanks for Sharona.

* * *

Robin sobbed alone in the Jamaican hospital room. She watched as the nurse pulled the sheet over Chuck's head and moved the gurney in the direction of the door. Gasping for breath through her crying, she tried to follow the nurse, but a doctor held her back.

"Ma'am, you cannot go. We are very sorry, but he is gone. You must focus on helping us to find out where this came from, so that we can now help you."

Robin couldn't catch her breath long enough to talk. An hour before she'd witnessed her husband stop breathing. Everything had been a blur.

Over the past days, she witnessed Chuck's condition worsen. However, neither she nor Chuck had been allowed to leave the room, so she wasn't certain what the doctors and nurses were saying. The red and white pustules that had formed all over Chuck's face and neck had terrified Robin. She thought she'd heard one doctor mention the possibility of adult chicken pox, but he'd said nothing directly to her.

The doctors had continued to ask Robin and Chuck where they'd been over the past month. When Chuck couldn't muster enough energy to speak, they urged Robin to answer for him.

"We've only been at home and here." She'd repeated her statement over and over. She recounted all of their steps ... where they'd been staying in Jamaica, the flight on which they flew to the country, their visit with her brother and where their home was. Even with this information, puzzled expressions never left the faces of the doctors.

Robin's requests to contact her family had been accepted, but not successful. They kept finding reasons for her to stay put, stressing that everything would be okay. The doctors seemed so wrapped up in their own concerns, that she felt like the staff had forgotten about the two of them locked up in that small room. Being in the island hospital was worse than jail. At least in jail she'd get one phone call.

* * *

Allowing the door to slam closed behind him, Tony entered his kitchen just in time to hear Jake's voice on the answering machine.

"Hi, Daddy." Jake spoke with loud, pronounced words. "Mommy said I could call to see what time you'll be here to get me on Friday. Bye!" Jake put the phone down. Tony could hear it sliding across a counter or table.

"Hi Tony," Karen said, joining in. "Jake just wanted to say hi, as you've noticed by now. He's excited about this weekend. I know you're probably still at work, but I told him he could leave a message. Give him a ring either later this evening or tomorrow. Okay? Talk to you then. Bye."

Under normal circumstances, Tony would've grabbed the phone to talk to his son before the end of the message. Today was different. At that moment, he could think of only one thing, and that was going straight to bed. The curtains were still drawn, so his room was dark and inviting. Still dressed, he fell into his unmade bed and closed his eyes. In a second or two, he was asleep.

* * *

Alexei lay awake. He'd attempted to turn in early, since he made it a habit to go to work at such odd hours. So far, he hadn't been able to sleep at all. Finding a way to protect his wife had monopolized his thoughts. His mind raced, and he wondered if President McAlister could help him. It was too late for that. How could he even begin to explain his fears?

However, he could hope that their plan might not work this time. With several of the terrorist leaders dead, the group may not have even materialized strong enough forces necessary to achieve a final initiative. So far, he hadn't heard of any outbreaks. But he couldn't help but to wonder about the mandatory inoculations. Maybe all of this worrying was for nothing. He prayed this was the case.

But what about Sharona if it wasn't? He had to find a way to make sure his wife was protected. He considered sending her to stay with her relatives. This might work, because they were far away from the celebration cities. He made a mental note to check into the idea first thing in the morning. After another hour of tossing and turning, his body rested.

Tuesday, September 5th

-10-

A shrill ringing caused Tony to stir. Uncertain if the sound was real or the component of a dream, he remained still. A repeat of the noise motivated him to open his eyes. Feeling the buttons on his shirt press into his chest as he rolled over, he realized he'd slept through the night in his clothes. His oxford was soaked with perspiration and his damp pant legs clung, twisted around his thighs. As much as he wanted to get up and take a shower, he felt as if he could hardly move.

What time was it? It must be three o'clock or four o'clock in the morning. Who on earth would be calling at this hour? He fumbled in the dark for his alarm clock. When his hand slid over the small black box, he turned it until the glowing digital numbers were in his view. Squinting to focus, he read the time as 2:35. The phone had stopped ringing. He closed his eyes and fell back to sleep.

* * *

George put the phone back in its handset and concentrated on the empty spot in the parking lot. Never, in the fifteen years Tony had worked for him, had his nephew not shown up for work. If he was going to be even ten minutes late, he would call. If he decided to leave early, George knew he would always stop by his office to tell him first. Genuine concern developed in George's mind. Had something happened to Jake?

He erased that thought and tried to focus on the paperwork in front of him. Of course Tony will have a valid explanation for missing work today. He'll call soon and explain everything. George did his best to remain positive. After thirty minutes passed, he reached for the phone again. Just one more time. Tony had to answer sooner or later.

* * *

The first ring woke him. This time, Tony became aware of the light that was seeping in through his vertical blinds. Was it morning already? He felt as if he'd just fallen back to sleep after the last phone call, and it had been two-thirty in the morning. Or was it? He was feeling uncertain about the day, or the week for that matter. The disorientation he was experiencing reminded him of the aftereffects of a big night out back in his college days.

In a daze, Tony rose, at a slow pace. He squinted at the light, which he now determined to be the sun. A second look at the clock confirmed the time as three-fifteen, apparently in the afternoon. How could he have slept until so late? The day was nearly over.

While stripping himself of his sweaty clothing, he proceeded toward the shower. After peeling off his damp clothes, a flash of cold air cut through his body like a sharp knife through butter. Scrambling, he reached for his robe to keep him warm while he waited for evidence of steam before braving his first step inside the shower. The wet heat felt soothing for a moment, but then he became dizzy and reached for the cold-water tap to cool the scalding spray. In a matter of seconds, his teeth were chattering again. Upon extinguishing the water flow, he plucked a towel from its home on a hook beside the top of the green shower curtain that outlined the tub. After drying off, he wrapped himself in his robe and headed to the kitchen.

Bright rays of natural light pierced Tony's sensitive eyes. He lifted his hand to create shade as he studied the wall clock in the kitchen, desiring one more confirmation of the time. Sure enough, the end of the workday was nearing. He was puzzled, to say the least. Was this the end-of-the-summer flu season?

The incessant blinking of the answering machine and caller ID box guided Tony to the phone, just steps past the breakfast bar. Successive taps of a button revealed at least five phone calls from work. He halted the call review after identifying the first set of numbers. Uncle George must be worried out of his mind, or maybe angry. Without a doubt, Tony's current behavior was uncharacteristic of his work ethic.

A push of the speed dial called his uncle's office. Tony carried the cordless phone to the living room and flopped down on the edge of the sofa. Even standing for a phone call left him short of breath. After half a ring, George answered the phone.

"Hello? George Lonitesci, what can I do you for?"

"Hey, it's Tony. I'm so sorry." He wasn't able to complete another sentence before George interrupted.

"Tony, what's going on? Are you okay? Is Jake okay? I'm sorry to call you so many times. I was just worried." George spoke in a rapid, frenzied voice.

"Uncle George, I'm fine. Well, I will be fine. I guess I must've turned off the alarm in my sleep. Geez, I haven't done that since college." Tony was still surprised at his own actions. "Anyway, I feel awful. I'm sure it's no big deal. If it's okay with you, though, I think I'll stay home. The day's just about over anyway. Are we still on schedule for shipment on Friday?" He hoped for a positive response. What the heck would he do if the answer was no?

"Yes, yes, we are," replied George. "Thanks to all of your hard work, everything's going to be shipped on time. So get some sleep and take some cold medicine. I need you to be ready to launch some fireworks on Monday, unless you want me to make alternate arrangements. What do you think?"

"George, I'll be fine by Monday. You can't force me out of this show that easily." Tony voiced a playful jab to his uncle. "Plus, Jake's going with me, and he'd be devastated if we had to cancel. Keep me on that schedule. In fact, I'll see you in the morning.

Now, if you don't mind, I have a date with the couch."

***

Feeling at ease with his worries, George decided to call it a day himself. Peeking around the corner, he saw the fireworks being packaged for shipment. His crew was ahead of schedule. It was all downhill from there. George sighed in relief. The last few stressful days were over, but he still needed to do something about all of the guys who'd been out sick.

***

Alexei was awake, replaying the day's activities in his head. He'd arrived at work at seven o'clock a.m. to find a fax from President McAlister on his desk. The fax was a friendly reminder that Alexei needed to gather help for the launch. He was certain that all UFW member countries had received similar letters. He was also confident that he had plenty of help lined up. As a precaution, all of his temporary aides had attended the governmental medical session last week.

With this thought, Alexei's concerns about his wife resurfaced. He knew he had to find a way to protect her from the possibility of any contamination following the celebration. The vaccines had been rationed and even family members of government officials had been eliminated from the list. No one had told Alexei that this decision had been made. He was bitter that his wife had been excluded. He knew for sure that the wives of his superiors had been present on the day of their inoculations. This act of unfairness surprised him.

"An inaccurate inventory of the stock led us to believe that we could accommodate all government workers and their families," Alexei's supervisor had told him.

Refusing to accept this explanation, Alexei cited examples of family members he'd seen during the inoculations. His supervisor informed him that this was a mere coincidence, and that they had not received the shot. Alexei knew this wasn't true, but he also knew better than to dispute the words of his superior.

"I can assure you that this inoculation has been nothing more than a precautionary measure," his supervisor had told him, in a patronizing tone. "The true odds rest in favor of a safe outcome. We're just paranoid. It's our nature."

This wasn't the time for jokes. Alexei wished he could believe this doublespeak, but he knew in his heart that no one had any idea what to expect. A party was being planned to celebrate freedom. For the first time in five years, his government's guard was down. The world terrorist organizations had spent years training, and losing even a large percentage of their operatives would not exhaust their desire to further their cause. And, as Alexei had just found out, they had resources.

The biggest concern weighing on Alexei's mind was the unknown. Even the heads of the Russian Federation had no definitive answer as to how much of a biological arsenal the terrorists had managed to stockpile. What the terrorists bought many years before was one thing, but what they may have taken from unguarded Russian facilities was a separate issue. With the knowledge the Russians had, they still had no true idea of how much or how little this could be. They only feared that something was going to happen on the day of that celebration, and they knew of at least one weapon the terrorists possessed. Was it really too late to warn the other countries? Alexei didn't think it was. But his opinion didn't matter.

He reflected on the Russian response to the United States when the Americans had voted to destroy the last remaining samples of the living smallpox virus. The Russians, in the privacy of their own offices, had referred to the Americans as foolish and ignorant to think that they had such control over nature.

"A virus cannot be beaten by man," a colleague of his had stated. Alexei had agreed, but not for the obvious reason that nature will always come out on top. Instead, he agreed because he knew that many more samples of that virus still existed, even though no one wanted to believe or to share this information. He was sure the product that the terrorists had purchased from the Russians in the seventies had not been lost or forgotten, but he couldn't prove it. He knew that one day it would surface, and everyone would pay for the greed of his country.

The feeling of doing too little, too late was overwhelming. How could something from so long ago come back to haunt his country and the rest of the world with such devastating consequences? Alexei closed his eyes and tried to remember a time before he knew anything about the terrors of the world.

He held a clear vision of when he was a young boy. Memories of a barren country existed foremost in his mind. The time following the Cold War had left his country in a state of poverty, and this was the dominant memory that he owned.

The pain that he felt when he learned of the death of his father also consumed him. His father had worked as a scientist for the Communist government of the Soviet Union. Not long after the country fell apart, so did Dmitri Gousev. As a boy, Alexei didn't understand what his mother meant when she said that guilt had killed his father. He understood now.

"Fight for your country, son," his father would say. "Our land is not a bad land, but an injured land. We must rebuild. Only time, dedication and money can make this happen."

Never was any direct blame placed on the actions of the United States for the fall of the Soviet Union, but the thought need not be spoken to be heard. Alexei had vowed to represent his land in their own battle. He vowed to make their dreams of recovering the power of what they once had come true. For the memory of his father, he was dedicated to fighting for this goal.

This lullaby had often rocked him to sleep. Tonight was no different. His eyelids closed, and his breath drew in and out in even rhythm. He slept with as much peace as he could feel through the numbness of his soul.

Friday, September 8th

-11-

Robin buried herself in the covers of her hospital bed, aware that this could be her last day of life. The scrambling of the doctors and nurses had been kept to a minimum for the past hour. She was sure they were waiting for her to die. She didn't blame them. They didn't know what to do, and the inevitable outcome was right around the corner. The consensus, it seemed, was that if they could rid their hospital of this infection, then their problem would be solved. The only method of ridding this hospital of the infection was to get rid of her. Lying in bed, she closed her eyes and focused on fond memories of Chuck.

She felt for the ring on her finger. Surprised the nurses hadn't stripped her of this, too, she slid the gold band off and cradled it in her hand. The sharp stone dug into her skin as she secured the ring on her index finger and clutched the diamond in her palm. So much for the family she wanted.

Family? Had hers been notified? How long had it been since she'd asked to call home? Hours, days, weeks? Rolling over, she craned her neck to find a calendar. What was the point? Why worry her family? It didn't matter anymore.

The tears came. In part, they were due to the painful blisters on her face. The salty droplets were symbols of her numb acceptance of what had happened. Robin held onto a slim hope that someone could help her, but at the moment she wished to live only if she could have Chuck back by her side. Aware enough to know that this wasn't going to happen, she closed her eyes again and prayed.

***

The fireworks were packaged and ready to ship. Tony had arrived at work early that morning to oversee the freight plans. He wanted to make sure all of the orders were correct. Everything had to be perfect. Clipboard in hand, he counted the boxes one last time and sat down on the final package to rest.

This was his first day back since he'd become sick, and his body sagged with exhaustion. When greeted by George that morning, he'd put on a front, insisting he was feeling much better. Visiting a doctor was a priority, as soon as the celebration was over. He'd promised. Only a few more days to go. He wiped the sweat from his brow and walked outside to wait for the delivery truck.

A beautiful Pennsylvanian fall day unfolded for Tony to enjoy. The afternoon sun had warmed the air just enough to take away the chill, but the evening promised a cool and comfortable close to the day. This would be a pleasant night to sleep with the windows open. Lately, he'd found himself thinking about sleep more often than ever. He checked the time. Once the shipment was on its way, he planned to head home.

The thought of canceling his weekend plans with Jake made Tony unhappy. Karen would kill him if he got their boy sick. In his mind, Tony rehearsed his conversation with his son, as the truck squeaked to a stop in front of the loading dock. From the driver's seat, a young red-haired driver hopped out.

His schoolboy appearance caught Tony's eye, creating concern. Could anything else go wrong today?

"Hey there, how's it goin'?" Tony called out to welcome the driver. "Where's Chuck today? Still on vacation?"

"Um, I'm not sure," the inexperienced driver answered. "I've been taking over part of his route while he was gone. To tell you the truth, I ain't never even met Chuck, so I wouldn't know if he was back or not." The young, scrawny guy rambled, as he fumbled with his computer pad. "Lemme see what you got here. Wow, it seems like a lot. Good thing I got a darn near empty truck. I should be able to get everything in one trip." He placed his electronic manifest on the concrete and started for the first box.

Tony interrupted his progress. "Hey, buddy, let me help you with that."

Less than forty-five minutes later, the truck was loaded and on its way. Tony breathed a sigh of relief. Now, he could go home. Saying good-bye to no one, he left through the back exit.

***

In anticipation of leaving early, Cheryl scrambled to finish her work. She'd already received approval to scoot early that afternoon. She confirmed that nothing had been missed.

She caught Shane watching her work herself into a frenzy. From the corner of her eye, she saw him snicker.

"What's so funny? I have everything under control. You might not think so, but I'm just about finished." Stopping to catch her breath, Cheryl noticed the pyramids of paper she'd built around her. Throwing her hands in the air, she laughed.

"Cheryl, why don't you get going before you bury yourself in paperwork. You are my right arm, but I promise I'll be fine while you're gone." With a gentle touch, Shane took her by the shoulders and turned her toward the hall exit. "Get your purse. Don't forget your trip itinerary. I've watched you staring at it all morning. We'll be fine around here. I promise."

Cheryl's gratitude sparkled through her blue eyes. Turning on her heels, she bounced off toward the door and officially began her vacation.

The ride on the Metro and the walk to her townhouse seemed to only take seconds. As she turned her key in the lock, Cheryl sang out for Hannah.

"Hannah, oh Hannah. I'm home. Where are you?" She took

light jogging steps up to the girl's room, but she went back downstairs when she heard talking in the kitchen.

Cheryl rounded the corner at the foyer. Kendra, Abigail, and Hannah stood at the kitchen counter, surrounded by a mountain of fresh vegetables, breads and pasta. A brick of cheese leaned next to an unopened bottle of wine and a two liter container of soda ... an obvious moment of weakness for Aunt Kendra.

"What's this, ladies?" Cheryl was surprised.

"We're making you dinner, Mom." Hannah's face lit up to display a wide smile. "It's a kick-off for our trip."

Cheryl squeezed her daughter into a hug and reached down to give her a kiss on the top of her head. "You sure are getting tall, young lady. Pretty soon, you'll be taller than me." She hid her face in her daughter's hair as one single tear escaped from the corner of her eye. Sometimes Cheryl found it difficult to think about the future. "Okay, now, what's for dinner?" As always, she made a rapid come-back from her silent moment of emotion.

* * *

With his head propped on an oversized bed pillow, Tony burrowed into the cushions on his couch. His conversation with Jake had gone as he'd expected. Nothing hurt him more than the sound of disappointment in the little guy's voice. Even Karen's support didn't help to cure Tony's sadness.

"It's just not fair, Daddy ... not fair." Jake had repeated the words through his sniffles.

Tony was trying to force the memory from his head when the cable TV news caught his attention with an interesting story. Without moving the remote from its balanced position on his stomach, Tony increased the volume for the set. He peered over his rounded abdomen to see the afternoon commentator as he spoke about how Celebrate Freedom was the event most widely covered by the international media.

"Media coverage in all countries has been following the planning

of this celebration. On September eleventh, many around the world will be waiting to witness this festivity."

The television anchor attempted to add spice to what was already being referred to as old news. The announcer went on to talk about a D.C. area high school that was planning to bury a time capsule following the commemoration.

"The students of Wakefield High School, in Arlington, Virginia are collecting newspaper clippings from September eleventh, two thousand one until present day. Their focus is on national freedom and the ways the war on terror has changed the world. Following Celebrate Freedom, they'll bury the capsule during an evening ceremony at their school. They hope the capsule will be uncovered years from now and that the contents will help to educate the country about the price of freedom."

That sounded like an interesting class project. Should the Lonitesci's donate something from the plant for memorabilia of the fireworks show that kicked off Celebrate Freedom? After finding a pen in the end table drawer, Tony grabbed a magazine from the coffee table and scribbled the information in the corner. He made a mental note to contact that school later.

Smacking the power button on the remote control, Tony used one arm to launch his body up from its horizontal position on the sofa. Having already changed into a fresh pair of boxers and a clean t-shirt, he was ready for bed. For a fleeting moment, he thought about making himself some dinner, but he decided he'd grab something at the airport in the morning. His plan to drive to New York was thwarted by the fact that he didn't think he could make it there without falling asleep at the wheel.

His plane was set to depart at four o'clock in the morning. With nothing else left to do in preparation for his trip, he retired to the bedroom. Closing the vertical blinds, he blocked any remaining evidence of daylight and settled in under the covers.

***

Once again, Alexei was awake when he should have been asleep. Sharona had been asleep for hours. In the morning, he'd meet with the launch crew for the Moscow celebration. Because their time was eight hours ahead of the U.S. East Coast, his local festivities wouldn't take place until September twelfth. He couldn't stop thinking about the celebration. What was bothering him so much?

Having come to regret ever having helped to plan Celebrate Freedom, Alexei felt immense anxiety regarding the event. How foolish were they to believe that such a widely announced celebration would not be a target of some terrorist act? How naive were they to think that the terrorists would view the death of their leader as a cause to abandon their mission? How could he have missed the clues that the terrorists were still out there? Did the active members of UFW really believe that only the obvious cells existed? Over the past month, Alexei had asked himself these questions countless times. He wondered how he could be the only one to see the potential danger that this blatant act of arrogance would bring.

If his assumptions were correct, the terrorists could have been planning an attack for some time. Their present desire for revenge made the celebration a perfect opportunity to strike. The rapid beat of his heart motored the movement of blood through his veins. He tried to calm himself from his silent rage.

Few people outside of his country knew of the extensive resources the terrorists had collected. His colleagues had done their best to try to forget the mistakes that they and their pred-ecessors had made. Nothing can be erased from history ... only accepted. His country had done what it had to do to survive in a time when poverty had threatened its own independent existence on the earth. They had done what they needed to do in order to have any hope of rebuilding. Again, this lullaby eased him to sleep.

Sunday, September 10th

-12-

From the airplane window, Cheryl lost herself in the distance between her body and the water below. What an amazing view. This was her first time on an airplane, and she'd been nervous about the flight. Regardless, her slender frame molded into the cushioned seat as if it were her couch at home. Her nerves having been calmed, all she could think about was getting to the beach. Before she knew it, they were landing in Orlando.

"Hannah, we're here. Wake up. You've got to see this view."

Hannah's grogginess suggested that excitement had kept her awake most of the night. "We are?" She tried to sound convincing, but her eyes were closed.

The plane was on the ground in no time. To the anxious girls, the taxi to the gate seemed to take forever.

Hannah and her escorts gathered their carry-on's and headed off the plane. Hollow sounding steps created a cadence as the little girl trotted down the ramp.

Wide awake, she was full of questions now. "Do you think Mickey or Goofy will be here to meet us?"

"Oh, sweetie, I don't think so," Cheryl answered. "I think they're probably all busy at work. But you'll see all of those characters at the park."

As they emerged into the airport, the sunshine hit them like a warm spotlight. Kendra grabbed Cheryl's elbow and pointed straight ahead. "I think they're here for us."

Next to the ticket agent's desk stood a group of four smiling individuals. One held a sign with Hannah's name. One guy was dressed in khaki shorts and a worn University of Florida t-shirt. He introduced himself as Joel, and called the rest of the welcome wagon by name.

"Hi there. We've got a car outside for you. Ready?" Joel motioned for one of his partners to head to baggage claim.

The three ladies followed their guide outside where a green SUV waited. The crew helped the ladies into their seats.

"Don't worry," Joel said. "The other guys will meet us at the house with your bags."

Once everyone was buckled up and comfortable, Joel climbed into the front passenger seat and instructed the driver to head to the Make-A-Wish house.

"Everyone comfy? We'll be at the house in a jiff. We're hosting three other families while you folks are with us, but you'll each have your own floor. You won't have to share the bathroom with anyone else." He winked. Looking over his left shoulder, he caught Kendra nudging Cheryl in the ribs.

"Okay ladies, we're almost there. We have lunch waiting for you. Once you're unpacked, you can browse through some of the Orlando Visitors Guide magazines and decide what you want to do first."

The driver signaled a right turn and entered a well-kept subdivision. Minutes later, they were at their destination. The ladies checked out their accommodations. This was Florida to the tee, complete with palm trees and oranges. Was that a pool in the back yard?

"I can tell you've noticed the pool." Joel paused for a minute to enjoy Hannah's reaction. Her enthusiasm made him smile.

"Are you the lifeguard?" Kendra kidded.

Cheryl tried to fight the flushing red from spreading across her cheeks, but it was too late. She looked down, pretending to search for something in her purse. A sideways glance to her sister prompted them both to giggle. This trip was going to be fun.

Joel gave the ladies a brief tour of their temporary living space.

"Ladies, if there's anything any of us can do for you, let us know." He focused on Cheryl as he spoke. "Oh, I almost forgot. We have pre-arranged transportation for all of our guests to get to Disney World tomorrow evening for Celebrate Freedom. Y'all are going, right?"

"Of course we are," Kendra answered for the group. "Are you going, Joel?"

"Oh, I'll be there. I wouldn't miss this show for the world. I can't wait to see the fireworks."

* * *

In front of the Westin Hotel, Tony waited for a cab to take him to meet the rest of the launch team. He hoped this meeting would last no longer than an hour, because he wanted to get some rest. His flu had moved into the muscle ache phase. Wishing he'd brought his own personal masseuse, he looked forward to doing nothing more than relaxing in the hotel room until the actual hour of the show.

Disappointed that his poor health was making this memorable show feel like nothing more than just another job, he couldn't wait for it all to be over. He'd given up all hope of feeling better any time soon, and his only goal at the moment was to make it through the next two days. He was anxious to get home and visit the doctor. From the corner of his eye, Tony watched as a glowing yellow taxi approached from his left.

Sitting back, he closed his eyes. His head fell to rest on the cracked faux leather cushion behind him. The honking and screeching from outside fell on Tony's deaf ears. He could've fallen asleep in the seat if he'd allowed himself.

The cab driver politely repeated the fare to Tony. He watched his passenger shake himself back into the moment. The impatient driver snatched the crumpled bills from Tony's jittery hand.

Using walls and rails for support, Tony guided himself through the guarded entrance to the platform that would be the setting for the following night. He showed his ID tag to the security men and took a seat near the front of the recently erected stage. Without success, he looked around to find the rest of his team. He figured he was about ten minutes early. Leaning forward, he made a pillow of his arms and relaxed. As he combed his fingers through his hair, he could feel the heat from his body escaping from his forehead.

Feeling a light tap on his shoulder, he looked up to find two men from his team awaiting instructions. Within minutes, the rest of the crew arrived and Tony began the meeting. With haste, he went through a review of the basic steps for the show.

"Guys, please go over the duty assignments I handed out earlier. If you have any questions, now's the time to ask. Remember to be here at 3:45. Be on time."

He escorted his team to the exact location where they'd be working the next night. Taking a deep breath, Tony exhaled through puffed cheeks. He inhaled slowly once more and watched the expressions on the faces of his men.

***

Sharona watched Alexei smile at her from across the linen-covered table. After returning an affectionate expression, she continued to eat her dinner. She couldn't remember the last time her husband had brought her to a fancy restaurant for a meal. Somehow he'd managed to sneak away from his work long enough to take her out for this pleasing, but late, dinner.

With no children, family responsibilities hadn't kept the Gousev's from frequenting restaurants. Alexei's work had been his offspring. He'd focused all of his energy on his job for as long as Sharona could remember. She knew that a successful career in politics had been his goal since childhood. Sharona remembered stories of Alexei in first level school. She'd been told that all he'd wanted to do was to be like his father when he grew up.

His respect of his father's work with the leadership of the Union of Soviet Socialist Republic was apparent. She knew that

Alexei viewed his father as a role model.

When his father committed suicide, Sharona had not yet met Alexei. She would've liked to have been there to comfort him during that hard time.

By focusing on his education, Alexei had fought his sorrow. His success at school had led him to the military after graduation. During his time stationed in Turkey, Alexei had met Sharona.

As a young girl in a discriminating world, Sharona saw the opportunity for a new life in Alexei's eyes. Within months after their meeting, she married him.

Since Alexei spent the majority of his time away in active military duty, the next years were lonely for Sharona. She knew that he missed her as much as she missed him, but an impressive military record was a necessary prerequisite for him to enter into a career in politics. She knew he'd succeed at whatever dreams he had, and she stood by him in his efforts to pick up where his father had left off. She always suspected that by plunging himself so deeply into his work, Alexei felt he could accomplish his father's unfinished dream of helping to build a unified nation.

Most of all, Alexei wished for his father to rest in peace.

Whatever his motivations were, Sharona knew one thing to be certain. Her husband loved her, and he would always take care of her. She had learned to overcome the feeling of the missed opportunity of never having borne children, and she'd accepted the life that she was given. Sharona Gousev loved her husband, and she knew he loved her. For this, she was happy and content. However, the different life she'd led as a child haunted her in her new world.

Again, she smiled at him. This time, she realized something had caught his eye at the door. She turned to look behind her, where she saw several of his colleagues speaking with the host.

With a soft kiss on the corner of her lips, Alexei excused himself. He placed his napkin on his chair and walked toward the back of the room. There, he was greeted by his supervisor, accompanied by two other military officers. He shook their hands and escorted them outside to talk. When he returned, he was distracted.

"My dear, are you ready to go?" He drank the last sip of wine from his glass as he leaned over to help Sharona from her chair.

"Alexei, you have not even finished your meal. That is not like you."

"I know, but we must go." Alexei motioned for the server to retrieve his check. "Put on your sweater, my love."

Only the humming of the car engine could be heard during the ride home. What had caused his mood swing this time? What had he been told? Sharona remained silent as she followed her husband through the door of their home and straight to bed. The enjoyable evening was over.

In his nightly ritual, Alexei tossed and turned, unable to sleep. Thoughts of the emergency meeting for the following morning occupied his mind. What could be so important that they hadn't already discussed and planned for? He wondered why his superiors had felt it necessary to interrupt his dinner for this. Would a phone call not have sufficed? Most important, he wondered if something had happened to change their plans for September twelfth. He wished that the latter were true.

He'd love nothing more than to take his Sharona and run far away before the celebration occurred. He didn't know what might happen, but he felt fear in knowing that anything could happen. He thought of his father. Alexei desperately wanted to please him.

With her back to her husband, Sharona laid on her side. Once she knew Alexei was asleep, she slid from beneath the blankets and left the room. Careful to be quiet, she glided down the hall and into the library, Alexei's office. Her touch of the computer keys created an illumination as the screen-saver flashed to the desktop. The connection went through in silence, and Sharona typed the familiar letters into the address bar at the top of the browser page. The travel time seemed longer for every visit she made. She was afraid of getting caught.

Turning to check the doorway for any sign of Alexei, Sharona nudged a book off the corner of the desk. The hollow thud of the wood floor caused her to jump. Her stray hand knocked a tin picture frame from its perch, and it clanged to the floor. She hurried back to the bedroom and felt relieved to find her husband still asleep. She hated having to hide from him. At least it would be over soon.

Monday, September 11th

-13-

Cheryl awoke to the morning sun and looked over at Hannah, who was still sound asleep. With dainty steps, she walked across the hard wood floor to find Kendra.

"Hey, Cheryl," Kendra said. "Grab some coffee and come out on the balcony."

After breakfast, they planned to hit the beach. They were already looking forward to the evening. The theme park had reserved front row seats for all of the Make-A-Wish children and their families.

Having coffee on the balcony with Kendra was a pleasant way for Cheryl to start the day. She pulled her feet up to the edge of her chair and took the mug in both hands, elevating it to the tip of her nose. A deep breath filled her inside with the aroma of fresh-ground coffee beans. She closed her eyes and took one more long, intentional breath. After a short meditation, she opened her eyes to see Hannah standing at the doorway.

"Hi sweetie. How long have you been up? Did I wake you?"

"No, Mom, you didn't wake me. I woke up on my own. This is nice out here." In a gentle movement, Hannah lowered Cheryl's feet to the ground and made a seat on her mother's lap.

Cheryl wrapped her arms around her daughter. "How are you feeling this morning, pumpkin?"

"I feel fine. I'm ready to go to the beach." Hannah bounded from her seat.

"Okay, dear. Go and get your bathing suit. We have time to

grab a quick breakfast. Our ride leaves at ten sharp."

* * *

Tony had been awake for an hour when he heard the phone ring. He considered ignoring it until he realized it was probably Uncle George. He rolled to the other side of the bed and decreased the volume of the television before he answered.

"Hello?"

"Hey Tony, how's it going? How's everything in New York? Is your team all set to go?"

"Everything's running according to the plan. We'll kick butt tonight, Uncle George."

"Good, good." George sounded satisfied. "How are ya feeling, Tony? You know it's not too late for me to get you some help. Just say the word."

"I'll get through it just fine." Tony told an innocent lie.

He bid farewell to his uncle and curled his body back into a fetal position. Why did he have to get sick at a time like this? He closed his eyes and went back to sleep. He was glad he had time to rest for a bit.

It seemed like only seconds later when the phone rang again. This time, one of Tony's team members was on the line.

"Mr. Lonitesci, where are you?"

Tony shot up and looked at the nightstand, mortified to see that it was nearly five o'clock. He should've been at the show site over an hour before.

"Oh, man, I'm so sorry. I must've dozed off. I'll be there in a few minutes." Before he heard an answer, he dropped the phone back into the handset and dragged his aching body into the shower. As he washed his face he rubbed his chin with the back of his hand. The rough skin caught his attention. He was way too old to have acne.

* * *

Shane strolled through the Mall, peering at the stage that had been set up on the capitol's lawn. He smiled as cameras shot candid photos of him and waved to the people who'd worked so hard to prepare for the celebration. Paces ahead of his Secret Service crew, he savored the time by himself. The sounds of guitars and drums played independently of each other as the entertainers worked to complete their sound checks. The fun was almost ready to begin.

Excitement was thick in the air. Early that morning, some of the staff had witnessed people already claiming space for their lawn chairs. The pride in the atmosphere generated an electrical current, and Shane knew that the citizens of the United States had long deserved this celebration. A photographer called to him from his far left, and he turned to force one last smile. Aware of the growing concern on his face, he headed inside before the media caught on to his mood.

Shane pushed his door closed and plopped down at his desk. Opening a lower desk drawer, he retrieved a fax that he'd stuffed under some other files. Securing his own fax machine had been one of many struggles with his security team, but, of course, he'd won. After all, that was part of his job. Why should he have to see his faxed correspondences secondhand? How dangerous could it be for him to have a fax machine in his office, anyway?

Phone in hand, he pressed a familiar speed dial button.

"Hey, Alan. Any chance you can come over here in the next few minutes? I have something I want you to take a look at." From his desktop, the fax stared at Shane as he waited.

Alan stepped inside the walls of the president's corridors and took a seat in front of Shane.

"What did you want me to see?"

"Thanks for coming over so fast." Shane passed the fax over to Alan to review. "It came in at eleven o'clock last night ... from an unidentified number. I can't find any way to determine its origin. I've been thinking about it ever since it came, but I thought it was probably a hoax. Something about it makes me uneasy, though. Can you find out who sent this?"

"I'll do my best. Confidential, I guess?" Alan asked.

"Highly. This is for your eyes only. I know this makes your job more difficult, but I don't want to incite an unnecessary panic over this letter ... not this close to the time of the celebration."

"Okay. I'll see what I can do. We don't have much time before the celebration. Do you think it's authentic, Shane?"

"I don't know what to think." Shane threw his hands in the air. His right hand fell to rest on his head, massaging his scalp with his fingertips. "I just want to take everything as seriously as we can at this point, even though I feel the odds are more likely that it's a sick joke. This brings me to my next request. Will you please go over with me, one more time, the security we've put together for each of our domestic shows? And, if possible, can we step it up a notch, at least here in D.C. and in New York?"

"I'll pull something together." Alan appreciated Shane's direct involvement in day-to-day operations. This president never took his position too seriously to care about the details. Alan reviewed the plans that had been approved and executed for the celebration's security.

Shane remained at his desk, unable to shake his feeling of uneasiness. The celebration couldn't be called off now. Too much time and money had gone into the planning of this day, and he owed it to the people to offer them confidence in their surroundings. He couldn't rationalize risking everything that he and all of his men had worked for because of a non-specific anonymous threat like this. What did this letter mean? Who was still out there? The terrorists? Tossing his copy of the fax back into the drawer, he went on about his business for the day. He had a speech to review and a celebration to lead.

"The war on terrorism has been won." He spoke aloud to convince himself.

* * *

Her parents were sad, but they understood. The phone conversation had been better than she'd expected, and she was glad to have said good-bye. Robin waited for the nurse to come back with the phone again. She had made her call home, right? Or had she been dreaming about it? Either way, Robin didn't think it mattered now. What could anyone do for her that hadn't already been done? She knew this wasn't home, yet she could barely determine where she was. Did Chuck know where to find her? What if he was worried? Maybe she should call him, too. Where was the nurse with the phone?

-14-

A cool, evening breeze blew through the Gousev house. While pretending to read a book, Alexei watched his wife prepare dinner. His mind wandered back and forth between the celebration that was to take place the following evening and the meeting that he'd attended that morning.

At six o'clock, the meeting was called to order. Alexei sat opposite the president of the Russian Federation, and the premier and his cabinet rounded out the table. A selection of other military officials filled in the perimeter of the tight space.

"Thank you for coming to this gathering on short notice," the premier announced. "After completing an ongoing investigation of old biological weapon arsenals within our country, we have determined that we cannot account for the contents of many of these arsenals."

After all of these years, Alexei wondered what had finally made them decide to check. He knew the truth. Most of the men in that room today probably did not even know the locations of all of the arsenals that had existed over forty years ago. The contents of the unguarded factories had probably been taken long before. No one knew for sure, but they were paid handsome fees not to care. How convenient it was that they now claimed to have no knowledge of this payment.

The anxiety that kept Alexei awake each night was due to his awareness of the inner workings of his government. He knew that they may never feel the guilt that he felt ... the guilt that he'd inherited from his father.

The missing smallpox virus that had created this sudden

awareness among the officials was only a drop in the bucket compared to the virus that had been sold outright nearly forty years ago. Either way, the truth was simple. The terrorists possessed more of the virus than anyone wanted to believe, and it was his government's fault. However, no one in that room today had offered to accept this blame.

As Sharona called him to dinner, Alexei removed his mind from the confines of that meeting. As soon as he finished eating, he thanked his wife for a good meal and left the table. With his book on his lap, he rested in his chair. Hours later, he remained on the same page. When he was finished reading, he escorted his wife to the bedroom to go to sleep.

"My dear, I have much to do tomorrow." Alexei kissed Sharona on the head. He planned to wake early in the morning to witness the kickoff of Celebrate Freedom in the United States. A heavy weight situated itself in the bottom of his stomach as he counted the hours until the first launch of the celebration.

Lying in bed, he wondered if he'd made the right choice. Was his fax in time to make a difference? At least he tried. Feeling like a coward for not identifying himself as the sender, he knew he wasn't prepared to give confidential information to outsiders. His head guided his judgment, but his heart controlled his actions. Now all he could do was wait.

At five o'clock in the morning, Alexei sat up in his bed, careful not to wake Sharona, and he turned on the television. As he expected, the news show was broadcasting the celebration.

"Launch time is in two minutes," the New York anchorman announced. His voice was followed by a delayed Russian translation.

The cameras followed Shane McAlister from all angles as he approached the stage. The sound of the American national anthem rang loud as the station showed side-by-side pictures of Washington and New York. After the music ended, Alexei listened as Shane spoke a few welcoming words. With the world watching, the first fireworks were launched into the air.

* * *

As the initial explosions of color erupted into the air, Cheryl tightened her grip on Hannah's sticky hand. Bright designs filled the sky above the crowd. Leaning her head back, Cheryl focused on the crystals of color bursting above.

Reds, whites and blues formed the flag of the United States. After waving back and forth, the flag appeared to have showered down around the spectators, like colored raindrops. Without thinking, Cheryl brushed at the imaginary ash she felt sure was on her shoulders. As a child, she could never be convinced that the remnants of the fireworks wouldn't fall on her. She giggled at the silliness of the whole idea. The next launch shot up into the air, and a bright turquoise green exploded with determination to fill the sky. Several yellow bursts broke out nearby, and another flag design formed in the midst of the fizzling out yellow. This time, the blue in the flag took on the color of ocean green, a creative vision of the American flag, but beautiful just the same.

A solid forty minutes of fireworks electrified the Orlando horizon. Cheryl, Hannah and Kendra watched with amazement at the beauty of the chemical magic.

"This is the greatest show I've ever seen!" Kendra wrapped her arms around her niece. A tight embrace connected them. "I've seen Lonitesci shows before, but they've outdone themselves this time."

"I can smell the fire!" Hannah exclaimed.

"That's not fire, honey," Cheryl said. "That's the smoke from where they're igniting the fireworks. It's all the way over there."

"Okay, but I can still smell it, Mom." Hannah took a deep breath and exhaled. "Yep, I can smell it."

* * *

In the finale, every color imaginable exploded one after another in the sky above. The brilliant turquoise green offered its viewers a subtle reminder that, in science, anything was possible.

During the show, Tony had difficulty keeping himself together. His appreciation of his team grew as he realized their dedication. The autumn air felt cold to him, but everyone around was dressed in short sleeves and shorts. Shivering, he pulled his baseball cap farther down over his eyes. Fashion being the least of his worries, he turned up his shirt collar to cover his neck.

The show provoked loud cheering from the audience. The ground vibrated with the wild movement of the onlookers. Pops and crackles created the percussion, the bassline for the dance in the sky. In the city of lights, this show offered its own unique dazzle and flair.

Tony was pleased with the results. He wished he could be charged by the energy from the crowd. Jake would've loved this. He could see the reflections of the colors in the faces around him as the vibrant hues appeared to rain down. The dazzling effects seemed to impress every member of the outdoor audience.

Tony noticed that the blue colors appeared to be more like turquoise and the reds somewhat like orange. That was his critical eye. Maybe Uncle George had achieved that turquoise green he'd been working for after all. Growing tired on his feet, Tony was relieved to set up the launch for the grand finale.

The final explosions bled through the air, blanketing the sky over New York City.

Without even staying for cleanup, Tony left once his role was fulfilled. He rushed to his hotel room and packed for his departure. Scheduled to leave before daylight, he requested a wake-up call. Already dressed in the clothes he planned to wear on the plane, he laid down on the bed. In a matter of hours, he'd be home. An appointment to see his doctor had already been made for the following morning.

***

The quality of the display satisfied George. His contact with the other cities during the show had kept the performances as coordinated as possible. He'd worried about Tony, though. Most of his discussions with the New York team had been made with the crew leader instead of his nephew.

The Mall was filled with people, shoulder to shoulder, as far as George could see. The smiles on their faces glowed with excitement. He was grateful his family had been chosen to be such a large part of this celebration. At that moment, he was proud of his company, of himself, and of his country. The emotion in the atmosphere was contagious. A tear rolled down the corner of his right eye, and he wiped it away. He genuinely felt that each and every one of the people present had been touched by his show.

He took a break long enough to enjoy the finale of his latest efforts. The fireworks exploded in planned succession, resulting in a piece of artwork in the sky. His eye focused on the bright turquoise green in the center of the display. A double-take confirmed ocean green crystals, which complimented the turquoise. The glowing balls of energy dispersed, creating the illusion that they'd fallen to the crowds below.

"Well, I'll be—" George spoke out loud. "How did Tony do that?" George had been working on that color for years.

* * *

On his television screen, Alexei watched the western celebrations take place. He'd been paying attention for nearly an hour, expecting the worst. To his pleasant surprise, the scene at each venue remained a positive display of celebration. Nothing seemed out of place, not that he would notice if anything was. As the news cameras flashed pictures from city to city, he convinced himself that perhaps his paranoia was unfounded after all.

Washington, New York, Orlando and Atlanta monopolized the East Coast news coverage. Only cheers of excitement and sounds of patriotic songs filled the air. This really was a celebration of freedom after all. He dressed for work and left for the office. Maybe his fears were unnecessary. He prayed for this to be the case, as he reviewed the plans for the Moscow celebration that evening.

* * *

Alan took the call from the West Coast during the second hour of the East Coast celebration. He spoke with sincerity to the show commander on the other end of the line, as his colleague explained the bad news.

"I'm not sure what to do," the Los Angeles show coordinator explained. "We have two hours until launch, and this damn weather pattern has thrown a real wrench in our plans." Pausing from the conversation, he barked out orders to his crew. Frustration coated his words. "Sorry about that. I know Las Vegas, San Diego and Seattle are all in the same boat. These storms aren't goin' anywhere before the morning. Should we grab some stadiums and move this inside?"

"Why don't you reschedule for tomorrow night? Indoor shows won't generate half the excitement without the fireworks displays. Plus, we'll have to set a limit for attendees. This has been such a hit so far. I hate to see everyone out there miss it. If you want, I'll make some calls to the other sites and pass along the new plan."

"Thanks, sir."

Alan called the affected cities. The change would be fine. The grand finale of the whole thing would be on the West Coast now ... even better.

Shane wandered to the festival, which was still in full swing. Making several calls to local security checkpoints, he confirmed that everything was all right. This was something else he'd have to apologize for. His Secret Service team hated when he took matters into his own hands, but they loved him just the same. That's the guy he was, and this was the kind of thing he did.

Each conversation gave him the right answer. After thirty minutes of phone calls and questions, Shane flipped his phone closed and buried it in his jacket pocket. He took only two steps before retrieving it again. He pressed a number assigned to dial a preset extension.

After one ring, a smile appeared on his face. Having confirmed a rendezvous point, Shane went to meet his wife.

Tuesday, September 12th

-15-

Tony listened as the pilot announced the time. It was 5:30 a.m. A complimentary airline pillow protected his head from the chill of the tiny windowpane. Comfort or germs? Tony gave up on his usual boycott of the covered foam rectangles. On this particular morning, this airline amenity was necessary for him to make it through the flight. Similar to every other morning over the past few weeks, he struggled to keep his eyes open. With the scratchy blue blanket tucked around his shoulders and the rim of his hat down over his eyes, he rested. Even the dim side panel lights in the cabin made his sensitive eyes water. At least the flight wouldn't be long. He focused his thoughts on getting home and getting some real medicine.

His body temperature burned through his blanket and layered clothing, yet Tony shook with uncontrollable chills. He declined the flight attendant's offer to bring him a beverage, although he thought hot tea sounded like a nice idea. Sitting up to drink something required too much physical effort. He tried to sleep, but his quivering body kept him awake.

"Good morning, folks. Sorry to disturb you, but please return to your seats and fasten your seat belts. We're beginning our descent into Pittsburgh," the pilot announced.

After an hour of fidgeting, Tony welcomed the information. Never before had he fallen victim to air sickness, but today he eyed up the white bag behind the seat in front of him, just in case.

Through heavy, intentional breathing, he controlled the

movement of air out through his mouth and back in through his nose. He flipped through the pages of a magazine, keeping his hand on the dreaded white bag. A few smooth bumps of the aircraft confirmed that the plane was on the ground, and Tony felt more confident that he could make it to the gate without being sick.

Minutes felt like an hour as the airline passengers stood hunched over in the aisle, awaiting their turns to exit the aircraft. Tony pushed his way into the line, breaking into a jog as soon as his shoes touched the exit ramp. After a few seconds at that pace, a quick walk was all he could manage as he hurried through the airport. His eyes located the nearest restroom.

Hurling his body into a stall, he plopped down on the floor in front of the toilet. Beads of sweat poured from his neck and forehead as muscle contractions in his abdomen caused severe stomach cramps. His mid-section continued to tighten in a regular rhythm for fifteen minutes. When he felt confident that he could stand without assistance, Tony grabbed his bag and headed outside.

Either forgetting or not caring about his car in the satellite parking lot, he threw himself into the back seat of a taxi. He positioned his bag on the center of his lap. With an exhausting effort to speak, Tony Lonitesci directed the cab driver to go to the nearest emergency room.

***

September twelfth, what a refreshing day. Shane was up bright and early. At his office, he checked for faxes or messages. A mild concern worried him that the news of an attack could still be on the horizon. A call to Alan confirmed that all had gone well. Shane leaned back in his chair and prayed a silent note of thanks. So far, everything had gone as planned. The celebration was a success.

Shane placed a call to his Russian colleague. The Moscow show was set to launch in just seven hours, and he wanted to wish

Alexei the best of luck. The phone rang three times before Shane heard his friend's tired voice.

"Hello?" Alexei's phone had an identification system that allowed him to prepare his answer in the language of the caller.

"Hello, Alexei." Shane greeted him in a cheerful tone. "How are things in the East? Are you anxious for the launch?"

"Yes. It will be good, no? Everything went okay?"

"Well, it's been a hit here. I was sure you'd be excited."

Alexei hesitated with his response, so Shane spoke again.

"Is this a bad time, Alexei? Did I catch you in the middle of something?"

"No. I was listening is all. So, the party was good? Everything was okay?"

"Yes. Everything was fine. The western cities had to postpone due to weather, but, other than that, everything was great. I'm sure it will be smooth for you, too."

"Yes, I think." Alexei sounded distracted.

"Well, I suppose you have a lot to do. I'll speak with you again soon, Alexei."

Wondering why Alexei had asked him at least twice in the conversation if everything was okay in the United States, Shane's nervous feeling returned. He called Alan.

***

Hannah was up first, even before her mother. She was tired from the activities the night before, but not too exhausted to start another day of vacation.

"Mom, get up. Let's go to the beach." Hannah shook her mother's arm as she whispered in her ear.

Straining to distinguish between her dream and the voice she heard, Cheryl rolled over and looked into her daughter's eyes. She motioned for Hannah to join her on her bed, and they snuggled together. "How are you feeling this morning, honey?"

"I feel fine, Mom. Can we go to the beach?"

"Yes, we can go, but first you need to eat so you can take

your medicine. Get your suit on. Do you know if Aunt Kendra's up yet?"

Hannah shrugged her shoulders. She swung her legs from the bed and pulled the covers down, signaling for her mom to follow. She grabbed her beach clothes and went into the bathroom to change.

Cheryl found her sister on the balcony.

"Kendra, what's our plan for today? Any ideas?" A few moments passed without any answer. "Let's decide while we eat. Come on."

At the entrance of the dining room, Joel greeted the smiling crew. "Mind if I join you ladies? It seems that we have a full house." He motioned around to the many diners before guiding them to an empty table.

"No problem," Kendra responded. "You might be able to help us with our plan for the day. Any suggestions?"

"Of course, I can help. If you'd like some company, I have the afternoon off. I'll drive."

***

Tony checked himself into the emergency room at the University of Pittsburgh Medical Center. With haste, he filled out the necessary paperwork. His arms remained tucked up inside the body of his sweatshirt as he waited for his name to be called. In a combined effort to stay warm and to conceal the embarrassing red bumps on his face, he kept his baseball cap pulled down over his eyes.

In the airport restroom, he'd noticed that the splotches on his face had multiplied. He feared the rash was an allergic reaction to something he'd eaten as opposed to the acne he'd suspected earlier. That would also explain the severe stomach cramping. Or worse, what if it was measles? He'd known someone who'd had measles a few years before. That guy had been laid up for weeks. Tony slumped in his chair and prayed for his name to be called next.

He couldn't remember the last time he'd felt so ill.

After forty-five minutes of waiting, the nurse called Tony's name and ushered him into an exam room. Without ever making eye contact, she asked him the standard series of questions and recorded his answers on her clipboard. She took his temperature and blood pressure in much the same lackadaisical manner.

"Wow, you've got one heck of a fever," she said. A look of shock filled her face as she noticed the rash on Tony's face. "Will you remove your hat please?" Pulling a latex glove over her hand, the nurse took the cap and placed it in a plastic bag. After making a few notes on the chart, she backed toward the door. "A doctor will be with you shortly."

Since sitting upright was a strain, Tony felt it necessary to lie down on the bed. Breathing had become difficult for him. In just a few minutes, a doctor entered the room. He was dressed in a yellow paper gown and wearing a mask on his face. That seemed like some serious precautionary measures. Maybe this was measles after all.

"Hello there, Mr. Lonitesci." The doctor read his patient's name from the chart. "I'm Dr. Brown, Chief of Emergency Medicine."

After reviewing the notes on Tony's chart, he snapped a pair of plastic gloves over his hands and began his examination. He started with the rash and spent several minutes looking at each of the red pustules, which were now coating Tony's face and neck.

"Open your mouth wide." He shined a light down into the back of Tony's throat. "Will you lift your shirt for me?" A look of concern filled the doctor's eyes at what his request revealed.

Tony looked down, but saw nothing on his chest to cause concern. Unlike his face and neck, he saw only sweat on his feverish body.

"What do you think is wrong with me? Allergic reaction? Flu?"

"Well Mr. Lonitesci," Dr. Brown began. "This looks to me like you've somehow contracted a case of adult chicken pox. Do you have any school age children at home?"

"My son, Jake, is five. He's in school." Tony thought about

Jake for a second. "But he doesn't have chicken pox."

Dr. Brown shook his head as he spoke. "He doesn't necessarily have to have it himself. He could carry the virus and never suffer through a breakout. However, for you, as an adult, this can be dangerous. We'll need to keep you here until I see some sign of improvement. Get comfortable. Odds are you'll be here for the next few nights. Someone will be here soon to take you to an isolation room. I'm afraid you're quite contagious. Don't worry, we'll take good care of you. I'll check in on you again in a little while."

The doctor left the room and Tony chuckled. Chicken pox? Who would've ever thought? Funny though, it didn't itch. He remembered having chicken pox as a child. The itching was enough to drive him insane. He'd read somewhere that children had higher tolerance levels of pain and discomfort. Not in this case. He tried to make himself comfortable while he waited for the doctor to return.

Dr. Brown left the cafeteria line with a diet soda and a turkey sandwich. He took a seat at the first table he saw and began to eat his meal. While reading the paper and enjoying his sandwich, he was interrupted by a group of third year medical students. He could hear their ongoing debate as they walked in his direction.

"Doctor Brown, can we ask your opinion about something?" the first student inquired.

"Sure, I have a few minutes." He was always willing to help with the students. "What's up?"

"Well," the first student continued, "if a person has a severe outbreak of chicken pox as a child, isn't it more likely that it would reemerge as shingles in his adult years? You know ... instead of adult chicken pox?"

"Usually, but it depends on the patient. People react in different ways," Dr. Brown answered. "Sorry I couldn't be of more help, guys." He was aware this wasn't the clear response they wanted. "Hey, why do you ask? Were you talking about the gentleman that came into the ER today?"

"What ER patient?" one intrigued medical student asked. "Is there someone here with chicken pox? An adult?"

"Yes. At least I believe so. He came in this morning. He's got an awful case. I admitted him for observation. That's not why you were asking?"

"Well, we didn't hear anything about that," the student said. "We were actually discussing this because another guy in our class just took a tour of the Latrobe Area Hospital. He told us they'd reported three cases of adult chicken pox in the last two weeks. He didn't seem to think it was any big deal, but I did. Anyway, I guess I was wrong."

Dr. Brown wrapped the uneaten half of his sandwich in his napkin and took one last, slow swallow from his soda.

"Thanks for the conversation," he said. He deposited his tray on top of the trash receptacle. Moving past the students, the doctor made his way to the administration office of the emergency room. "Get me the Chief of the ER at the Latrobe Area Hospital. Please, call me as soon as you have him on the line."

"Is this an emergency?" the receptionist asked.

"It could be. I sure hope not, but it could be."

* * *

The nurse gathered the last remaining sheets and shoved them into the plastic bag. Stepping outside of the room, she stripped herself of her clothing covers, removing her gloves last. With a clean towel, she scooped up the pile and dropped it all into one last plastic bag. The cleanup crew would be back soon. They hadn't wasted any time in getting the body to the crematorium. She pitied the person who would make the call to Robin's family.

-16-

After contemplating other possibilities for forty minutes, Dr. Brown decided to do a further examination of Tony Lonitesci. In the meantime, he instructed the front desk personnel to contact him as soon as anyone at Latrobe returned his call.

After properly covering himself, he entered Tony's room, hoping to get more information from his patient.

"How long have you been sick?"

"Oh, about two weeks, I guess," Tony answered.

"Tell me again how this started. What were the first symptoms that you felt?"

"I thought I had the flu. You know ... I was extra tired and run down. I felt crappy. Sorry Doc, I know you want details, but I don't know how to explain it any better."

"Have you been out of the country lately? Say, in the last month?"

"I haven't traveled out of the country in over six months. I'm long overdue for a vacation." Tony tried to make light of the serious line of questioning. "Why are you asking? What would that have to do with anything?"

Reluctant to comment on his speculation of what the problem could be, the doctor danced around answering Tony's questions. His mannerisms had turned from casual during his earlier visit to more serious, and he felt his patient could sense his present state of concern. Taking care not to create any anxiety, he made some notes and excused himself from the room.

"I'll be back in a few minutes to run some more tests. Try to relax while I'm gone."

Before he could ask any more questions, Tony watched the doctor disappear into the hallway. Too weak to follow him to the door, he rolled over on his side and closed his eyes. At least he could wait in a comfortable bed. He drifted off in no time. His slumber kept him from noticing the bright red sign the nurse positioned on the outside of the isolation room door.

A managed chaos erupted in the ER. Janitorial employees draped yellow caution tape from the entrance of the emergency room to the elevators at the far end of the hall, blocking passage into the wing from outside or from the other areas of the hospital. Several doctors gathered together at the ER desk and participated in quiet, solemn discussions.

"I don't want to jump the gun here, but my gut tells me that we need to dig a little deeper into this Lonitesci case. I'm giving Latrobe ten more minutes to get back to me, or I'm calling them again." Dr. Brown pointed to the telephone as he spoke.

As if it could obey orders, the phone rang. The nurse at the desk transferred the call to his office.

After fifteen minutes, the doctor emerged, ready to initiate a new plan. He gathered his co-workers with him in a tight circle and explained what had to happen next. A heavy curtain of alarm fell upon the medical professionals as they scattered in different directions, following a plan they'd only read about in emergency management protocols before that day.

A call was made to the Pennsylvania State Health Department, and the state of medical emergency officially began.

Dr. Brown wiggled his fingers into a fresh pair of gloves and secured a facemask tight behind his ears. He slipped into yet another yellow paper cocoon and returned to Tony's room.

This experience was a first in his medical career. He'd never before had to tell a patient that he might have an infectious, deadly disease that was thought to have been eradicated over thirty years before.

Until now, smallpox was a disease that medical students read about in courses on the history of modern medicine. Medical doctors all over the world were convinced that they had not only eradicated the disease, but that they had destroyed all remaining traces of it a number of years earlier.

The events that had played out in front of Dr. Brown over the past twelve hours had knocked him off balance. Wishing to take a minute to collect his thoughts, he knew he couldn't spare the time.

* * *

Alexei walked to the center of the stage at the Moscow venue for Celebrate Freedom. He peered at the crowd that had assembled for the evening, studying each and every face. His purpose was twofold. His primary objective was to remain on the lookout for danger. He knew he couldn't single-handedly thwart the efforts of terrorists, but he felt that his keen judgment of character could help to identify trouble before it could strike.

With the introduction of suspect profiling, Russian officials had made legal the act of offensive attack if probable terrorists were identified. They'd realized that the success of terrorist operations most often stemmed from their unpredictable nature.

Alexei knew he had one leg up on these guys. He was sure they'd strike somewhere, somehow during one of these celebrations. He took it upon himself to protect his country.

Second, he was intent on confirming that Sharona and her family had stayed away from the celebration. His request had not gone over well when he told his wife that he didn't want her to be present for the festivity. He made his best effort at explaining that he didn't feel that this crowd would be appropriate for her or for her aging mother. He also stressed that the evening was a blatant reminder of the battles that had just ended, and he felt it impossible to put the memories of terrorism behind him. This would be a difficult night for him to celebrate.

As an example to his wife, he used the painful memory of his father's guilt in connection to terrorist activity.

"See, Sharona, I can only think of despair. We can now rest at night, and that brings peace. But, we still have far to go."

Without hinting at his present fear of yet another attack, he'd tried everything to convince her not to come without alarming her. He could hear the disappointment in her voice as he left her at the door, but she didn't seem as upset as he'd expected. Although his wife had never disobeyed his requests before, Alexei feared he might find her in the crowd that night.

The horns played and the launch team gathered at their starting point. Alexei noted his signal to begin.

"Welcome, everyone, to Celebrate Freedom."

Allowing himself to be intoxicated by the cheers, Alexei took a moment before he spoke again. When the crowd quieted, anxious to hear his words, he grew wary of the silence. The quiet before the storm. With a quaking voice, Alexei made the introductions of his colleagues. He rushed through his welcome speech and turned the show over to the launch team to start the opening fireworks.

The pyrotechnic rockets shot into the air in a planned succession. The opening of the show was the same as it had been in the American shows. The American flag symbolized the conception of the plan for the United Free World, so it was fitting in any UFW setting. The flag of the Russian Federation exploded in the air, straight up and high above the faces below. The spectators embraced the moment, appearing to be inhaling the glittering remnants of the designs. The flag of the United Free World erupted with such force and vigor that it solicited wild cheering from underneath its wave. Again, the reds appeared to be orange, and a deep ocean green accented the design. The slight imperfections of color went unnoticed.

An excited Alexei ducked through the crowd to the nearest exit. From his mobile phone, he called several of his colleagues to inquire about the activities of the night. Receiving no word of any questionable events, he realized he had little support from his peers to investigate any further. He decided to head home to his wife.

Alexei found humor in the fact that his colleagues held enough concern for this night to receive smallpox inoculations, yet they relinquished the notion of a possible terrorist attack with such ease. He forced his frustrations away and entered his home.

On the side of their bed, he sat next to Sharona. Her rigidity gave him the distinct idea that she still harbored some disappointment from their earlier discussion. Her coldness was a small price to pay for her safety. Peeling off the layers of his dress uniform, he tossed his clothing on a chair and crawled into bed. His body welcomed sleep, but, as usual, anxiety kept his mind awake.

Terrorist activity had not been recorded for nearly two years before the discovery of the body of Mohammed Atif. Had he even died at all? Was the identification of the body foolproof? What action would be more suited to a terrorist leader than falsifying his own death? Alexei's stomach grumbled at the thought. He knew that somewhere in the world these men were mocking the UFW in a celebration of their own.

***

Tony woke to the sliding steps of paper-wrapped shoes around the perimeter of his bed. He opened his eyes, a bit at a time, attempting to avoid the bright exam light above him. A few seconds were necessary for him to focus on the face in his view. Behind the mask and protective gear that covered his visitor's face, Tony could only see eyes. The seriousness in his observer's expression suggested that something was wrong.

In his hospital bed, Tony lay in nothing but a thin cotton gown. He'd watched the nurse dispose of his clothing. At least he thought she'd thrown it away. She'd shoved it all in bright orange plastic bags.

The aching in his arms and his legs had worsened, and his stomach continued to convulse in painful contractions. Tony rubbed his hand over his abdomen to soothe the pain, and he realized that the rash had spread. The lack of itching still puzzled him.

Dr. Brown looked Tony in the eyes. After helping his patient to lie back down after his examination, he wheeled a stool from the corner of the room over to the side of the bed. He drew in a long, deep breath as he steadied the rotating seat and straddled the cushion.

"Tony, I don't know how to tell you this, but I'm afraid you don't have chicken pox after all."

"Well, that's okay, Doc, I was hoping for a food allergy anyway. I could stand to lose a few pounds." Tony made a desperate attempt at a joke. When the doctor failed to respond with a laugh, he quieted and waited for more of an explanation.

"Preliminary tests and observations have led me to believe that you've somehow contracted a case of smallpox." Dr. Brown unleashed the news in a weak, but direct, voice. "I know this is difficult to digest, so I'll give you a moment. But when I return, I need to work with you, Tony, so we can find out how this happened. I need to get some answers so I can help you. Do you understand?"

Tony could only nod. He watched the doctor leave the room. Disbelief was all he could feel. Smallpox had been non-existent in the world for over thirty years. Right? This had to be a mistake. How could he have gotten smallpox? Could this be something that just seemed like smallpox? There was a vaccine for this, wasn't there? It could be treated, right? This couldn't be happening. Was his son in danger? Thoughts and questions ran through his mind. They escaped, one after the other, in the form of a crying scream through his lips. The empty room filled with his outrage.

Dr. Brown waited until Tony recovered from his emotional outburst. He heard a one-man conversation coming from the inside of the hospital room. When the noise quieted, he returned to his patient's side.

"We're going to do everything we can to help you, Tony. You're not in this alone. But, first, we need to try to figure this out." Dr. Brown paused for a response. He wasn't surprised by the silence. "Let me share with you how I came to make this preliminary diagnosis. I defined your situation as being a high probability smallpox case after a call to the Latrobe Area Hospital verified three other patients in their area who'd been treated for adult chicken pox in the past few weeks. These numbers are extraordinary in nature, so they warranted an investigation."

"What's our next step?" Tony stared through his doctor's eyes as he spoke.

"Since I have you right here, I've decided to send a lab test to the State Health Department for their verification. There's no sense waiting for Latrobe to get back to us before we move forward. We should have the results in a few hours." The Doctor leaned closer to Tony. "This might hurt a little. Hang in there." Dr. Brown scraped at a pustule on Tony's neck. He contained the sample and propelled his stool away from Tony. "The result is necessary in order to determine a definite diagnosis. In the meantime, we've got some serious work to do. I need your help in finding out how, when, and where you may have contracted this disease, if you have it. Someone will be in to draw some blood. Other than that, we're done poking at you for a while."

The spinning in his head prompted Tony to lean forward and reach for the waste can. After several powerful, heaving motions, he realized that he didn't have to vomit after all. His stomach cramps continued, but the onset of nausea was more likely due to the fear and stress stemming from the impact of the news. He slid back farther on his bed, curling into a sleeping position. The doctor encouraged him to sit up.

"Tony, I can only imagine how you're feeling right now." Dr. Brown offered genuine compassion. "I'll do everything I can to make you comfortable and to help you through this, but I need for you to focus with me for a while. Can you do that?"

"Yes." Tony replied in a low voice. "What can I do?" He gasped for a breath and started to cry.

Once enough time had passed for Tony to regain his composure, Dr. Brown spoke again.

"Are you in any way connected with military actions in this

country or in any other country?"

Tony shook his head. He looked Dr. Brown in the eyes and gestured for him to continue.

"Have you been in any other country in the last several months? Have you, or anyone else in your household, received any strange unidentified mail in the last month?"

With each question, Tony's answers remained consistent. "None of this makes sense."

"Tony, I know we can get to the bottom of this if we work together. Try hard to think of anything out of the ordinary that you've encountered in the past month. I want to help you, and I want to stop this thing before it gets out of control. I'll be back to check on you in a few minutes. I'm going to make sure your lab test has been sent out." With true sincerity, Dr. Brown locked his eyes onto Tony's. Without words, he stressed the importance of the job ahead of them. The doctor got up to leave.

"Doctor, am I gonna die?" Tony watched his physician halt in his steps.

"I'm going to do my best to make sure that doesn't happen." Dr. Brown answered with honesty.

"Doctor?" Tony called out once more. "Are there any other cases … of smallpox?"

The doctor shook his head.

"Not yet." He waited for more questions, then made his exit.

Thoughts ran rampant in Tony's mind. He thought about Jake, his Uncle George, and the guys at the plant. When a vivid picture of his funeral developed in his head, he forced himself to stop thinking. He lay back on his bed and rolled to his side. He had to call George and Karen and let them know where he was, what was happening to him. He decided to wait to make those calls until his diagnosis was certain. There was no reason to worry them without confirmation. Maybe this would turn out to be measles after all. He prayed for the latter to be true.

In order to make the sign of the cross, Tony closed his eyes and reached into the depths of his memory of his days in Catholic school. His right hand worked its way through the motions. A stream of tears ran from his eyes as he recited the Lord's Prayer.

* * *

A hard-covered binder held the reports that had been compiled for Shane. As the clock struck five, he reviewed the latest update, searching for any hint of alarming activity at any of the Celebrate Freedom festivals to date. As far as he could see, the Russian celebrations had gone well. Not having heard from Alexei made him believe that everything abroad was okay. Noting the time, he realized the end of the workday had arrived, and he hadn't eaten his lunch yet. That would explain his dizziness. He decided to step out for a bite.

Before he could move from his desk his phone rang. The identification of the incoming line confirmed the caller as Alan.

"McAlister."

"Hi, Shane. Have a minute?"

"Yes. What's on your mind?" Something about Alan's tone didn't seem right.

"We've received word from the Pennsylvania State Health Department of a possible smallpox case in Pittsburgh."

Shane took a second to process the information before he spoke. He swallowed the lump in his throat. "Probable? Do you think it's for real?"

"I don't know what to think, but they're taking it pretty seriously. They've followed their emergency protocol straight down the line. Will you hold for a second? I have a call coming in from the CDC now."

"Sure, Alan." An hour or thirty seconds could have passed while Shane waited. He was numb.

"Sir?" Alan returned to the line.

"Yes, Alan. What was that about? The same case?"

"Yes, Sir. The CDC has made a request to send a three-person Epidemic Intelligence Service Team to confirm the diagnosis and administer vaccines. I told them to move forward."

"Okay, Alan. We've got some work to do. How long will it take for you to round everyone up and get over here?"

"I'll see you in a few minutes."

"Hey, Alan?"

"Yes?"

"Do they have any idea where this originated?"

"Not yet."

"Okay, I'll see you in a bit. Thanks, Alan."

After the conversation ended, a dial tone droned on in Shane's ear. He was numb with shock. The strongest prayers in the world couldn't make this go away. He put forth his best effort anyway. Once a minute of silence passed, he was back to work. Shane knew that reaction time was crucial here. Moving through the unfamiliar motions as if they'd been rehearsed, he was thankful that the brain could take over when emotions threatened to shut down human performance.

How did this happen? Questions ran laps through his mind. The doubling of security teams and the best intelligence of the free world hadn't prevented this attack. It had to be an attack. How else would someone get smallpox in this day and age? The UFW thought they'd won.

After making urgent calls to the necessary people, he instructed his staff to meet him for an immediate discussion of the handling of the media and the protocol for the first stages of vaccinations. The Homeland Security protocol manual was transferred from its home on a bookshelf to Shane's desk. If they stayed on track, they could figure this out. At least Shane hoped so.

Shane felt confident that this was not the result of any action that took place at Celebrate Freedom. That couldn't be the case. People were watched and faces were screened during all stages of planning for that event. No plan existed that could've gotten past the security for that celebration. This had to have happened earlier. Smallpox had a two-week incubation period. The celebration was only yesterday.

Was this was a single act of domestic terrorism? This was the question of the hour. As horrific as that idea seemed, Shane felt comfort in believing that it might be the case. If this turned out to be an isolated situation, then the nightmare would soon end. He mustered up a strong front and went to meet his staff.

-17-

The Epidemic Intelligence Service Team arrived at the Pittsburgh International Airport in record time. A team of FBI agents surrounded the gate, waiting for the three passengers to exit the plane. They were the first to emerge from the doorway. Without any words, the five men walked fast to an exit where a car waited to take them to the hospital.

"What's going on here?" one member of the team asked an agent as they approached the facility.

"I'm not sure," the agent answered.

A man stumbled down the steps as he was escorted from the hospital. He was a visitor who obviously didn't want to leave.

"I have a right to know what's going on in there," the angry man shouted. "My mother's in there."

"Don't tell me something's already leaked out," the agent mumbled under his breath. This would be a long night.

A short time later, the Epidemic Intelligence Team was escorted to the roof of the building where an army helicopter rested on the helipad. Their next stop was the Andrews Air Force Base. With samples in hand, they boarded the chopper and took off.

A military aircraft would carry the samples and the team members to the Centers for Disease Control and Prevention in Atlanta, Georgia.

Returning to the hospital entrance, the agent noticed a

gathering of onlookers. The ejected visitor stood preaching to the crowd about what he thought was happening inside. Some information was correct, but most was exaggerated. Exhaling through his mouth, the agent turned to his partner.

"This could get ugly." Long strides of his athletic frame carried him to the disgruntled man in a matter of seconds. With a firm hold on the guy's shoulder, the agent pulled him to the side.

"What's the problem, sir?"

"Who are you? You're my problem right now." The irrational man wiggled to free himself of the agent's hold. "Let go of me. My mother's inside, and I heard there was a terrorist in there. I want her out of there, and they wouldn't let me take her."

"Sir, I'm sorry for your concern, but we have no confirmation of any serious problem inside," the agent said. "In the event of an emergency, you will be notified. Please, go home. You're doing no good staying here."

He encouraged the rest of the crowd to leave.

"I'm not sure we can handle these people without some help," one agent said. "Look, here comes a reporter. That's all we need." He stumbled to the side as a camera man tried to push his way by. "This is nuts. We'll need backup." Reaching for his cell phone, he made the request.

The call had barely disconnected when the phone rang back. This time, the FBI agent slid around the corner, slipping into a more silent area.

"Yes, General."

After a short conversation, the agent clapped his phone closed and made his way to his partner.

"The viral samples are on their way to Atlanta. We can expect a final confirmation of the test results by eleven-thirty tonight."

Like moths to a bright light, the media trucks appeared at the hospital. The news personnel created an additional hype by broadcasting as truth the possibility that an unknown virus was present inside.

"Ebola is present within the walls of a local Pittsburgh

hospital," one anchorman announced.

"A victim of meningitis awaits treatment at a nearby Pittsburgh hospital," another uninformed broadcaster said.

"These guys have no idea what they're talking about," an agent said. "This is the kinda crap that will make this situation spin out of control."

The chances of calming the growing chaos seemed hopeless.

At eleven-thirty, Dr. Brown answered a call to the emergency phone line. Nodding, he accepted the instructions that were delivered to him. Placing the phone back into its receiver, he called to his team.

"We have a conference call to set up, and I need everyone's help." The doctor wiped his moist forehead with the back of his hand. He knew he needed to remain calm.

"All members of the hospital administrative staff who are not currently in the building must be present for this conference call." Dr. Brown rattled off the people to reach. "Also, we need to contact the Pittsburgh Chief of Police, the State Health Commissioner, the State Attorney General, the Governor, the CDC, the FBI, the Assistant Secretary of Health and Human Services, the staff of the National Security Council and the White House. These numbers are in the Official Index of Medical Emergency Protocol. If you run into any problems, call me. Let's move, people. We have a confirmation of our diagnosis. We're the chosen staff who's stumbled upon the first confirmed case of domestic smallpox in over thirty years."

His orders left his crew silent, but they moved forward with determination.

"Doctor, is this a national emergency?" one nurse asked. "I mean, it seems like we're treating this as a terrorist attack, but there's no evidence of that, right?"

"That's right," Dr. Brown confirmed. "But the men in the White House don't want to take any chances with this one. It's not like we see smallpox everyday. Let's get going." The doctor gripped the nurse's forearm and offered a gentle squeeze. He wished he could tell her that everything would be okay.

"Our first objective in this conference call is to determine whether or not to make this news public," an FBI agent explained to Dr. Brown as he escorted him to the conference room. A brisk pace made it difficult for the men to walk and talk at the same time. "If the president decides to go ahead with the announcement, then we have to decide how and when. We need to be careful not to incite a panic. This situation will only worsen with a heightened state of alarm."

Before taking his seat, Dr. Brown passed a look to each member in the conference room. He was waiting for direction of when to begin, when the lead FBI agent motioned for him to speak. Commencing the meeting, Dr. Brown asked the emergency room administrative director to initiate all of the necessary phone connections. Once all parties were confirmed to be present, they began.

For two hours, the members of the newly formed Emergency Relief Committee spoke out on what steps to take next. Debates arose over how, when, and if to address the public. A collection of other concerns where brought up through a collage of voices.

"We have to prepare for the irrational behavior that could erupt once this announcement is made," the Chief of Police said.

"The protocol needs to be followed for inoculating the health care teams and patient contacts," a CDC spokesperson stated.

Just as a plan had materialized and was nearing the stage of execution, an urgent call was patched through to the correspondent in Atlanta. The conference room and its satellite connections were placed on hold as the CDC officer took the call.

Silencing the crowd with his entrance back into the conversation, the top official from the CDC returned to the Pittsburgh conference call.

"I'm not sure where to find the words to announce this, but I'll do my best," the senior representative began. "I've been informed that samples from three patients in the Latrobe Area Hospital in Pennsylvania have all been confirmed as the smallpox virus. This is not a contained situation."

At once, all parties on the other ends of the phone lines grew silent. Dr. Brown watched as the expressions on the faces of his colleagues turned from intense concentration to devastation. This was not an isolated case as they'd all hoped. He was certain that the people on the opposite ends of the phone lines wore identical facial expressions at that moment. He waited for someone to speak.

The advisor for the CDC continued. "We must move forward with our plan at once. We need to execute this with tact and confidence, because it's imperative that we set the bar for this protocol. Each of you will be role models. Decide on the exact number of vaccines that we need to get to you, and I'll send a team." Without wavering, the advisor spoke his words. In the privacy of his office, he feared his heart would beat through his chest.

Following the conference call, each member of the emergency team went on to follow through with his orders. First, Dr. Brown had to check in on Tony. His primary goal as a physician was to do whatever he could to save his patient. Second, but close in range, was to find out where Tony had come in contact with this deadly disease. An answer to this question existed; it just needed to be found. Once uncovered, Dr. Brown knew that this information could be the key to a solution for this problem.

The hospital issued protective coverings had never felt so flimsy before. Dr. Brown was sure he could see right through the paper gown, and his facemask seemed too light to filter anything from his breath. Now, as he suited up to visit Tony, he wondered how effective these measures were. Shaking his head, he forced himself to remain rational. Before entering the room, he grasped the wall to steady himself. Was he coming down with something now too? He refused to allow his mind to play tricks on him.

-18-

Shane was scheduled to address the nation the next day. How many gut wrenching speeches would he have to make while in office? Just when he thought the worst was over, another blow would come from behind—a sucker punch.

Once again, he had to announce the possibility of a domestic tragedy in his country. No evidence existed that this was an attack, but he knew the people would jump to the worst conclusion. Would they be so far off base? He didn't believe so. He felt guilty for not having foreseen the attack ... if it was an attack. How could he have allowed this to happen?

He loved his country, but the hatred that the terrorists represented outweighed his love. Their loathing of the United States always seemed to beat him. He'd vowed to put an end to their terror, and he would make good on his word.

Overwhelming emotions plummeted Shane into an immediate thinking session. Attempting to trace the steps of the four smallpox victims, he took a notebook and charted the events. First, he listed the information that he knew to be fact. All four victims were located in Pennsylvania. One victim was in Pittsburgh, and the others were in a neighboring suburb. Was there a connection?

Shane was anxious to find someone who would confirm his suspicions. Peeking into an open meeting room, he spied two other members of the Anti-Terrorism Task Force. After some brainstorming with his colleagues, Shane thought he might have found a connection between the four victims. Percolating the information through his mind, he headed back to his office.

Plopping down on a sofa, he leaned forward and thought out loud.

"Tony Lonitesci is a manager at Lonitesci Fireworks. The other victims are all employees of the Lonitesci factory. Someone sabotaged that factory. That has to be it. We need to order a quarantine of that plant, and we have to vaccinate all the employees and their contacts." Shane knew this could be premature, but it was better to be safe than sorry. In the heat of the action, the obvious hit him like a ton of bricks, and he snapped into an upright position.

Scrambling his way to a phone, he requested an urgent line out to any West Coast celebration site.

When the phone wasn't answered, Shane turned on the television. His heart sank when he realized he was too late.

The fireworks were already in the air. Even if his theory was correct, nothing could be done now. Was it even realistic to think that the virus had been spread through the fireworks? Or was his paranoia and eagerness to solve the problem taking over his typically rational mind? It didn't matter now anyway. The final phase of the celebration was well under way.

In the western states, the finale lit up the sky. Side-by-side television screens captured picturesque views of the San Diego beaches and the Los Angeles skyline. The bright lights of Las Vegas offered an additional scene featuring the pyrotechnic magic consuming the sky above.

Shane watched as the colors exploded and floated through the air above the crowds. The reaction looked like a colorful rain shower. The spectators exuded happiness and delight. Their wide smiles appeared to swallow the bright drops of electricity. The party was in full swing. If his hunch was right, he was too late.

Ending the call, he realized that a day of celebrating couldn't hurt at this point. Celebrate Freedom could only cushion the pain that would follow with the morning newscast. With sullen strides, he returned to his seat and the investigation of his theory.

At noon the following day, he was to address the country with the announcement of a plan for dealing with the known cases of smallpox. His speech would be precluded by the news release about the outbreak early in the morning. Shane had asked the mayor of Pittsburgh, the Governor of the state of Pennsylvania and the State Health Commissioner, collectively, to make this announcement. His second request was for an additional statement to be made by the FBI, to cover the subject of the safety of the city and the threat at hand. Later, he was scheduled to present his *plan*.

He perused the written words in front of him. The eloquent tones of the speech had been well thought out. His writing staff had worked hard, and their performance reflected their extreme concentration during such an emotional time. However, Shane was certain that no words could soften the blow of the news that was about to break. Even though the speech would make no mention of a terrorist attack, his constituency was smarter than that. They'd figure this one out. No speech could ease the fear of an already frightened and battered country. He'd spent years working toward his personal and professional goal of combating terrorism in the world, and his efforts had yielded an even bigger disaster.

His guard had not been let down. He'd continued to observe reports of intelligence and constant profiles of questionable characters within the country. The United States had successfully avoided domestic acts of terrorism for years, and this was what they had to show for all of their hard work. Finding a reason to believe that *good* always won in its battle against *evil* was getting more difficult for Shane each day. His job now was to remind the American people that this battle wasn't over. Good would always win, hands down. Scribbling some notes in the margins, he continued to work on his speech. He *hoped* good would win this one.

-19-

Dr. Brown attempted to manage an hour of sleep. Tony had stable vital signs, at least for that moment. He'd received CDC reports at the break of the new day, confirming that all four known smallpox victims had been employees of Lonitesci Fireworks. Any information that he was able to extract from Tony was crucial in the attempt to determine the origin of the virus. While waiting for his patient to wake up, he tried to rest as well.

A few minutes of sleep would do him good. Lying in the empty patient room, he forced his eyes shut. The doctor found the nature of the human mind to be a living paradox. Without proper physical rest, the psyche can't function to its highest capabilities. However, with too much overwhelming the mind, the body can't achieve valid sleep. In frustration, Dr. Brown straightened his clothing and returned to the administrative area of the ER.

The past hours blurred together in the doctor's mind like memories of a bad dream. The patients and guests who'd been in the hospital at the time of the diagnosis hadn't taken kindly to having to stick around for a while. There wasn't an alternative. These people had to be interviewed and, in some cases, inoculated. It was all for their own safety, but they weren't thinking clearly. It wasn't until after most of them left that the surroundings had quieted. If the media hadn't been made to leave with them, who knows if the madness would've ever calmed.

The CDC team was set to arrive at the hospital no later than six a.m. They'd bring a supply of vaccines to start inoculations for the hospital staff and patient contacts. The new, revised plan also called for a team from the CDC to go to the Latrobe Hospital to execute the same plan. The team would assist the state epidemiologist in a statewide surveillance and case investigation.

Once this investigation was underway, the hospitals were assigned the task of helping to develop a registry of all face-to-face contacts of their smallpox patients. These contacts needed to be monitored daily for the fever and flu-like symptoms associated with the virus.

For this effort to prove successful, Dr. Brown needed Tony's cooperation. He'd allow him to rest for a few more hours, but then he needed his patient's help.

The report that had been faxed from the CDC waited for him in his office. The fax noted that the test was positive for smallpox.

...microscopic differences are thought to be identified between the sample which had been taken from patient 1-S. Lonitesci and test samples of the smallpox virus. The differences were noted to be minor. More tests are being run on the sample to identify the exact characteristics.

This information intrigued Dr. Brown. Had the virus been altered on purpose? How would this affect the protocol for containment and treatment? The questions festered in his mind like an irritated rash. He wondered why these points hadn't been broached during the conference call earlier the last evening. He knew the reason. No one knew the answers, at least not yet. He made notes on his copy of the report and placed it in a private desk drawer. This was not something that should go uninvestigated. Before he left his office, his phone rang.

"Hello, Dr. Brown?" the female caller said. "I'm calling on behalf of the statewide hospital phone tree. I realize that your hospital is the origin location, but will you please continue the chain with your calls to complete the awareness effort?"

"Sure, of course," he answered.

The caller questioned him about any other patients who'd been treated for fever and flu-like symptoms in the past several weeks.

"The purpose of these questions is to identify any other suspected patients so we can further isolate the outbreak," she explained.

After answering each inquiry to the best of his knowledge, Dr. Brown hung up the phone. He made himself comfortable and carried on with his assigned phone tree calls.

"Excuse me, Dr. Brown –" A nurse poked her head in the door. "Do you have a minute?" At the doctor's positive response, she sat down on the chair next to his desk.

"I need some advice on what to tell Tony Lonitesci's family and contacts when we call them. We need to get hold of them soon and ask them to come in for observation and vaccinations. The press conferences are scheduled for first thing in the morning, and the president's address will be at noon, if I'm not mistaken. Outside of our isolated emergency state, the rest of the world is not even aware of what's happening yet." Having stated everything in one breath, she paused to replenish her oxygen supply. She continued, in a quaking voice. "I think we need to call Tony's family now. What do you think?"

The doctor sat quietly, processing her concerns.

"I tend to agree with you, on all counts. I think we should get in touch with his known contacts right away and bring them in for vaccines. They should be here, waiting, when the vaccines arrive. I'll go to Tony as soon as I finish these calls for the phone tree, and we'll put together a list of people to contact." With a compassionate look, Dr. Brown reached out to his nurse. In a mutual squeeze of gratitude, his hand met hers.

Through cloudy vision, Tony focused on the face of his only visitor. He tried to sit up, but Dr. Brown encouraged him to remain comfortable. His effort to remove his oxygen mask was also met with resistance. Tony placed the mask back in its position.

"Tony, if you can, please tell me the names of your closest contacts, family members and co-workers. I need to know who you've been in contact with since you've been sick. This is important, so that I can make sure they're okay." Dr. Brown watched as a tear rolled down his patient's cheek and around the perimeter of his oxygen mask.

"My son, Jake—" Tony's immediate response showed his concern. A complete list of names followed. "Karen, Uncle George—" He instructed the doctor to gather a list of Lonitesci co-workers from his uncle. Not yet aware that other victims of smallpox had been identified, he had no idea that some of his co-workers had already been diagnosed. He continued to name everyone who came to mind, when an embarrassing thought occurred to him.

"I'm ashamed to tell you this, but just yesterday morning I was on a plane full of people from New York. I came here directly from the airport. I felt so terrible ... I never even considered I could've been contagious ... at least not with something like this."

"Thanks for your help, Tony. This gives us a good start." The doctor attempted to hide his growing concern.

Once outside Tony's room, he stripped himself of his protective mask, gloves and gown. This ritual had grown quite tiresome over the past few days. He called for assistance, and a member of the administrative team ran to his side.

"I need you to call the state health commissioner right away. Tony Lonitesci was on an airplane only twenty-four hours ago. They'll need to contact every person who was on that flight. Heck, they should try to reach anyone who was in that airport yesterday morning." Dr. Brown rubbed his forehead and closed his eyes. "Actually, it's time for us to call the New York State Health Commissioner. They'll want to start their statewide phone tree, too. After all, Tony was in New York for several days before he found his way to us."

***

Shane gulped his coffee, hoping for some quick energy. Once

again, he replayed the latest call in his mind. Privately, he wished he'd never picked up the phone. He knew that any biological attack would affect a large regional area, but the potential for this to spread from state-to-state was daunting. He'd just given approval for an emergency CDC Epidemic Intelligence Team to head to New York City. Where would he have to send them next?

He pondered why a terrorist organization would've identified a fireworks manufacturing company as a target, and his only explanation bothered him even more than the question. Those bastards meant to contaminate the actual fireworks. What a sick way to reach a mass population. Effective though. Could an employee of the Lonitesci company be guilty of this? The simplicity of this scenario was unlikely. If that were the case, then finding the perpetrator would be easy. Terrorists didn't work that way. They tried to be more complicated and elusive than that. But he needed to have the employees interviewed and investigated anyway. Maybe the answer was right there in the factory after all. He made a list of questions for his staff to get working on.

Any new employees at the Lonitesci plant?
Any employee currently on vacation?
Was anyone gone at the time of the celebration?

From his desk, he watched for the first hints of sunrise. At six-thirty, he would initiate another conference call between the agencies participating in the investigation. The purpose of the call was to make the positive identification of a bioterrorism attack and to determine whether or not a regional quarantine needed to be set up. Also, Shane wanted to enlist support for a similar call, which would be set up for the New York area later that morning.

He'd come to the conclusion that if one bioterrorism attack had been executed in Pennsylvania, then evidence of other attacks could soon surface, especially if his theory about the fireworks transmission proved accurate. He wanted to be wrong in this case, but his heart and his head argued that the odds were he was correct. Why else would the only three victims of the virus all work together at the very same plant that had produced the fireworks for the celebration? This would be far too much of a coincidence if the fireworks weren't involved in this mess.

Shane realized that he had only three hours until the first scheduled conference call. Getting some sleep before the explosion of morning activity was imperative, but he had other personal dilemmas to sort through. He knew his staff would be waiting for his initial thoughts about what had happened. They were always ready and willing to help, but he liked to think things through on his own first before talking with his advisers. That's the kind of guy he was.

At the moment, he believed he was the only person to have made the connection between the known smallpox victims and the fireworks shows. Should he even bring it up? He decided to wait for Alan's opinion.

His dilemma was whether he should wait until his hypothesis was proven correct before releasing the news. Inciting a panic based on unsubstantiated theories wouldn't be good. However, should his theory be proven correct, the rest of the country and the world needed to act with speed to save lives. He prayed that the answer to his predicament would come to him by daybreak as he allowed his head to fall on his desk.

*** *

The CDC Epidemic Intelligence Service Team arrived at the University of Pittsburgh Medical Center at five-thirty a.m., thirty minutes ahead of schedule. They entered through a guarded door near the helipad on the top of the hospital building. At the same time, a security team ushered Tony's relatives into the facility through a side door on the ground level.

With her groggy son slung over her shoulder, Karen entered the Emergency Room. She tried to conceal her obvious concern, as she responded to Jake's questions about his father with vague one-word answers.

The nurse who'd called had been brief in her explanation of why they needed to get to the hospital with such haste. What was Tony doing in Pittsburgh? The nurse had stated only that he was sick and that the doctor had made an urgent request for them to come in for preventative testing. Karen couldn't even begin to guess what this could be about. Since the call, her stomach churned with anxiety.

Karen took a seat in the waiting room chairs. She observed an official looking group of men and women walk past them.

"What's going on?" Karen realized she was speaking aloud and peered over Jake's head to see if he was awake. His silent body lay still, fast asleep. "Everything looks so official ... so intense. What's up with the caution tape and security guards everywhere?" She continued to speak out loud, hoping that someone would stop and answer her questions. "This feels more like a police station than a hospital."

The silence seemed incompatible with the hustle and bustle that was going on around her. Karen stood to walk to the administrative desk when she heard a familiar voice calling her name.

"Karen, is that you?" George called from the doorway. The blockade of security uniforms hid his body from her view. "Karen, I'm over here." This time he waved his right arm in the air.

"Oh, George, what's goin' on? So, they called you too?" She gave Tony's uncle an endearing look.

George bent down and squeezed Karen into a hug. He smiled at his great-nephew, who was asleep on her lap.

"Yeah, they called about an hour ago. We got here as soon as we could." George released his grip and pulled his wife closer to his side. The couple followed Karen back to the chairs and found two additional seats. "Do you have any idea what's wrong with Tony? I knew he was sick, but this seems serious." Careful not to disturb Jake, he spoke in a soft voice.

"I don't know what to think," Karen answered. "I've been told as much as you have, and that isn't much. I hope someone will be out to talk with us soon. I'm so worried that I can't even think straight. They told us they needed to run tests on us," she whispered. "What on earth could they possibly need to test for? And why couldn't they tell us more on the phone?"

"I haven't heard any more than you," George said. "I have to say, this whole ordeal has given us quite a start. To top things off, they haven't told us anything about Tony's condition."

Just as they began to feel anger mixed with their fears and concerns, Dr. Brown entered the sitting area.

"Hello, everyone. I'm Dr. Brown, Tony's physician. Thank you all for coming. If you'll follow me around the corner, we can talk in private."

As they exited, another group was ushered to the now empty seats. Tony's co-workers welcomed each other, as they entered the sitting area one by one. The voices of the men grew louder, with the rise of their level of frustration. They demanded to know why they'd been called in.

In the exam room, Karen, George, and Marian sat in shock at what they had just been told.

"I need to go and find Jake," Karen said.

"He's fine," Dr. Brown promised. "He's playing with some of the nurses in another room. I don't see any reason to startle him. It's not a good idea for him to be present for this conversation. We can fetch him later, when we're ready to run the tests."

"Okay, I guess you're right," Karen agreed. She began sobbing, and her words trailed off. "How could this have happened?" She spoke between broken gasps for air. "Are we all in danger? Is Tony going to die?" Before the doctor could respond, she posed the question that every party in the room was afraid to ask. "Was this a terrorist attack? I don't mean to sound extreme, but how else would he have gotten smallpox?"

"Karen, I'm sorry, but I don't know how this happened. I hope that, with Tony's help, I can get to the bottom of that. All of the tests we need to administer are precautionary at the moment, so the strong possibility exists that you're not in danger at all. We're trying to keep Tony comfortable until we can figure this thing out. We're doing our best. He's in critical condition, but he has a fighting chance."

Before answering Karen's fourth and final question, Dr. Brown paused. Then, in a weakened voice, he answered with honesty, for he saw no other proper way to handle the moment. He knew that the president would be addressing the nation at noon, and the FBI, governor and health commissioner would be making their statements that morning. The media would take it from there with their own take on what had happened. These folks deserved to know the truth.

"It's likely that this was the direct result of a bioterrorism attack. But I can't stress the point enough that we have no proof of this right now."

Within seconds, Karen felt a burning sensation in her throat.

"Excuse me." She made a rapid exit, finding her way to a restroom just in time.

Kneeling in front of the toilet, she heaved her early morning coffee into the bowl. She rested her head on the cool porcelain and sobbed. A mental image of her son gave her the strength necessary to stand. An overwhelming urge to hold Jake in her arms propelled her from the bathroom stall. She felt her way to the sink and splashed cold water on her pale, white face. After drying herself with a handful of coarse paper towels, she left the restroom.

-20-

The conference call went just as Shane had expected. The majority of the participants had agreed that a quarantine of entire cities or states was unnecessary at this point. They felt that airports and public transportation outlets could continue to do business as usual for the time being. For these reasons, Shane felt no urgency to offer any details of his theory about the attack. After the call, he discussed his thoughts with the Anti-Terrorism Task Force, and they made a plan to focus on finding evidence to prove or disprove his theory.

"Issue vaccines to the hospital staff and patient contacts of the four victims," Shane directed. "The FBI will accompany the State Health Commissioner and governor in their speeches at nine o'clock. I'll follow with my press conference at noon. In the meantime, you guys in New York wait for further instructions in the event that an outbreak does occur in your area. However, any known contacts of Tony Lonitesci in New York need to get to a hospital for testing and vaccines. Don't forget, we have to get the passengers from his flight to come in for vaccines, too."

Everything fit into the plan as if it were all tied up into a neat little package. But Shane knew that in a few weeks, days or maybe even hours, the scare was going to take on a whole new face. He was afraid that this would be an up-close and personal look directly into the face of terror.

He reviewed the preliminary report from the CDC. They'd helped the Pennsylvania state epidemiologist establish a statewide surveillance and case investigation system. Simultaneously, the FBI agents were working to determine the origin of the attack.

This composite of thoughts rotated through Shane's head. Although he feared letting his country down, he understood the importance of keeping his own feelings of desperation from filtering through in his speech. He'd fought for years to keep his constituency safe, and he was not about to change directions now. This setback could be overcome, and this was the message that he was prepared to deliver.

The Pennsylvania press conference was underway when Shane turned on the television. He sat in the privacy of his office and waited for the events to play out.

The three hours after the announcement of the smallpox outbreak filled the White House with crazed activity. Shane ordered all administrative and minimum-security clearance employees to stay home from work until further notice. The Anti-Terrorism Task Force set up shop within the Pentagon and began to compose a plan for retaliation.

All the while, Shane anticipated the next phone call from the CDC identifying more domestic cases of smallpox. Butterflies danced in his stomach as he waited to address the nation. Pacing in his office, Shane rehearsed his words, stuttering with the opening of his speech. Moving back to his desk and fumbling with the phone, he knew he needed to calm his nerves before he took the stage.

"Hey, Alan?" Shane was glad to hear the general's voice. "Can you come over here before we go on the air?"

"I ask you all today to lend me an ear, as I deliver a speech that I've prayed I'd never have to make." Shane began in a somber voice. "Together we face the distinct possibility that the threat of a domestic bioterrorism attack has become a reality."

Fighting to repress the tears that choked him from inside, he paused. Finding the strength to play the role of the country's fearless leader proved a difficult task at that moment.

"If this is a terrorist attack, I'm certain that the commanders of our armed forces will find the cowards who've once again attacked our nation. The preliminary protocol for dealing with a biological attack of this nature calls for all citizens to cooperate one hundred percent with the requests of our health officials. Thank you for your attention. God bless you all."

In a blur of passion, Shane's words were spoken. Marred by a range of emotions, the speech lacked his typical eloquent delivery. In a subconscious movement, he held his mid-section as he exited the stage. He had never before cut his public remarks short.

* * *

Karen acknowledged the nurse who called her name. She stood and offered a half-hearted smile to George and Marian as she followed the nurse down the hall. Taking a seat on a chair, she watched as the nurse prepared the vaccine.

"Okay, ma'am," the nurse said. "This won't hurt at all. Just stay still for me."

Karen flinched as the nurse approached.

"I'm sorry," Karen said. "I'm just nervous. Can this vaccine hurt me at all? You know, are there any side effects?"

"There are a fair amount of possible side effects, but this is necessary for your own preventative care, ma'am. Didn't the doctor explain this to you?"

"Yes, he did. I've just read so many articles about the side effects of this vaccine. I'm letting my fears get the best of me. I apologize." Karen turned her face to her side, deleting the nurse from her view. Closing her eyes, she made certain not to see anything. A vision of Jake popped into her mind.

"What about Jake?" Karen asked.

"Excuse me?"

"My son, Jake. Will he be having this vaccination as well? I should be with him if he does. He'll be scared." Karen looked back in the nurse's direction, witnessing the final steps of the vaccination process. She shivered, feeling the hair on the back of her neck pointing out.

"You'll have to ask the doctor about that," the nurse explained.

"Where is Dr. Brown? Will I have a chance to speak with him

again?" Karen watched the nurse swab at her arm. The shot had-n't made her feel any more comfortable with the situation. She still felt vulnerable.

"I'll find him for you, ma'am. Why don't you take a seat back in the triage area, and I'll have him come to you."

"Hi Karen. I was asked to come and see you. How are you holding up?" The doctor examined the gauze pad that was taped to Karen's arm.

"I'm holding up fine, I guess. I wanted to ask you about Jake. When will you be giving him the vaccination?"

"Jake won't be having the inoculation, Karen."

"What do you mean? Why won't he?" Karen felt her eyes tear-ing up as she waited for the doctor to respond.

"The state health commissioner and the CDC have decided that children under the age of ten shouldn't be inoculated." He could see the disappointment in Karen's eyes. "The adverse side effects could prove themselves to be even more dangerous for a child. Plus, Tony hasn't been in contact with Jake for several weeks, so he was most likely not exposed to the virus during the conta-gious period."

To her shock, Karen felt relieved that lately Tony had neg-lected spending time with his son. She wasn't sure how she felt about the idea of Jake being excluded from the vaccine, but she lacked the energy to put up a fight.

"Dr. Brown, do you believe that this is the best thing for Jake?"

"Karen, I have to confess that I've never been in a situation to make any recommendations for the treatment or prevention of smallpox, but I do feel confident in the rationale behind the deci-sions of the CDC."

Something about Dr. Brown's demeanor made her feel at ease.

"I have to pay Tony a visit now. I'll have someone bring Jake back to you soon." The doctor stood from his seat. "The nurses can reach me if you have any more questions."

"What I need now is for you to think hard, Tony," Dr. Brown began. "I need for you to think about everything and anything that may have seemed out of place in your life over the last three weeks. When did you start to feel ill? Had anything different been added to your daily activities? Did you come in contact with anyone with whom you weren't familiar, you know, who may have spread this virus to you? Please think, Tony. Your memories could be important."

"I can't think of anything out of the ordinary, Doc." Tony concentrated. "I'm sorry. Really, I am." He turned his head to the side to hide the tear that escaped from the corner of his eye. Through his oxygen mask, he inhaled long, slow breaths. In the silence of the room, the sound of his labored breathing was deafening. "I'll keep trying. I promise."

"Okay. Keep thinking, and call for me if you come up with anything else." Dr. Brown placed the call button within Tony's reach. Halting at the door, he spoke again. "Tony, think about your activities at work. Think about the last three weeks at the plant."

The reference to the plant sparked a question from Tony.

"Why do you ask about work? Is there something going on at the plant?"

"I'm sorry to have to deliver more bad news, Tony." Dr. Brown regretted having brought it up, but he knew it would've come out sooner or later. If it could help, sooner was better. "But three of your co-workers have also been diagnosed with smallpox. The FBI has narrowed the origin of this mess to your place of employment. So think hard, Tony. Call me if anything comes to mind."

Once again, Tony turned his head. This time he allowed the tears to flow freely.

Before he broke down as well, Dr. Brown left the room. He dreaded having to tell Tony about his co-workers. He feared the news would aggravate the status of his patient's health. At least he was able to give Tony some information to keep his thoughts on track without having to tell him the whole story. He breathed a sigh of relief that he'd avoided having to inform Tony that two of his co-workers had died earlier that morning.

Dr. Brown was a mere four paces down the hall when he noticed a nurse heading toward Tony's room. He reached out to stop her.

"Are you headed to Tony Lonitesci's room?"

"Yes, his call light rang. I was on my way to get a gown, so I can see what he needs."

"I'll save you the trip," Dr. Brown replied. Had he thought of something already?

Upon entering the room, he found Tony leaning forward in his bed. He helped to prop his patient into a seated position.

"Tony, what is it? Did you think of something?"

"I thought of something that was different," Tony said. "We had a new delivery driver. It was some young kid. I think he said he was just filling in. Before him, I'd always had the same driver. Maybe this is the missing link that everyone's looking for." For the first time since he'd arrived at the ER, Tony showed signs of life.

"Okay Tony, when do you remember seeing this driver? Do you remember the date?"

"Actually, I do remember," Tony answered. "He came to pick up the fireworks on September eighth."

"Tony, I do appreciate your help. You're doing a great job. Now, get some rest. Call me if you think of anything else."

"Don't you think this could help?" Tony asked.

"Maybe, but on September eighth you were already sick. Remember? You had to have come in to contact with this virus at least a week, or maybe two weeks, before that date. You know, based on your symptoms. Keep thinking, though, Tony. You could be on the right track. Plus, it's good medicine for you to keep your mind on other things right now."

"Okay, I'll call you if I think of anything else." Frustration overwhelmed Tony as he tried to force his pillow down to support the small of his back. He couldn't do anything right.

Before Dr. Brown left the room, he turned and moved back in Tony's direction. His wrinkled brow suggested he had more questions. Plopping down on an exam chair, he wheeled up next to Tony's bed. "Tony, why did you say you had a substitute driver?"

"My normal driver, Chuck, was going on vacation. He must've gone on quite a vacation, because the sub guy was around longer than I expected. In fact, I asked him when Chuck was supposed to come back." Tony stopped to take in a long breath of oxygen. "He said he didn't know when that would be, didn't seem like he cared."

"Tony, I have one last question before I leave you to rest. What was his name again? Your regular driver?" On his prescription pad, he scribbled Chuck's name. "Thanks, Tony. I'll be back in a bit. You've done great. Now get some rest."

Almost forgetting to remove his protective clothing, Dr. Brown hurried to his office to call the FBI. This could be something to work with.

* * *

The words of Shane's announcement left Alexei stunned. Fear gripped his heart, and he felt a sudden pain in his chest. Not wishing to concern his wife, he excused himself and prepared to head to his office.

As he'd expected, he was not alone when he arrived. Upon entering, he was approached by a number of his superiors. They had questions.

"Have you heard from President McAlister regarding the recent smallpox outbreak in the States?" Their inquiries fired at Alexei in a panic-stricken unison.

"No, I am sorry, but I have not. Did you expect that I should? Gentlemen, if you will excuse me, I have some phone calls to make. But I think we all know that our own actions have determined that we will most likely be left in this situation alone."

Alexei observed his colleagues' expressions as they looked at each other with shock at his blatant statement about their past misdeeds. He made his way to his office and prepared for the next step. He'd always known that the day would come when the only way to survive in the world would be for each man to take care of himself. That time had arrived. He checked for any correspondence from Shane. As he expected, he found nothing. After gathering his personal files, he left for home.

Once in the safety of his house, he headed straight for the library and drafted a long letter. As he wrote, he checked to be sure Sharona was still busy with her sewing. Concealing his writing from his wife was difficult, but necessary. He didn't want her to worry. What she didn't know wouldn't hurt her. Alexei's love for his wife blinded him from seeing how the letter he scripted affected her more than he knew.

From his memory, he retrieved all of the times, places and dates that he'd stored for so long. Using documentation from his father as a reference, he explained his beliefs regarding what had happened. Alexei dug deep into his inner core and regurgitated information on which he'd taken oaths of silence, risking severe penalties should anyone find him afterwards. When he finished, he sealed the envelope and placed it in a desk drawer. Addressed and ready to send once the time was right, the letter remained hidden.

Sharona watched from the doorway as Alexei closed the desk drawer. Hurrying, she disappeared down the steps before he noticed her.

"Sharona, I think it is time for bed. Come along, darling," Alexei called downstairs to his wife.

Taking her place alongside her husband, Sharona closed her eyes. Years of practice had taught her just how long to wait before Alexei would be asleep. Thoughts racing through her mind helped to pass the time as she waited. Distracted by her own concerns, she lost track of the time that had expired since they'd gone to bed. This had to have been long enough. By moving her toes outside of the sheets, she tested the moment, to see if he was awake. Noticing that he didn't move, she slid all the way out of the bed. Alexei's only movement was the steady rhythm of his breathing.

Light steps guided Sharona to the library, where she took a seat at the computer. Her fingers danced over the keyboard in trained motions. As she typed, she looked over her shoulder for any sign of Alexei. The return message shocked her. Why did she have to get involved again? She thought she'd done her part. Her brother's money belonged to her. She shouldn't have to fight for it.

-21-

The Pittsburgh FBI team had been working for hours on the lead that Dr. Brown had brought to them regarding Tony Lonitesci's possible contact with the virus.

With little effort, they'd reached a manager of the delivery company who'd confirmed that Chuck Lyons had not returned to work following his vacation. However, this liaison had also confirmed that this wasn't unusual behavior for their drivers.

"This happens with one of our drivers at least every six months," he'd said. "But I will say that this wasn't normal behavior for Chuck Lyons."

The agents found their contact to be cooperative in turning over all of Chuck's employee information. At this point, the investigation team waited with patience for the return call from Robin Lyons' family.

The phone rang. "FBI task force, Agent Anderson, how may I help you? I see. Yes. Do you have that number, ma'am? I'm very sorry for your loss. I appreciate your help. I'll be sure to contact you when we have more information. Thank you again, ma'am." Charged by the information he'd uncovered, he called to his team. "I think we've got something here. Thomas, I need you to call this hospital in Jamaica. Harper, please arrange for the bodies of Chuck and Robin Lyons to be examined right away. They're still in Jamaica. We've gotten lucky, guys. The Jamaicans were waiting for permission for cremation." He handed slips of paper to each of his agents.

Reading the notes from his pad, Agent Anderson shook with energy.

"Robin and Chuck left for a week's vacation in Jamaica, due to return on September first. On September third, Robin's mother received a phone call from a hospital in Montego Bay. The nurse told her that Robin was ill. When she asked if she could speak with her daughter, she was told that Robin was in quarantine for a highly contagious illness. She wasn't told what the illness was, but she was told that it was considered to be terminal."

Anderson flipped the page in his notebook.

"Before she could finalize her travel arrangements, the hospital called her back. This time was to inform her that Robin had died. Later, she found out that Chuck had died soon after being admitted. The doctors and nurses in that hospital weren't much help with information. Robin's mother still doesn't know what caused their deaths. The death certificates listed communicable disease or adult chicken pox virus for the cause of death for both Robin and Chuck. She's made efforts at getting their bodies sent back to the states, but the Jamaican physicians have insisted that they should be cremated. I told her we'd help with this."

"Does she know we'll have to autopsy them both?" A second agent asked the obvious question.

"Yes, and she gave her consent. She gave consent for Chuck's body too, since he doesn't have any living family members."

Agent Anderson knew the results of the tests would uncover something. He remained disturbed by the fact that the information to date still hadn't led to finding the origin of the virus. He felt confident that Tony Lonitesci would provide the missing piece to the puzzle. Picking up his cell phone, he called Dr. Brown.

***

Following the familiar hall to Tony's room, Dr. Brown felt as if he'd worn a path in the flooring over the past few days. They were getting closer. He could feel it.

***

The most recent report from the CDC monopolized Shane's

attention. To date a total of ten cases demonstrating flu-like symptoms had been reported at the Latrobe Area Hospital. This number was in addition to the original three diagnosed cases of smallpox, of which two victims had already died. The information stated that the ten feverish victims were being held for observation and watched for any evidence of rash, muscle aches or stomach cramping. So far, they hadn't presented the latter symptoms. For this reason, the Atlanta crew believed that the scope of the outbreak might be smaller than first expected.

With a sweep of his hand, Shane moved the report to a pile on the side of his desk. He longed to feel the confidence that the CDC possessed. Logic stood between him and the temporary comfort of underestimation. A bioterrorism attack would not be executed on a small scale. The possibility for mass destruction was far too great when it came to smallpox. Those guys wouldn't approach their opportunity to shine with such a poor attempt, only affecting a few people. Folding his hands in front of his chest, he rested his head on his fingers, massaging his chin with his thumbs. Just then, Alan approached the door with another fax. Shane could tell by the look in his friend's eyes that his own fears were fast becoming a reality.

Without saying a word, Shane took the fax. The ink appeared faded, the sign of an overused toner cartridge. The insignia on the top of the page was easily identified. Shane attempted to clear his mind with a long blink of his eyes before he read the latest report from Atlanta. Limited words described their most recent findings. For Alan's benefit, Shane read aloud.

"Four of the ten suspected cases in Latrobe have presented a rash—face, neck and hands," Shane announced. "They've experienced severe muscle and stomach cramping, and their fevers have escalated. Samples have arrived in Atlanta, where they're awaiting testing." He tossed the page aside. As he exhaled from a deep breath, Shane watched for his colleague's reaction. "Alan, will you please gather the task force for another meeting?"

Alan nodded, aware that the information to date supported the fact that this tragedy had just begun.

"We need to identify how this virus got into that manufacturing plant. This outbreak is no coincidence. That virus was released in that plant with the intent of spreading it to others," Shane said. His strong voice cracked. "Those fireworks were contaminated. I know it. But how?" He waited a second before reminding Alan of the obvious. "And, Alan, we need to figure this out soon, so we can make an attempt to contain it before it spreads out of control."

Alan waited for Shane's silence before he asked his question. He wasn't even sure he wanted to know the answer. "If that's what happened, then won't we be finding cases of smallpox cropping up all over the world?"

"I hate to say it, but I think that's the precise problem that we're up against. The CDC has stated that the incubation period for smallpox is seven to seventeen days. We've only just begun to see the effects of this attack. We need to prepare ourselves for the worst-case scenario. We might see a flood of victims over the next two weeks. We don't have any time to waste."

***

Hanging on every detail, Tony listened as Dr. Brown discussed his views regarding the latest report from the CDC. He wasn't shocked to hear that two of the other victims from the plant had died, but his heart sank as he heard the words. In his mind, he detached from his body. He watched the doctor cross his legs and uncross them again as he groped for the right words to say. He watched himself as he lay still, without reaction to the news he was being told. Who were the other victims? He didn't need to know. He'd meet up with them soon enough. From above, he observed his eyes closing. He heard the alarm sound on the monitor next to his bed as the green line went flat.

Dr. Brown jumped to his feet and executed emergency procedures with a calm methodical approach. Although placid in his emotion, he moved with urgency. Within seconds, help arrived. His crew of doctors and nurses worked with persistence until Tony's heart pumped on its own again.

Tony opened his eyes to find the team of doctors staring him in the face.

"What happened?" he asked.

"You gave us a start," Dr. Brown answered. He dismissed the rest of the team and returned to his stool, next to his patient.

"Tony, are you up to talking with me for a minute? I know the FBI can use your help. If you want me to come back later, I will."

"No, now's better, Doc," Tony said. He spoke with a soft voice. "What can I do to help? Please tell me how I can help."

"Tony, it seems you may have been right about your change in delivery drivers having something to do with this. Only the agents don't think it was your driver who spread this to you. He also may have been a victim. Do you remember what he delivered on his last visit to you?" He prayed this information would lead the investigation in the right direction.

"Umm, I guess so. We get so many deliveries at the plant. Let me think ..." Tony spoke through slurred speech. He paused and drew a long breath from his oxygen supply. "I remember that day ... the last day he delivered before his vacation. He talked my ear off, but I just wanted to get back to work. Nice guy, though. He was worried because the packages were marked *hazardous material*. That's it! He was worried about the potassium perchlorate. I even remember one of the boxes being damaged. And, they were packaged differently than I'd ever noticed before."

Dr. Brown scribbled notes and waited for Tony to finish.

"Tony, where do you get that, uh, potassium perchlorate?" He read the chemical name from his note pad. "Is it a local vendor?"

"No, not for this order. I needed too much. I ordered online from a company in China. George can give you the web site." Tony's voice trailed off. His eyes closed again, and he rambled on about something else.

Dr. Brown couldn't make out the words, but he did hear Tony mention the name Jake. He wished with all of his heart that Tony could visit with his son. They both knew that wasn't possible. He turned to leave.

"Dr. Brown?" Tony called out in a weak voice. "Tell that driver, Chuck, is it? Tell him I hope he feels better soon."

"I'll do that, Tony. Now you get some rest." A tear escaped from the doctor's eye as he left the room. He rushed to his office to call Agent Anderson.

Reminding himself that staying calm could help to save lives, he remained focused. After a brief conversation with the agent, Dr. Brown withdrew the papers from his lower desk drawer and read the contents again.

The lab reports from the CDC were the same for each recent documentation of the disease. Smallpox had been identified in each victim, but this strain possessed some altered characteristics. Different from usual strains of the virus, this sample was given a temporary name of smallpox four, or SP4. This information intrigued him.

Why was it different? How would that affect the patients? He hoped for answers soon, because they could affect the treatments. With the probability of an increased number of victims, Dr. Brown made it his business to call the CDC.

He pushed the numbers into the phone and waited for a representative to answer. The call took forever to go through, and he wasn't surprised to be placed on hold. The phone lines to the CDC had been tied up for two days. While listening to the recorded message, he waited. When his pager beeped with an emergency call, he slammed down the phone and rushed from his office.

The nurse covered the body of Tony Lonitesci. In silence, she recited two prayers. One prayer she said for Tony and the other for the rest of the world. Her hand shook as she turned the doorknob to leave.

Frustration overwhelmed the doctor as he returned to his office. He knew he'd done everything he could for Tony, but he hated to lose any of his patients. Was there something else that could've helped? Did the presence of SP4 cause the treatment to fail? This was a stretch, because most smallpox patients died, and he knew that. But, he still wanted to find out what he could about SP4.

Connecting to the number again, Dr. Brown was determined to stay on hold until someone answered his call. Finally a voice spoke to him. Excited, he took the opportunity to ask the questions that were on his mind. The answers he received were less than satisfactory.

"Yes, Doctor. They've confirmed that the samples were smallpox," the CDC representative stated. "However, these specific samples show slight differences from traditional smallpox. Years ago we participated in an international agreement to destroy all remaining samples of the virus. Therefore, we don't have access to any true samples for a comparison. We've used the vaccina virus to continue vaccine production. We don't have an explanation for the differences that we're seeing in this current strain."

Dr. Brown's mind spun in circles much like the words of the conversation he was witnessing. "As a doctor, I'm concerned with these uncertainties. I'm afraid that we may not be equipped to fight the unknown."

"Doctor, I appreciate your concern. We'll notify you when we have more information to share. Thank you for your call."

The dial tone droned on in the doctor's ear. Slamming the phone down, he surprised himself by the force he exercised.

Friday, September 15th

-22-

As usual, a fresh pile of data awaited Shane's return to his office. The majority of the pages were printed on CDC letterhead, announcing new and suspected cases of smallpox. In New York City alone, fifteen possible cases had been identified. They were all thought to have come from contact with Tony Lonitesci. At least twelve more suspected cases of the virus had been reported in the Pittsburgh area. The samples from these patients awaited final test results.

Shane cringed at the prediction of ongoings for the upcoming days. The Lonitesci plant had been closed by the CDC and tested positive for contamination. Trace amounts of the smallpox virus had indeed been found in what remained of the company's potassium perchlorate supply. Those fireworks were constructed by innocent men for a celebration. Instead, they were used to spread a deadly disease around the world. He slammed his fist into the pile of papers. The pain that raced up his wrist only helped to mask the emotional rage that he felt inside.

"A plan of this proportion is incalculable," he mumbled.

With the press of a speed dial button, he called for Alan.

"Did you read the reports?" He was already talking before Alan could complete his greeting.

"Yeah, I read it. I don't get it though," Alan answered. "Is it the chemical company that did this? That seems too easy to figure out—and way too obvious."

"That's my point. It can't be that easy. An executive from the

Chinese supplier claims that his company had never received or filled any order for the Lonitesci's. What do you make of that?"

"How hard is it to prove shipment of the order? Don't the Lonitesci's have a record of that?" Alan asked. He regretted speaking, after he realized he'd stated the obvious.

"Invoices that were delivered with the product are authentic, but this guy refuses to comment on the origin of the order. He says their office doesn't have any record of this sale or delivery. I'm not sure if he just doesn't want to be involved or if he's keeping something from us." Shane moved in the direction of the window. "The leaves are starting to turn. Won't be long before they're all gone."

"We can do something about this, Shane. If that company isn't involved, then why don't they prove it?"

"I've tried to get my contact to approve an inspection, but he won't budge. He flat-out refuses to cooperate, and I'm not surprised. I don't have much leverage to enforce this on my own."

Alan deliberated how to broach the next subject at hand. He played on the heat of the moment and decided to dive right in.

"I hate to add insult to injury, Shane, but have you reviewed the last report I sent over? It's about our foreign support."

"Haven't gotten to it yet. It must be toward the bottom of the pile. What does it say?"

"Nothing surprising, but it's not good. Our resources abroad have weakened, to say the least. Our allies are pulling away. They're worried about their own domestic issues. Can't blame them, but it defeats the whole idea of strength in numbers," Alan explained. "I feel like UFW is a thing of the past, down the drain. And they're all hoarding smallpox vaccines."

"Afraid they won't have enough to meet their own needs?" Shane finished Alan's thought. "I know what's going on. I expected as much. They want to know who did this, so we're back to trusting no one. Jesus, Alan, I can't say I blame them. You know, we are talking about an attempt at world disruption here. We want to know, too. I don't trust my allies either. What kills me is that I know they all think that somehow this is our fault."

"Come on, Shane, That's emotion talking. They might denounce you and our country for being arrogant, for celebrating too early. Well, let's not forget that they were right there with us. Hell, this whole thing was Gousev's idea."

"Either way, five years of coalition building have just gone down the tubes. At least we have each other, right?" Shane's wisecrack broke the tension in the room. "Thanks for listening to me vent. We'll figure this out. I just wish we had one lead to go on."

"We'll find them, Shane," Alan promised. "And when we do, they'll wish to God ... whatever god they want to pray to ... that they'd never messed with us."

Shane maintained one goal—finding the people who were responsible for this plan. He knew that terrorism couldn't be defined by one individual or even by one group. But these people took human lives, and they needed to be stopped. Although he acknowledged that he could've been premature to believe in the success of the United Free World, he didn't regret the celebration. Freedom was worth celebrating. He knew there had to be a light at the end of the tunnel. He prayed for a glimmer to lead him in the right direction.

Standing, he gathered his notes for the meeting with the task force. He reminded himself of a time when a committee of this nature hadn't even existed. Things had changed over the years, just as they always did. Now, attending these meetings was second nature for Shane. He prayed for the day when the workload of this committee could be reduced.

With all White House employees having returned to work, Shane could feel the murmur of a quiet whisper circulating through the halls as he navigated the corridors on his way to the conference room. Certain they were dying to ask questions, Shane was thankful that they didn't. As soon as he entered the conference room, he called the meeting to order.

"All right, everyone, give me what you've got."

Listening, he prayed for good news. While waiting for the first voice to speak up, he glanced at his watch to see how much time he could spare before his meeting with the CDC and the World Health Organization. The minutes were ticking away.

He already knew what they had to announce. Several suspected cases of smallpox had been identified in other Celebrate Freedom host cities and some abroad. The celebration had borne a demon, and the monster was growing every day.

Forcing his thoughts back on track, he passed the latest CDC report around the conference table.

CDC Report to: White House Officials, World Health Organization and Federal Bureau of Investigation. September 15

Confirmed cases of Smallpox*

Pennsylvania: 25 cases confirmed
New York: 18 cases confirmed

Suspected cases of Smallpox
not presenting rash as of twelve noon 9/15

Washington, DC: 13 cases of flu-like symptoms
Atlanta, GA: 7 cases of flu-like symptoms
Orlando, FL: 6 cases of flu-like symptoms

* All victims have tested positive for a faintly mutated form of the smallpox virus now referred to as SP4 – smallpox four.

That meeting, like most recent gatherings, left Shane exhausted. Fearing that the CDC report represented the start of an unwelcome tradition, Shane read over the numbers again. The quantities of smallpox cases seemed to have multiplied with the hour. These cases were all somehow connected to Tony Lonitesci or other plant workers. The people who'd been present at the fireworks shows had not even begun to present symptoms. He dreaded the moment when those cases would appear.

Shane felt guilty for not publicizing his belief of how the true attack had been carried out, but he saw no valid reason to do so yet. The disease had already been unleashed. By offering the explanation of the magnitude of such an attack, he would only assist in escalating a level of panic. This wouldn't serve the needs of the public.

With the illness manifesting itself in New York, the request for vaccines had doubled. New York wanted a supply equal to or greater than that which had been sent to Pennsylvania. Following the confirmation of more cases, the governor of Pennsylvania had made a request to double the initial quantity of vaccines his state was to receive. Two other states and the District were waiting for test results, so the requests for vaccines were expected to grow.

Shane sighed at the result of the math he'd worked out in his head. In a simultaneous gesture, he ruffled his hair with his right hand and crumpled the report in his left. In a country with over three hundred million people, the supply of smallpox vaccines would be inadequate.

Digging through his files, he retrieved an attack scenario that had been written for him by an analyst who was working with the Anti-Terrorism Task Force. In a fifteen-page report, the analyst had documented his model of how domestic events would play out following a bioterrorism attack that used smallpox as the weapon.

The text was grim. The author described the initial detection of the virus and the positive test results from the CDC. The report walked Shane through the onset of more cases and the growth in number of requests for vaccines. In the setting of what appeared as an eerie screenplay, the writer designed a scenario that led straight through the guts of a horror story as the cases continued to multiply. With the identification of more cases came the desire for more vaccines, and with more victims came the need for the public to see justice for their killers.

Panic is sure to take hold of even the most level-minded citizens. Children will be pulled from schools, and hospitals will be plagued by break-ins from desperate souls seeking preventative vaccines. Shane threw the manuscript into the trash. Chills ran the length of his spine as he thought about the writing in the report. This was just like a *Farmers Almanac of Terrorism* – only worse. He saw no reason to read any more. This was one man's take on how things would happen, and he refused to let it paralyze him. His reality was paralleled in the first paragraph, as if it had been written word for word about the attack that the world had just suffered. He had to get through this one day at a time. Besides, he felt confident he could change the ending.

Saturday, September 16th

-23-

While gathering her stuff, Cheryl helped get Hannah packed. Lazy afternoons on the beach, relaxing dinners in the evenings, and two trips to Disney World had filled their vacation time. Without doubt, Celebrate Freedom had won the unanimous award for their favorite activity during the trip. Photos from that evening had covered three rolls of film from Hannah's camera, more than she'd taken during the entire rest of the week. Cheryl rubbed her thumb over the black leather camera case. She knew her daughter would remember the celebration forever.

"Do you have everything, sweetheart?" Cheryl turned to face her daughter.

"Yes, Mom, I have everything." Hannah answered in a monotone voice. "How much time do we have? Can we walk on the beach before we go?"

"I'm sorry, sweetie. We don't have time. Joel's waiting to take us to the airport."

Hannah dropped her head and stuffed her clothes into her suitcase.

"Hannah, I'm gonna grab us some bagels for the ride. Do you want any special kind?" Kendra tried to bring a smile to her niece's face.

"No thanks, Aunt Kendra. I'm not hungry."

"But, honey, you should have something. You have to take your medicine, and it'll be hours before you get the chance to eat again," Cheryl said.

"Mom, I'm not hungry. My head hurts, and my stomach feels a little weird." With a hint of defiance, Hannah turned away from her mother.

With an instinctive motion, Cheryl moved to her daughter's side and reached for her forehead. She slid the back of her hand down toward Hannah's cheek, while feeling her own head with her free hand.

"Hannah, let me take your temperature. How long have you been feeling this way?" Cheryl fumbled in the medicine bag for a thermometer.

"Mom, I'm fine. I just started feeling crappy this morning." She hated when her mother overreacted. There was no reason to worry. "If it makes you feel any better, I'll eat a bagel. Blueberry's fine, Aunt Kendra."

Kendra nodded and started downstairs to the kitchen.

"Hannah, come here for a second." Cheryl halted her daughter from packing and sat her down on the bed. "Are you sure you're okay, honey? Please tell me the truth. Maybe we should postpone our flight and go to see a doctor."

"Mom, relax. I've felt a lot worse before. Maybe I'm just feeling sad because we have to leave."

"Okay, sweetie, but take your medicine." Cheryl spoke her order in a sweet but stern voice. "You sit next to me on the plane. I want to keep an eye on you." She felt her daughter's head one more time as she placed the thermometer in Hannah's mouth. "Now stay still until this beeps three times."

Through her emerging smile, Hannah held the thermometer in place. Rolling her eyes in a goofy expression, she made it clear that she knew when to take it out. She'd been doing this her whole life.

Cheryl wondered where the time had gone. Worlds away from the problems she'd left at home, this vacation had left her in sheer bliss. Still, part of her was ready to return to a familiar place. She was looking forward to seeing Abigail, and she knew Kendra was anxious to see Gerry. Getting back to work even sounded okay.

The television flashed a glimpse of a news report that mentioned the smallpox outbreak in Pennsylvania. Cheryl stopped to listen to the anchorman speak. She expected to find a somber atmosphere at the office when she returned. Thoughts of work occupied Cheryl's mind the entire ride to the airport.

"Hey, dreamy, we're here." Joel nudged Cheryl. He jabbed at her in a playful manner. "Hello ... are you with us, Ms. Williams?"

"I'm here now, but I won't be for long," Cheryl answered. She turned the corners of her mouth down in an exaggerated frown.

"Here we go, ladies." Joel unloaded their bags. Looking up from the luggage, he caught Cheryl watching him. He felt energized by her stare. "Hey Brian, give me a hand getting these over to Skycap, will ya?" He spoke to the driver, but his eyes remained focused on Cheryl.

"I can help too," Cheryl offered. She brushed past Joel to lift the smaller of the three suitcases.

In minutes, the luggage had been checked. All that was left for the ladies to manage was a small pile of carry-on bags.

"Joel, we can't thank you enough," Cheryl said. "We had an outstanding time." She watched as he squeezed Hannah into a bear hug.

"You send me a postcard from Washington, ya hear? It's not every day I meet a young lady from the nation's capital." He slipped his address in her hand and she accepted it with a smile. After giving Kendra a quick hug good-bye, he turned to Cheryl. He'd saved the best for last.

"I really enjoyed the time you ladies spent with us at the house. I hope for the very best for all of you. If you're ever in Florida again, give me a call." Joel pinched Cheryl's cheek. He outlined her silhouette with his thumb. His hand slid from her chin to her shoulder and along the length of her arm. His fingers stopped, briefly, as they met her hand.

"Thanks again. I do hope we'll hear from you sometime, Joel. I know Hannah would like to send you some photos from our trip." Stuttering forward, Cheryl leaned into a hug with her new friend. A rosy glow bled across her cheeks. In a rapid move to hide her red face, she slipped from Joel's embrace and bent to retrieve her carry-on bag.

Joel and Cheryl had already discussed staying in touch. Although he was younger than she was, she'd found him to be pleasant company. She was confident he felt the same. Several of their evenings had been spent sitting on the deck, drinking lemonade or enjoying an occasional glass of wine.

"Well, I've got classes to head off to, if I'm ever going to become a doctor." Joel walked backwards toward the SUV. "So, if you all don't need me anymore, I'll be going. Have a safe trip, and write soon."

As the Explorer disappeared from their view, the exhausted young ladies started off in the direction of the gate.

At the waiting area, Cheryl found three seats together. Snuggling in between Kendra and Hannah, she took the middle chair. To her left, Hannah dropped into a seat and rested her head on her mother's shoulder. Within minutes, she was asleep. Cheryl stroked her daughter's hair and let her own head fall back onto the neck support.

* * *

With every passing hour, the volatile situation escalated. Data confirmed a national shortage of smallpox vaccines. Although this wasn't new information, Shane was saddened by its definitive nature. Word of suspected smallpox cases in several New England cities had made its way across his desk. Theory held that these victims would be categorized as first generation cases, resulting from their visits to New York for the celebration. In addition, a report had also been confirmed that three suspected cases of smallpox had appeared in London. Atlanta had been inundated with samples for testing. What was the point? It was all a mere formality now.

His phone rang again. "Hello, McAlister."

"Hi, sir. It's Alan." The general's voice sounded even more serious than usual. "I just got off the phone with Agent Anderson, in Pittsburgh. We have a situation there that I need to discuss with you. Do you have a minute?"

"Of course. What's going on?"

"They had a break-in at the hospital last night. The agents caught three men trying to force entry in the early morning hours."

"Okay, so they didn't succeed?" Shane wasn't clear why the agent had called Alan about the trivial situation.

"No, they didn't succeed. They were stopped, but that's not why Anderson called. He was bothered by the reason the guys said they were breaking in."

"And, that reason was..." Shane tried not to get frustrated.

"The men were looking for vaccines. After they were denied vaccines from their family doctors, they lost it. Agent Anderson sounded pretty upset. He said things were getting out of control."

"Was this an isolated case, Alan?"

"I think it was the first situation. But Anderson said they seemed like decent men. Sir, he said they were begging for the vaccines. He's afraid they're heading toward a large-scale panic. I think he's nervous of what's next."

"I understand his concerns, Alan." Shane replied with a canned response. He squeezed his eyes closed tight in a juvenile attempt to erase the world around him. "Please tell him that we'll make it a priority on the task force agenda to discuss how to handle situations like this."

"That's what I told him, but I said I'd keep you abreast of the situation."

Shane shook his head in disbelief. This was only the beginning. What would happen when the virus broke out in the magnitude that was expected? The vaccines could be gone in no time.

Attempting positive thinking, Shane focused on the latest reports from the task force. They'd been working around the clock to find the men responsible for this crime. Some believed that finding the terrorists would also uncover a hidden supply of smallpox vaccine. They wouldn't attack with such a deadly virus unless they felt protected. The strength of the terrorist organization had plummeted with the capture in August, and they couldn't afford to wipe themselves out by being careless.

To date, the task force hadn't found many answers. This terrorist group had effectively concealed themselves from the United States government. This was hard for Shane to swallow, since the U.S. military had prided themselves on finding anyone, at any time and in any place. This cell had the obvious support of a much larger institution.

Shane called Alan back.

"Hey, Alan, can you come over here? I've got some other things to talk to you about." Shane waited with patience for his right-hand-man to arrive.

In no time, he appeared at the door. "Hey Shane, what do you need?"

"Alan, can you find out for me the names of any countries or large cities that have ordered the smallpox vaccine in the past year? And find out if they've administered these vaccines to their government employees or civilian population within the same time frame. A country who meets this criteria might provide the map we need to direct us to the terrorists. Do we have any more information on the company that shipped that potassium perchlorate to the Lonitesci plant?"

"Not yet. We're still working on it, Shane. I'll get the men on the vaccine question right away. I wouldn't think that should take long. We'll do our best."

"Thanks, Alan." Shane swiveled in his chair to view his most recent mathematical calculations. Before he could double-check his work, his newly installed personal fax spit out yet another memo from the CDC. He glanced at the lengthy paragraphs, but his eyes rested first on the list of *New Confirmed Smallpox Cases.*

New Mexico - two confirmed cases.
Arizona - three confirmed cases.

Shane called out to stop Alan from leaving.

"Hey, Alan. Will you find out how these latest smallpox victims wound up in New Mexico and Arizona? Let me know as soon as you hear something. Thanks." He was reluctant to read the rest of the report. More cases in Pennsylvania and New York were recorded on the list. When the phone rang, he answered right away. That was fast. It seemed like Alan had just left his office.

"Hello? Yes, Alan. Okay. I see, and the Arizona cases? Okay, thanks. Let's get another committee meeting put together for the next hour. Thanks."

"New Mexico victims were on the plane with Tony Lonitesci," Shane mumbled and scribbled notes on the most current CDC report. "And the Arizona victims were at the Orlando Celebrate Freedom show." The lead snapped from the tip of his pencil. Throwing it in the trash, he took a pen from his desk drawer. Next to the notes, he wrote the following in parenthesis:

Phase Two - 2nd Generation of Outbreak.

The report found its place in his leather bound notebook. Shane left his office to gather some more information. His fax machine beeped as the door slammed shut behind him, and another CDC report printed.

Immediate Attention - New Findings

This report sat face down on the table, awaiting his return.

Following the task force briefing, Shane remained in the conference room, wishing to take a few minutes with his closest advisors. The meeting had gone as expected. A growing number of smallpox cases had been reported throughout the infected states, in addition to the introduction of the virus in several other areas. The suspected cases in London were confirmed as smallpox. The Russian government added the icing on the cake, though, by sending a written correspondence stressing its concern over the outbreak. They blamed the United States for the attack. One thing after another. This situation gave a whole new meaning to the term *domino effect*.

> *The overwhelming arrogance displayed by a worldwide celebration could only ask for an attack by evil powers and terrorist cells ...*

"Can you believe this, Alan?" Shane threw his hands out in disbelief. He pointed to the Russian correspondence. "How can they blame us for this? We've been in this together for all this time, and now they act as if we're their enemies. Even our foreign *friends* have abandoned us to place their domestic concerns first. The foundation of support that we built with these guys has crumbled right beneath us, just when we all need it most." He tossed the document back on the table and shook his head in frustration. "Christ, Alan, we can't even get China to cooperate by questioning that chemical plant. Don't they realize they could be at risk for this thing, too, even without having had the celebration? If the chemical plant was involved, then they've been exposed, too. I don't get it. What the heck happened?" Shane took a deep breath. His venting had brought some relief, but not enough.

"I know, Shane. We're going to figure this out ... I know it. All we need is a little more time."

"Yeah, but time is the one thing we don't have." Shane sighed and gathered his notes. Patting Alan on the back, he started to the door. "Let's get some people working on determining the probable origins of these smallpox cases that are cropping up all over. Are they first or second generation cases? Also, we've got the CDC setting up satellite labs to make diagnostic testing more timely. Let's make sure we're using those. Call me if you hear anything."

"Will do. I'll be in touch."

"In the meantime, I'll be working on a plan to control our other impending outbreak ... panic. Talk to you soon. Oh, hey, Alan—"

"Yes, Sir?"

"Give Agent Anderson a call and let him know that we're working on a plan for panic control."

"Okay."

"I hope things have calmed down out there." Shane knew he was hoping for a lot.

*　*　*

Alan listened while the agent explained the current situation in Pittsburgh.

"General, everything's gotten worse. Parents are refusing to send their kids to school. Other parents are sending their kids to school wearing facemasks. The military supply store is the only business having a positive quarter, because the local restaurants and shopping malls have been darn near empty. Some nights they just have to close. Then you have the grocery stores, which have been cleaned out of everything they had in stock. They won't order more stuff, because they're afraid to have any incoming goods. I can't believe what's going on. We need to do something."

"Do you think the economic damage has been limited to the local restaurants and shopping centers?" Alan asked.

"No. The city of Pittsburgh has had to cancel all conventions and trade shows as well as concerts and professional sporting events. This has put a number of people out of work. I bet New York's feeling this, too, probably even worse. On top of all of that, we have the pharmacy break-ins to contend with. It's getting out of control."

"Listen, don't give up on us yet. We're working on a plan to settle this craziness. Trust us." Alan prayed the task force could deliver on his promise. "I think the only way we can calm these people is to demonstrate that we've found and dealt with the men who've done this. We're working hard to do this."

"Thanks for your call, General."

Sunday, September 17th

-24-

Cheryl sat on the sofa, watching cable news. She couldn't believe the turn of events the nation had witnessed since she'd left for vacation. Just one week ago, the station had been preparing to cover a worldwide celebration of freedom. Now, it was broadcasting the latest breaking story about a possible international bioterrorism attack. Cheryl listened to the anchorwoman announce the news that the World Health Organization had confirmed several cases of smallpox in London. She shook her head in disgust. She was just about to turn off the television, when another news broadcast caught her attention.

"In Arizona, a young couple and their six-year-old daughter have tested positive for the smallpox virus. A source tells us that CDC officials have stated, off the record, that the three victims were thought to have contracted the virus while visiting Orlando, Florida for Celebrate Freedom."

Cheryl stared at the television. This couldn't be right. Her instinct was to call Kendra. She knew her sister would tell her that this was all a mistake. Before she could dial the number, her phone rang. The Caller ID revealed that Kendra had beaten her to the punch.

"Hey Kendra, are you watching TV?" Cheryl spoke before her sister could say hello.

"Not right at the moment," Kendra answered. "Why? You sound upset."

"I *am* upset, Kendra. Cable news is showing a family who's

tested positive for smallpox, and they said they think these people caught the virus in Orlando, at Celebrate Freedom." The volume of her voice grew louder with each word. "Sorry, I don't mean to yell. I just don't understand why on earth a visit to Orlando would make these people high risk. Thousands of people were at that celebration, maybe millions. Listen, let me call you right back." She hung up the phone before her sister could ask any questions.

Her heart started to beat faster as she dialed the number to her office. She didn't have to report to work until Monday, but she needed information now. The phone rang four times, before her own recorded voice answered. Remembering it was Sunday, she hung up. Waiting until Monday to find out what was going on would be difficult, but she didn't have another choice. She called her sister back.

"Sorry, Kendra, I thought maybe I could get some info from people at the office. This news just scared me, that's all. I'll let you go. Call me if you hear anything else."

Heading to the kitchen to clean up from breakfast, she realized it was already noon. She knew Hannah was tired, but twelve o'clock was late to sleep in, even for a ten-year-old. On the weekends, she usually woke up early, anxious to spend the day with her mom. Maybe she'd had enough of the mother-daughter thing for a while. Rounding the corner at the top of the steps, Cheryl pushed her daughter's bedroom door until it swung open.

Hannah was curled up in bed with her covers pulled up to her chin. What Cheryl could see of her face appeared flushed, pink in color.

From the doorway, Cheryl could hear her daughter's labored breathing. Was she congested? She moved to the edge of the bed and placed her hand on Hannah's forehead. The heat that escaped to her hand alarmed her, and she went to find the thermometer. When she returned, Hannah hadn't moved. She shook her daughter, trying to wake her. After ten seconds, Hannah opened her eyes.

"Hey, Mom," Hannah whispered. "I'm still tired."

"I know sweetie, but you've been asleep for fourteen hours. Your head's burning up. I'm sorry to wake you, but you have to let me take your temperature." She slid the thermometer between her daughter's dry lips and stroked her forehead. She watched as Hannah closed her eyes, allowing the thermometer to hang in its place.

After three minutes, the beeping sound prompted Hannah to open her eyes and her mouth. She handed the thermometer back to her mother.

"Come on, sugar. We need to get you dressed." Cheryl urged Hannah to sit up.

"Where are we going?" Hannah would rather not have moved.

"We need to have Dr. Watters run a quick check on you. Let me see if she's available." Cheryl spoke in a casual tone. "You know, she hasn't seen you in over a week, and I promised her I would bring you in after our vacation. She wants to make sure you're okay. I go back to work on Monday, so I thought we should go today."

"But do we even have an appointment?" Hannah knew that her doctor wasn't available for casual walk-in visits, and it was Sunday.

"Of course, sweetie. Abbie took care of that. Now, get dressed." Cheryl walked across the hall to her own room.

After closing her bedroom door, she dialed Abbie's phone number. Her legs shook against the side of the mattress, as she counted the rings of the phone. "Please be home, please be home," she mumbled.

"Hello?" Abigail sounded out of breath.

"Abbie, hi, it's Cheryl."

"Oh, hey, Cheryl." Abbie responded with enthusiasm. "How was the trip? I can't wait to see the photos."

"Abbie, I need your help," Cheryl cut in. "I need you to call Dr. Watters' answering service." She paused for a quick breath. Her voice was trembling. "I need you to make an emergency appointment for Hannah. I would do it myself, but I told her we had a pre-set routine appointment, and if she hears me on the phone—" Cheryl's voice trailed off into crying.

"Please, stay calm. I'll find Dr. Watters," Abbie promised. "Cheryl, stay in control ... for Hannah." She waited for a response. "What's the problem? What should I tell the doctor?"

"She's got a temperature of a hundred and two. She's been in bed all day, and she won't get up. Thanks, Abbie. Call my cell phone to let me know what's going on." Cheryl waited for Abigail to call back.

* * *

Shane sifted through the stack of faxes that had accumulated. He'd allowed himself only minimal time out of the office the day before, and he already felt as if he'd fallen way behind. He read one fax after another. London, Russia, France and Ireland had all begun their own protocols for smallpox quarantines and treatments. Each country had reported at least nine confirmed cases of the virus.

Within the United States, seven states plus Washington, D.C. had confirmed cases of smallpox. Four new states had reported suspected cases, and the end of the initial incubation period had just been approached. The West Coast still had a day or two before its cases were expected to surface.

Shane decided that the time had come to announce the theoretical origin of this virus. He was prepared to explain the suspected contamination in the fireworks and the possible use of the pyrotechnic show to spread the virus across the world. He'd hoped to have more information about the people responsible for the act. He'd come to terms with the fact that, for this announcement, he wouldn't have the answers to the inevitable questions of who and why.

Fearing panic on a large scale, Shane molded his words carefully. He reminded everyone in his circle that the important message to send was that the world had eradicated this disease once before, and they could do it again.

He counted the minutes until airtime. From the depths of his soul, he mustered up all of the confidence he could find. Several intentional swallows provoked deep breathing through his nose. While waiting, he flipped through the unread faxes, resting on the bottom page in his stack. The words startled him. Reaching for the phone, he scrambled to make a call in the time he had left.

"Alan? We need to delay this announcement. I know it won't look good, but I need thirty minutes. Get everyone in the conference room, now." Uncharacteristic of his usual tone, Shane barked the orders.

Once he reached the conference room, he threw the fax toward the middle of the table. The light paper floated from the air to the wooden surface and landed, right side up. Each man glanced at the fax as he entered the conference room. The words were large and bold. The call letters stood out in the memo as if they represented a logo or trademark for a new popular retail brand.

SP4 - a new strain of smallpox demonstrates shorter incubation period.
This variance of smallpox is not inhibited by the traditional smallpox vaccine.
Differences in new strain make treatment questionable ...

Shane began to speak, even before everyone had entered the conference room. He needed to make the most of the thirty minutes he had.

"Well, we've been thrown yet another twist of events in our subject at hand. SP4 is more dangerous than we thought. It's more deadly than smallpox." He paused for comments.

When silence filled the room, he went on. "So, the good news is this—we may not have to be concerned at all about the insufficient vaccine we have available to our citizens. The bad news is the vaccine probably won't work anyway."

The room became a vacuum, sucking the air from all of those present. One after another, the standing men took their seats and prepared for the most important brainstorming session of their careers.

"We need to find a way to announce this as a positive, and not as the terrible negative that I believe it is. Any suggestions?" Shane was desperate.

"Sir, do they have any reason to believe that traditional vaccines will work for this strain?" Alan asked.

"No, they don't think so. In fact, the CDC fears that the vaccines might actually make the virus stronger—at least that's what preliminary testing has shown. However, they are working around the clock to identify anything that might stop this monster in its tracks."

Shane stared at the paper on the table. How could the terrorists have succeeded in mutating the virus? Their means of planning couldn't reach this level of sophistication.

***

With Abbie and Hannah by her side, Cheryl sat in the ER. She was thankful the doctor would see Hannah on such short notice, especially on a Sunday. Choosing Hannah's physician had been difficult, but Cheryl had known right away that Dr. Watters was the right choice. She was dedicated to her career, and she made herself available whenever possible.

In another effort to make progress, Abbie moved from her seat next to Hannah and approached the administrative desk.

"Excuse me, ma'am?" It was another failed attempt to get someone's attention. With no luck, she returned to the waiting area, but this time she settled down next to Cheryl. "They won't even look in my direction."

"I know, Abbie. Once they have your insurance information, they seem to forget you're here."

Abbie's tone calmed. "I just hate to watch her sitting here, burning up, when Dr. Watters hasn't even seen her yet. I hope they don't keep her waiting much longer."

"I know." Feeling Hannah wiggling in her seat, Cheryl leaned to the side to allow her daughter to get comfortable. Once her little girl was situated, Cheryl moved her hand up to stroke her daughter's forehead. Her fingers combed through Hannah's perspiration-soaked hair. She remained calm for Hannah's benefit. Inside, she began to panic.

When Hannah's diagnosis had been altered from HIV positive to a confirmation of AIDS. Dr. Watters had stressed the importance of a positive attitude in dealing with this prognosis. In separate conversations, she'd explained to both Cheryl and Hannah that the best medicine for any disease was a healthy soul. To date, both young ladies had taken her advice to heart and had acted in accordance with that plan. Their positive attitudes had rubbed off on everyone around them. Hannah lived in an environment filled with strength, faith, and positivity.

At that moment, Cheryl found it difficult to exude strength. With the latest diagnosis having come about less than a year earlier, she expected to have had more time before having to deal with such a deterioration in her child's health. Hannah had been doing so well. Cheryl believed she'd prepared for the day when her daughter's health took a turn for the worse, but this was far too soon. She wasn't ready yet, and she refused to accept this now. She appreciated having Abbie to turn to for support.

"Abbie, will you take my seat next to Hannah for a few minutes? I'll be right back."

Abbie positioned Hannah's head on her shoulder, just as Cheryl had been sitting with the sleeping girl seconds before.

Once she was sure they were comfortable, Cheryl walked to the restroom.

She found an empty stall, turned the handle on the door and entered. Forcing the metal lock bar into its place, she let her body fall against the cool aluminum wall in an immediate motion. Crying like she hadn't since she was small, she released years of pent up emotions. Her heaving breaths caused her to lean forward. She slid down the length of the door until she landed in a seated position.

Pulling a piece of toilet paper from the dispenser, she dried her eyes and wiped her nose. Tossing the paper in the bowl, she flushed and left the confines of the stall. The stained porcelain of the community sink welcomed her, as she splashed cold water on her face. Spending some time replenishing her makeup helped her to disguise the fact that she'd been crying. A powerful inhale propelled her to exit the restroom.

As she approached the waiting area, Cheryl could see Abigail and Hannah sitting, as she'd left them moments earlier. Before they saw her, she retreated in the direction from which she'd entered and stopped by a vending machine. Some change from the bottom of her purse bought her a small bag of cookies, Hannah's favorite. Snack in hand, she returned to the waiting area to join her crew.

"Hey guys, any news?" Cheryl forced a cheerful voice.

"No, not yet." From over the top of Hannah's head, Abigail studied her friend's colorless face. With her eyes, she asked Cheryl if she was okay.

With silent words, Cheryl's glance answered that she'd be fine.

"Mom, I thought I had an appointment. What's taking so long? What time was I scheduled? Why is she seeing me here, at the hospital?" Hannah wrinkled her eyebrows in question. Impatience was uncharacteristic for this ten-year-old.

"Sugar, you did have an appointment. I'm not sure what's taking so long." Cheryl struggled for a plausible explanation.

"I think someone had to come in for an emergency visit, Hannah." Abigail chimed in at just the right moment. "Maybe that has set Dr. Watters back a bit. I'm sure she'll get to you as soon as she can."

Satisfied with the explanation, Hannah turned her focus to the goodies she spied in her mother's hand.

"Are those cookies for me, Mom?"

"They sure are, my love. Are you hungry?"

"A little –" Hannah knew she'd make room for a sought after snack. "Besides, they're my favorite kind."

* * *

Cheryl made Hannah comfortable in the hospital bed.

"I still don't understand why I have to stay here, Mom. I've been sick before, but they never made me stay. Where's Dr. Watters? I don't want any other doctors to come in here and ask me a bunch of questions." Hannah was more upset than usual.

"Sweetie, Dr. Watters will be back soon. The other doctors won't bother you. If they have any questions, they can ask me."

Very soon, Hannah was fast asleep in her bed. Cheryl tucked the sheets around her daughter's chin, afraid that the fever would make her cold in the air-conditioned hospital. When she felt confident that Hannah was comfortable, she took a seat in a chair in the corner of the room and closed her own tired eyes.

Thoughts zipped around in her mind and kept her from resting. In their discussion, Dr. Watters had reminded Cheryl how they'd been preparing for the day that Hannah's condition could worsen. However, she hadn't confirmed that the time had come. More tests were needed first. But, she'd explained in her most compassionate voice, the symptoms could point in that direction. Cheryl had managed to fight back her tears, but she'd taken a few minutes to herself before facing Hannah.

With a desperate desire to know what would happen next overwhelming her, all she could do was wait. She'd spent many nights lying awake and wondering. How would it all play out? Would Hannah get sick and then better, a seesaw of stable and poor health? Or would she become ill and only spend a short time longer with her? Cheryl fought the urge to feel bitter at God, at the doctors that had delivered Hannah, or just at anyone who would listen. She knew that faith and a positive attitude were imperative now, and she refused to give in to the weakness.

She moved her weight to her right side and pulled her knees

up to her chest. Clasping her hands in front of her shins, she positioned herself to watch her daughter sleep. Maybe this was just a case of the flu. But even the flu could be too much for Hannah's weakened immune system. Her eyes bounded around the room, searching for a clock. She wondered how much longer it would be before Dr. Watters would arrive.

After another twenty minutes of trying to rest, Cheryl crossed the small hospital room and found the television remote on the table next to the bed. Careful not to wake Hannah, she enacted the mute function as soon as the power came on. A news report caption decorated the screens of every channel she saw. She settled on the news and disabled the mute. Lowering the volume, she strained to hear the faint dialogue of her boss.

***

Shane spent the evening determining his next move. His announcement to the nation had gone over as he and his team had expected. The outcome was one step shy of chaos.

People throughout the country felt the attack was the direct result of an ill-prepared government, and they felt compelled to speak their minds. Words were spoken that reflected the belief that the CDC was ignorant of how to do their jobs during the time of an emergency.

Any attempt to contact other members of a United Free World had proven pointless. The question of how this attack had happened had deterred the other countries from a cooperative effort.

The mutation of the smallpox virus had set back years of preparation. The country had been well prepared for a smallpox outbreak. However, the introduction of a new strain of the virus had thrown a wrench in the plan, a variable for which no one had planned. Had the terrorists planned the twist in the conventional attack? He didn't believe they were that scientifically endowed. How could they have known of such a consequence? He smiled, aware that he'd just stumbled over what could prove to be the free world's ace-in-the-hole.

Shane called an emergency meeting of the task force. Over the past month, Sunday gatherings had become a regular part of the week's schedule. Finally, though, he felt he could offer some information, which would lead his men along a productive path. Perhaps they'd been looking in the wrong direction. Maybe the terrorists didn't create this mutation after all.

Enthusiasm welcomed the men and women who entered the conference room.

"Hello, everyone. I have some new information to share. Some fresh news from the CDC has sent my theory in a new direction." Shane paused for a sip of cold water.

"The latest reports from the CDC have suggested that early effects of the smallpox vaccine have proven disappointing when used for treatment in our current situation. This vaccine seems to result in worsening the effects of the SP4 strain. Vaccinated patients in Pittsburgh are showing high fevers, reoccurrences of the rash and intense stomach cramping and nausea. The Pennsylvania State Health Commissioner's office has reviewed numerous calls regarding this situation. In an attempt to assist the state health offices, the CDC has requested advice from our task force on how to deal with such inquiries."

The faces around the table wore identical blank stares. Unsure of how to respond, Alan spoke first.

"Okay, so help me out, sir. Why did you say this was a good thing?"

"I'm glad you asked, Alan." Shane was anxious to continue. "When I received this information, I began to look at things in a different way. If our own Center for Disease Control is struggling to develop a protocol for handling this scenario, then how could those damn terrorists have prepared for this outcome? SP4? No way could those guys have been ready for this. Our CDC housed a sample of the smallpox virus for years after the disease's eradication. They studied it inside and out. They've developed protocols for every possible scenario out there. They have protocols for imaginary viruses we've never even seen before. If they weren't ready for this, then I don't see how anyone else could've been either. No way in hell."

Alan listened until Shane had finished talking. He was surprised by Shane's use of curse words while speaking to the group, but he knew Shane's candid speaking demonstrated his excitement.

"I see what you're saying, Shane, but I don't understand. How could the lack of planning by the terrorists help us now? We're suffering, whether they planned for this or not."

"I understand, and I agree that we're suffering, but I think we can use their inadequacies to find them." Shane's eyes were smiling for the first time in a week. "They were planning for a smallpox outbreak. They had the virus, so we have to assume that they also had the vaccine."

As he took a breath, Shane saw his weary team members coming to life around the room. He watched for signs that they followed his point so far. "So if they'd planned for the outbreak by vaccinating themselves, they are now suffering the consequences. The vaccine will cause the virus to effect them in a more severe manner, killing them or forcing them to come crawling out wherever they're hiding. They'll wander out like intoxicated insects after an extermination, and we'll be waiting for them."

"So, any domestic terrorists should be developing the illness now, along with the people who were exposed at the celebrations. Right?" Alan asked.

"That's the way I see it, Alan." Finally Shane felt his efforts were on the right track. He retreated to his office to regroup.

Since he hadn't gotten much sleep over the past few days, he'd begun to feel weak. He took a seat on the couch and attempted to rest for a bit. If he was aware of the warmth escaping from his head, he didn't acknowledge the problem.

Monday, September 18th

-25-

Monday morning greeted Shane with shock, as he realized he'd been sleeping in his office since the meeting the evening before. Although the rest was warranted, he scolded himself for having taken such a long break. After washing up, he changed his shirt and took his position at his desk. At least he had an hour or so to work before anyone else would show up.

Shane sifted through another pile of faxes. More reports from the CDC informed him of their experimental attempts to treat, or at least contain, SP4. To date, they had little to go on.

Across the country, the reports were all the same. Doctors wanted information on what to do next and were growing agitated with the lack of solutions.

A coughing spell halted Shane's progress. His discomfort prompted him to massage his forehead with the top of his hand. He'd slept a long time the night before, yet he felt as if he'd been sleep deprived for a month.

He fumbled in a desk drawer for a fever reducer. The sound of pills rattling against the plastic container brought about an anticipated feeling of comfort. A gulp of lukewarm water chased three tablets down Shane's throat. He continued reading through the faxes.

From the bottom of the stack, one fax caught Shane's immediate attention. This notice differed from the others, because the heading didn't begin with *CDC Special Report* or *State Health Commissioner Alert*. Instead, the contents of this fax were handwritten in neat lines on plain paper in the style of a personal letter. The letter was addressed to *Mr. Shane McAlister.*

Shane gathered the three pages of the fax. Page three was signed in the bottom margin. His focused effort revealed the scribbling as A. Gousev.

* * *

Again, Cheryl had called out of work for the day. She was concerned about jeopardizing her job, but her desire to be with her daughter outweighed those worries. She sat in the chair adjacent Hannah's hospital bed, writing a list of things she'd ask Kendra to pick up.

Over the past few hours, Hannah's condition had worsened. Her fever hadn't broken, and she had increased cramping and nausea. These symptoms were typical of the AIDS virus, but Dr. Watters had warned Cheryl not to jump to conclusions about which phase of the disease her daughter was experiencing.

Lately, Cheryl spent her hours alone praying. She prayed for the Lord's will, and she prayed for Hannah to be comfortable should the Lord's will be to take her.

Cheryl's faith was strong, but she felt conflicted. She questioned why an innocent girl like Hannah should be tormented by this disease when other healthy people in the world were capable of killing others for no reason. Promising herself not to question, she focused on finding the answers.

Over the past hours, Cheryl's movements had become robotic. She preserved all of her energy for when Hannah was awake, saving her smiles for the time spent with her daughter. Once Hannah was asleep, she relapsed, returning to her quiet self.

Hannah stirred, as she opened her eyes. She reached in the direction of the shadow of her mother.

"Hey, Mom, how long have you been here?"

"Sweetie, I've been here the whole time. I haven't gone anywhere." Hannah seemed groggy, probably from the fever.

"What time is it, Mom?"

"It's only eight-thirty."

"In the evening?"

"No, in the morning. We stayed the night."

Hannah moved the covers up around her chin and closed her eyes again. Cheryl returned to her seat and went to work on a crossword puzzle.

An hour later, Kendra appeared, carrying several bags. Placing the bags on the floor, she threw her arms around Cheryl.

Kendra knew Cheryl had always been the stronger sister. But as she pressed up against her sister now, she felt sure she could feel her older sister's heart crumbling in her chest. She saw the sadness in Cheryl's eyes, and she wished there was something she could do to help. Aware that her niece's health was beyond her control, she moved the focus to another topic.

"Look what I have here." Kendra encouraged Cheryl to watch her as she reached into her oversized purse. She pulled out an envelope and waved it in front of her sister's face.

"My mail? Your plan is to cheer me up by bringing me my bills?" Cheryl laughed. Kendra always managed to make her smile.

"No, silly." Kendra was pleased to witness the smile on Cheryl's face. "I mean, yes. I did bring you a letter. But not a bill. I happened to notice one piece of mail that I thought you might be interested in reading." Kendra taunted Cheryl by waving the letter in the air and hiding it behind her back.

Cheryl jumped to her feet and reached for the envelope, following its movement through the air. She was just about to win the childlike game, when she heard a crying sound coming from Hannah. Sidestepping Kendra, Cheryl forgot all about the fun she'd been having.

"Hannah, what is it honey? What's wrong?" She stepped closer to her daughter and listened for a response. From under the covers she could hear Hannah mumbling.

"Mommy, it hurts." Hannah spoke in a weak voice.

"What hurts, honey? Your tummy? Does your tummy hurt?" She untucked the covers from around Hannah's face and leaned closer to hear her daughter's voice.

Cheryl welcomed the daylight Kendra added to the room by opening the blinds. She watched as Hannah drew back from the light, as if it hurt her. Cheryl gasped as the sunlight fell on her child's face. She pressed the call button several times.

Dr. Watters took one look at the white pustules that had formed on Hannah's face and demanded that everyone leave the room immediately.

-26-

The *do not disturb* button on Shane's phone came in handy at times like this. He turned off his mobile and made himself comfortable at his desk. Days had passed since his last communication with Alexei, and he was anxious to read what his Russian friend had to say.

Shane read the letter with an open mind, but he couldn't ignore the news he received. Smallpox vaccines had been administered in Moscow almost two weeks before Celebrate Freedom.

Alexei's penmanship was difficult to read. Executed in broken fragments, his English writing skills were rudimentary. Nonetheless, the three-page letter had an obvious point to make.

Dear Shane,

I have not spoken to you in days. I guess I will start from beginning. I beg you read all the way. Please do not make assumptions cause you to stop reading. I have much to say, and I wish you to hear all that I say. Please, I ask, do not mention this letter to my government. I will be gone before you get this, but they will make me disappear sooner if they know I send this letter.

My life in Russian government has been rewarding in many ways. My father was military man. He worked hard in science development. His work with Soviet government and later Russian Federation developed sense of loyalty in me. This loyalty I cannot fully explain. The Russian

*government is old institution, and our country is strong
entity. I am proud that my family played a part of this
history.*

*My letter is sincere, but with all of this explanation in
mind, I know not if this is right thing to do. But I cannot
decide anymore between right and wrong. I feel one way
and have been asked to act in another. I struggle, my
friend, with the questions and doubts that haunt my mind
...the same questions that haunted my father's mind, his
heart and now his soul.*

*For many years, I worked in divided world in Russia. One
side of our world is free world. This free world is guided by
group of democratic leaders who believe that freedom is the
only way to exist in this world peacefully. However, this
same group of men have seen that freedom comes only with
price, and this price was too high for the Russians to
afford.*

*With the fall of the Soviet Union, the Russian government,
and therefore its people, suffered in many ways. Once
superpower and leading nation of the world, our country
fell to the lowest depths in no time. Poverty stricken towns
developed from what were once fruitful organizations. The
government could not lead its people toward positive
future, when they couldn't see light at end of tunnel. And
all along, our allies, so they were called, had left us without
anything to rebuild. Our allies left us alone and
devastated. Russia could not rebuild, not without help.*

*My father explained to me once that Russia wanted help
from free world. But this help came with strings attached,
and that help later caused devastation within our home
land. Our people, and my father's comrades, were left to
recover anything that could be salvaged. I will tell you this*

... I do not fault his actions now, nor will I ever. Just the same, I do not fault my own actions, nor will I ever. This world is about survival. We all do what we need in order to survive. My country has only tried to stay alive, and even outcome of this effort is questionable now.

Shane wiped the sweat from his brow and placed the first page behind the rest. Why was the office so hot? He picked up where he'd left off.

My father felt worst about effects of their struggle to survive as they affected people in the country. He suffered in his heart whenever things would go wrong that hurt his people. That is why they worked so hard though, to save the people. They only wanted people of Russia to have good lives, like Americans.

My father, Dimitri Gousev, would lie awake at nights and cry. I hear him sometimes, but he never knew. Sometimes he would cry out in his sleep, the only time he felt safe talking about things, I guess.

The worst time was when anthrax was released in several small cities along the West Coast of the sea. It was only test. This was test that went wrong. Something didn't work, and weapons meant to be only tested detonated too early. They spread farther than expected. People died. Many people go to hospital over the weeks after that happened. My mother was nurse. She saw them. Dead bodies piled up in corners of hospital, and dying men and women were in hospital beds right next to dead bodies, waiting to join them. I heard my mother crying to my father about this experience. I heard her beg him to do something. He held her, but he did nothing. He couldn't, he later wrote. He couldn't unless he wanted for all of us to die. He could do nothing. They never knew that I heard them that night.

They never knew that I heard conversation every night following. They might know now that I hear their words often. In fact, I can hear them now, as I write this letter.

Shane flipped to the final page, hoping to gather some obvious idea of where Alexei was headed with his words. Unusually tired, he feared he'd fall asleep before finishing his reading.

My father's letter was left for me to find. He wrote it by hand, just as I write this to you. He told me about everything ... all of the demons that haunted him. He told me why he felt so ashamed to leave me, and he asked for my forgiveness. I now ask for you to try to understand the things I have to say, and I ask you forgive me and all of the innocent people of my country. I need for you to do this, in the spirit of freedom.

After the fall of the Soviet Union, my country was left in poverty. The government wanted help, but received none. The lack of support from the rest of free world left our leaders feeling betrayed, and also paranoid. They felt that if they were not going to be offered help, then they needed to watch out for themselves. Really, can they be blamed? The government feared the massive bombs of destruction that the United States was producing in record time. I am aware that the idea was raised that both the US and Russia were to stop the production of the biological weapons, but it seemed that no one ever made solid this deal. The United States kept producing, or so we were told, so our country needed to work just as hard. It was work of one factory that finally forced my father over edge. He was manager leader in Stepnogorsk biological warfare weapons plant. To most people, this plant appeared as manufacturing plant for pharmaceuticals. So it was, I suppose. But, the manufacturing was more than medicines. My father was in charge of manufacturing and

*planning of defensive weapons of mass destruction ...
biological weapons. His main focus was using the smallpox
virus as weapon.*

*He told me in his letter that he was scared. They all feared
what would happen when day would come that the United
States would attack – when you would come for us and
threaten to take over everything our country had worked so
hard to have. They built the weapons with one thing in
mind, defending our country.*

*When agreements were made to stop production of
weapons, government successfully convinced military
workers, like my father, that to believe that this was over
was to be naive. The government insisted that to let their
guard down was only to invite domestic destruction. So,
they kept building and multiplying what they built. Before
anyone knew it, it was end of the twentieth century, and
tucked away in many manufacturing plants throughout
Russia was enough smallpox to conquer world.*

*In start of the twenty-first century, the government began
to believe that perhaps this threat was diminished. So far,
United States had not threatened security of Russia. Also,
our country had been successful in making enough
weapons to defend its fate, if necessary. However, poverty
continued. Money that had been spent over the years to
continue manufacturing took away from helping to cure
the poverty that had infected our world. Someone had to do
something to fix this problem. They acted fast and never
talked about it again. I only know of their actions because
these actions were what killed my father.*

*The government needed money to survive as independent
nation. Do you see? Prospective buyers stood on the
doorstep, waving many funds. They came in secret, and*

they left the same way. No one knew exactly who they were, and they tried to maintain this ignorance. My government, the leaders of my nation, sold ingredients of biological weapons to outsiders. They made several transactions over number of years. They allowed themselves to sleep at night by telling each other that money was necessary for survival of their nation. They even went as far as to make themselves believe that the people who pur-chased the smallpox virus were not capable of turning raw material into anything too harmful. This allowed them to sleep at night. It allowed my father to sleep, but he chose to never wake up. They slept okay until September 11, 2001. Until then, they never saw any repercussions of their ignorance. They knew then that they were just waiting for time to reveal stupidity of their actions.

I write to you now in an attempt to offer a clear understanding of what has happened to our world. I need to tell you now, but I will never be able to talk with you again. Speaking of such information is subject to extreme penalty in my country. Plus, I can no longer sleep myself. The guilt of knowing haunts me, as it did my father.

Please don't misunderstand my words. My country did not act in an offensive or malicious manner. My country is a free country and wishes for genuine survival of freedom. My country knows not the consequences of what it has done, and it chooses to remember only why it had to do what it did. I do not imply that my country had anything directly to do with this latest attempt at destruction.

I only ask that you use this information to track the paths of those who are responsible for these actions. They made secret purchases from my country, but they worked not with any member of the Russian Federation in the planning of this act. Russia has made mistakes, and Russia wants not

*to allow United States to come in and identify these
mistakes. For this reason, do not attempt to approach my
colleagues with this information. They will deny all that
has been said. I care not what their plans may be for me,
because I will not be here to learn of my destiny. The
protective shot which I have received will not save life of my
beloved wife, and I cannot continue without her.*

*For your benefit, use this information to trace path of
virus an vaccinations. They may lead you to true
criminals, and I am confident that your persistence will
bring about victory of freedom. I have listed origins of
virus, and I have named manufacturing plants below
that housed smallpox in large quantities. Vaccines were
sought after by responsible parties. It will be by following
leads to sales that should lead to perpetrators.*

*Good luck. I have gone as far as I have strength to go. I ask
you for forgiveness.*

In truth,
A. Gousev

In Shane's mind, confusion mixed with amazement like a well-blended cocktail. He read the pages again, this time skimming through most of the paragraphs. His reading slowed, as he covered again the parts about the sale of the smallpox virus and the use of tracking recent vaccine requests. The theory sounded simple, but how could he even begin to track stolen vaccines? He doubted the terrorists had been that obvious.

His frustration grew, and a feeling of resentment overcame his emotions. How could the Russians, supposed allies of the free world, have participated in such an act? How could he take anything that Gousev had to say as truth? How did he know that this wasn't all part of the game? No one could be trusted at this point, especially the Russians. He tossed the letter to the side. He watched as it missed landing on the corner of his desk and fell to the ground. Each of the three pages floated to the floor and took its own position face up, next to his feet.

Bending to collect his faxes, in the far corner of his view he caught the words of one paragraph from Alexei.

... the protective shot which I received will not save the life of my beloved wife ...

Alexei didn't know about the mutation. He didn't know that the traditional smallpox vaccine wouldn't protect him from this new strain of the virus. Did this mean that the terrorists didn't know, either? This could be the confirmation Shane was waiting for.

As he pieced together the events in his mind, his energy sent him soaring. This mutation could be the one thing that could lead the United States to the terrorist cells. In a flurry of motion, he circled portions of the fax as he called for Alan.

Scheduling a public broadcast of the information about SP4 and its interaction with the smallpox vaccine was imperative. He hoped this news would calm the people who were desperately trying to obtain vaccines. At the same time, he was confident that this announcement would cause the terrorists to seek help for themselves.

Moving his right hand from shoulder to shoulder, he performed the sign of the cross. He bowed his head and expressed silent words of thanks. He began to map out his strategy.

Reaching for the aspirin in his desk drawer, he realized the magnitude of the job that waited before him. He knew one thing for sure. If he was going to accomplish this next course of action, he'd have to rid himself of the daunting headache and fever that he'd been experiencing over the past few days.

***

Cheryl and Kendra were escorted from Hannah's room. All the while, Hannah called for her mother. Cheryl fought to stay, but

Dr. Watters insisted that she leave.

Unaware of the moist blood on her hand, Cheryl hadn't even felt the pain as she'd chewed the skin around her thumb. Like an antennae tuning in to a radio wave, she twisted her head to face the sounds of voices approaching from behind her. She slumped back in her chair when she realized it was only a clean-up crew.

With her right arm around Cheryl's shoulders, Kendra leaned in and stroked her sister's golden hair with her left hand.

"Dr. Watters will take great care of Hannah. You know she's the best."

"I know, Kendra. But I can't believe this is happening. I'm sure of what I saw – a rash on Hannah's face. It looked like the pictures we've seen on television – you know, the pictures of smallpox. Do you think she caught it on our trip? I heard there were some people from Orlando who've gotten sick."

"Cheryl, don't jump to conclusions. The rash you saw could've been lesions from Hannah's condition. You've always known this could be a part of her illness." Kendra tried to soothe her sister's nerves. "Please try to relax until Dr. Watters comes out here to talk with us. I'll stay with you ... just stay calm."

By squeezing her sister into a tight hug, Cheryl expressed her appreciation. She kissed Kendra's shirt sleeve and allowed her head to fall limp on her sister's shoulder.

"By the way, don't you want to see what I have in my purse for you?" Kendra hoped to lighten the heavy emotion of the moment. "Don't you want to see?" Again, she waved the letter in the air.

Cheryl snatched the letter from her sister's hand and turned it over to reveal the return address in the top left corner. Priority mail? The Florida street address piqued her curiosity as she tore the envelope open and unfolded the letterhead inside.

She had an idea who the sender might be, but it wasn't until she followed her finger to the bottom of the second page that she realized his identity. Joel had kept his word and stayed in touch. At that moment, Cheryl welcomed the words of a warm, casual letter from a new friend.

"Who's it from?" Kendra bent down to see Cheryl's facial expression. She'd been eager to see her sister's reaction to the letter.

"It's from Joel, as if you didn't know." Cheryl rolled her eyes into a goofy position. "My guess is that he's writing to see how Hannah's doing and to see how our trip home was. If you let me finish, I'll let you read it when I'm done." She gave her sister a playful elbow in the side.

After a few minutes, Cheryl had finished reading the letter. As she expected, Joel had inquired about Hannah in his note. His letter also spoke about events at the Make-A-Wish house. He wrote about his work at the hospital, and he touched briefly on the smallpox outbreak. His hospital had treated a few suspected cases, and there were rumors that his facility could be chosen as one of the smallpox treatment centers.

His words communicated how much he'd enjoyed the company of Cheryl and her family during their visit. He expressed an interest in visiting Washington, D.C. He encouraged her to write soon. She smiled as she folded the letter and returned it to its envelope. She tossed it back to Kendra.

"He's a good catch, Cher." Kendra caught the envelope and pointed it at Cheryl. "Don't miss out on getting to know him. I mean it." She scolded her sister in advance. "And, he seems to adore your daughter ... and your sister for that matter." She spied a glow on Cheryl's cheeks.

Dr. Watters walked into the waiting area. Cheryl felt a rock drop to the bottom of her stomach.

"Dr. Watters, how's Hannah?"

Cheryl fired out the questions one at a time, leaving little opportunity for the doctor to answer. When she paused from her frantic outburst, she watched as Dr. Watters took a seat on a stool, waiting to speak. The doctor drew in a deep breath and began to explain the situation.

Tuesday, September 19th

-27-

Standard practice for the task force now involved early morning committee meetings. Shane prepared for Tuesday morning with anticipation. He was glad to be presenting a solid plan, something he'd been without for too long.

Copies of Alexei's letter were passed out. Not unlike reciting prose, Shane explained his interpretation of the message. The correspondence was an obvious attempt for Alexei to gain closure before he moved on, possibly to commit suicide.

"We need to set up a task force to locate Alexei as soon as possible. His life and his knowledge are too valuable for us to let him disappear. Plus, he's a colleague, and he deserves to be helped." Refreshed by a rejuvenated confidence, Shane announced his plan with enthusiasm.

A yellow highlighter spotlighted the excerpts that had prompted Shane's plan for identifying and uncovering the terrorists. The yellow lines shined in the fluorescent illumination of the room like small rays of sunshine.

"Gousev suspected a biological attack, but he's not aware of the mutated strain of the smallpox virus. If the Russians aren't aware of the mutation, then they wouldn't know about the effects of the smallpox vaccine on SP4 victims. If the guys who sold the virus to the terrorists didn't know about SP4, then it's a safe bet that the terrorists aren't aware of the mutation, either. It's a strong possibility that this mutation was not intentional, but in fact, an accident." Shane believed that this accident could be just the key he needed to open the door to answers.

After his lengthy explanation, he paused to drink a glass of water. His heartbeat accelerated as if it were entered in a race against the functions of the rest of the organs in his body. Waiting for the questions to come pouring across the conference table, he glanced around the room to see who his first taker would be. Shane called for Alan to start.

"I follow your points regarding Gousev's letter." Alan began with a hint of confusion in his voice. "However, I'm not sure I follow how this information can help us to find the terrorists. This mutation is killing our people, and we don't know how to stop it. Our vaccines don't work, and somehow you feel this is the brass ring we need to grab. How is this a lead?"

"Okay, you're with me so far." Shane positioned his hands into a parallel alignment, pointing them in Alan's direct line of vision. He created the semblance of a path to follow. He made intense eye contact with his colleague, as if he were the only other person in the room. Capturing his attention, he encouraged Alan to follow him along the road in front of him. "Now, stay with me, Alan."

Shane spoke in slow, annunciated words. "I believe that this mutation of the virus is a coincidence. I think the intent of the terrorists was to disperse the smallpox virus in an attempt at mass destruction. This plan was altered by the formation of SP4." Once he was sure they were following his logic, he looked around the room, making eye contact.

Before continuing, Shane paused again to sip his water. His stomach had joined the race with his heart, and he feared the results of this ongoing event would lead to his being ill. He waited another moment to make sure the water would stay down.

"My belief is this: the terrorists think they're safe because they inoculated themselves with smallpox vaccine. This is the same vaccine that I believe the Russians had sold them. The Russians had also administered vaccines to their government leaders prior to Celebrate Freedom. From Alexei's letter, I believe it's clear that they are all under the impression that the vaccine will protect them."

The faces in the room brightened with each additional word that Shane added to his statement. Heads nodded in agreement and in comprehension of his theory.

"We've learned that this SP4 virus spreads faster than the traditional smallpox virus. Also, the CDC has noticed a shorter incubation period with SP4. They've used the incubation periods from the early victims at the Lonitesci plant as the litmus test for this theory. It seems that the virus may have been slightly altered when it was mixed with the potassium perchlorate, resulting in the Lonitesci plant victims. However, the chemical reaction involved in the detonation of the fireworks resulted in a more defined mutation – SP4. The medical researchers have shown that the incubation period for SP4 can be as short as four days, compared to the traditional seven to seventeen days. We expect to see the shorter incubation period for those victims who contracted the disease during a celebration show. We can be fairly certain that the terrorists who actually tampered with the chemicals have already died, but their partners in other countries who thought they were safe will witness an unexpected turn of events. In fact, the probability is that the vaccinated terrorists will become ill faster, and they'll experience more extreme symptoms."

Silence marked the unanticipated surprise that filled the room. The nodding came to a screeching halt as those present were hit by a terrifying realization. As military officers, they'd also been vaccinated against smallpox.

Shane didn't feel the need to state the obvious. Instead, he elected to focus on the positive.

"So, you see, this is where our plan comes in to effect." Shane spoke again, before his colleagues had the chance to shift the emphasis. "The terrorists are vain. Their existence is vital to the survival of their cause. With the extermination of the majority of their cells in the past several years, they are all that is left of their group. They can't afford to die. I know they'll attempt to seek help. They'll get sloppy, and we'll be ready for them when they do. We just need to be prepared to intercept their SOS. When they come out, we'll be there waiting."

Concealing his pain, Shane fought to ignore the cramping in his stomach. Witnessing the reactions of his colleagues, he was pleased with the support and energy he felt growing within the walls of the conference room. Ideas and suggestions filled the conversation as he excused himself and retreated to the restroom, leaving Alan in charge of the brainstorming session.

* * *

Cheryl tugged at her twisted hospital gown. She rolled her head to the right and watched Kendra sleeping in the next bed. Sleep would've been nice. But was it worth it to wake up?

The activities of the night before lingered in her mind as if they were a recurring bad dream. Cheryl had tried to listen to the delicate words that Dr. Watters used to explain the situation. The doctor had commented that Hannah was a fighter, despite her weakened immune system. She'd encouraged Cheryl to remember that her daughter was only ten years old, and that children were strong.

Like racecars flying by a checkpoint, the night's activities had blurred together in Cheryl's mind. Time was difficult to measure when she had yet to absorb the reality of what was happening. What day was it, anyway?

Cheryl couldn't remember how long the doctor had spoken. She'd stopped hearing anything after the word *smallpox*. As if AIDS wasn't enough for her daughter to suffer, Hannah had been inflicted with another deadly virus, and the prognosis was grim.

Dr. Watters hadn't come right out and said that she couldn't treat Hannah, but Cheryl refused to be naive. She knew from her contacts at work that this current outbreak was driven by a new form of the smallpox virus which they didn't know much about. Nothing that Dr. Watters, or anyone, could do would help her daughter now.

She didn't care about her own health. The doctors and nurses had done their best to make her and Kendra comfortable. By CDC protocol, Cheryl and her sister had to be tested and observed for a period of time, since they'd been in contact with the victim. *The victim.* The words made Cheryl shudder. Hannah had been referred to as the victim more than once in her life.

Since last speaking with Dr. Watters, Cheryl had slept little. She'd fought to stay in Hannah's room, but the doctor had refused her request. Through the night, she contemplated sneaking down the hall, but she decided against the idea.

The doctors had made a decision not to tell Hannah about the smallpox infection. She already knew she was sick. Why shatter her positive attitude? Dr. Watters had explained to her that her mother was waiting in another room until her immune system was stronger. She lied to the ten-year-old by telling her that her mother and aunt had come down with a stomach flu, and they didn't want to risk passing the germs along to her.

Telling this lie pained the doctor. Hannah had accepted the news and asked if she could write notes back and forth with her mom. This little girl didn't allow much to hold her back.

In her right hand, Cheryl held a note from her daughter. The message was written in a light-hearted tone. She asked if her mother was comfortable and if she had thrown up in the hospital bathroom. Cheryl knew Hannah was poking fun at her typical response to having a stomach flu. It was no secret that throwing up was a fate worse than death for Cheryl, especially in a public restroom. She smiled at Hannah's teasing words.

Cheryl drafted six different letters before she settled on her exact words. Who would ever imagine that writing a simple note to her daughter could be so difficult? With every sentence she worried about passing along a hint of her sadness. In the end, she chose a note of few words, all enclosed in a large heart. She clutched the note in her hand, waiting for the nurse to stop by for morning rounds.

So far, neither she nor Kendra had heard the results of their lab tests. She felt fine. This waiting period was unnecessary.

Cheryl knew her sister had been unhappy to be forced into the series of tests, but Kendra had agreed to stay in the hospital room without putting up a fight. Cheryl was certain she would've stayed the previous night anyway, just to support her.

Kendra had been sleeping for a while, though. Most often an early riser, this was uncharacteristic of her. Cheryl looked for a clock. The sunlight outside offered evidence that it was at least six-thirty. Her thoughts were confirmed as the morning nurse poked her head in the door.

"Good morning, ladies." The nurse softened her voice as she noticed Kendra's motionless form in the bed. "I guess someone's still sleeping. Did you get any rest last night, Ms. Williams?" While waiting for a response, she moved to Cheryl and felt her forehead.

"Yes, I did. Well, for an hour or so," Cheryl lied.

"You should try to get some more sleep. You won't do your daughter any good if you get sick, too." The nurse delivered her warning in a motherly tone.

"I know. I'll try." Cheryl had every intention of keeping her word. "Can you please take this to Hannah? I've been waiting all night to get it to her."

"No problem." The nurse pocketed the folded note. "Are you hungry?"

"Actually, I am, a bit." Cheryl leaned forward, trying to iden-tify the familiar smell. "Anything good?" She made her best attempt at sounding upbeat.

"Of course, only the best for our guests." The nurse stepped into the posture of a French maid as she carried the tray to Cheryl's bedside. "We have fruit, eggs, toast, and juice, Madame. Interested? You need to eat."

"Oh, toss me a tray. To tell you the truth, I'm pretty hungry. It's a rare day that I lose my appetite." Cheryl wiggled to a seated position, and the nurse rolled the portable table in front of her.

"Well, I'm jealous. I don't know where you put it. Give a call when your sister wakes up, and I'll bring her breakfast." Her wave functioned as a good-bye as she moved toward the door.

"Please don't forget the letter." Cheryl called after her.

The nurse nodded and tapped her pocket.

Minutes later, Kendra opened her eyes. She squinted toward the parted curtains.

"Do you want me to close the blinds, Kendra?" Cheryl noticed her sister's sensitivity to the light. "I'd opened them so I could see what I was eating." In a playful expression, she squished up her nose.

"No, that's okay." Kendra turned away from the window.

"Hey, press your call button." Cheryl pointed to the side of her sister's bed. "The nurse said she'd bring you a breakfast tray as soon as you woke up."

Kendra wrinkled her nose and shook her head. "No, thanks, I'm not hungry."

"What? Are you kidding? You're always hungry." Cheryl was joking, but she felt a hint of concern. Something was wrong.

"I'm fine, Cher." Kendra answered with little energy. "I think maybe I just had a rough night's sleep. I still feel tired." Fluffing her pillows under her head, Kendra situated herself on her side, facing her sister. "I think I might try to get some more sleep."

Cheryl watched Kendra as she closed her eyes again, falling back to sleep within seconds. She prayed that her sister was just exhausted. Pushing her tray table away, she reached for the letter from Joel.

On flowered stationary from the hospital gift shop, she started the reply three times before she was satisfied with the words she'd chosen for the greeting. At that rate it would take weeks to write the letter. In addition to her desire to stay in contact with her new friend, she also felt a certain freedom and relief in discussing Hannah's situation with Joel, even if it was limited to written correspondence.

Communicating with Joel felt natural to Cheryl. His medical background gave him the intellectual foundation to discuss Hannah's health. Also, he'd met Hannah, and he'd taken a genuine interest in her well-being. Most of all, Cheryl had spent ten years trying to make her daughter's life as normal as possible, at the risk of living an abnormal life herself. She felt something special in her new friendship with Joel.

During a break from writing, she scribbled a note to call Abigail. The past twenty-four hours had been a blur, and she was certain Hannah's nanny was worried.

Cheryl noticed her sister's labored breathing. Long and raspy breaths made it sound as if Kendra's lungs were working overtime to move the air in and out.

"Are you okay?" Excessive sleeping was unlike Kendra, and Cheryl was starting to worry.

"I don't know." Kendra answered her sister with honesty. "Do you think it's hot in here?"

Cheryl felt anxiety building within her stomach. "Kendra, let's call the nurse to check your temperature. Maybe you're coming down with a fever."

"I don't think so," Kendra argued. "I just think it's warm in here." She pushed the covers to the bottom of her bed and moved one foot from under the sheets. "Aren't you even a little hot?"

"Kendra, I think it's cool in here," Cheryl answered.

Kendra took a deep breath and pulled the blankets back up to her shoulders. She was afraid to tell her sister that now, she too was cold. In an instant, the beads of warm sweat that had formed along her hairline caused her to shiver, and she reached for her call button.

"Okay, I'll have the nurse check my temperature, but I'm sure I'm fine."

-28-

Hours of web research had led the Anti-Terrorism Task Force to another brick wall. Their studying of seized web tracking reports pointed in the direction of a number of possible web site destinations that could've been potential homes for terrorist activity and messaging. Hackers of all varieties worked with diligence toward the goal of identifying the one site that might be the vehicle for worldwide terrorists to communicate.

Multiple disappointments encouraged some task force members to consider moving their efforts to other projects, but Shane wouldn't support such actions. One theory remained amidst all of the frustration within the walls of the research room. These terrorists needed to communicate in order to stay alive, and the one vehicle for communication that could be heard around the world was the Internet.

A group of web specialists and well-known hackers were assembled in secret. Once they passed final clearance checks, workspaces were converted into quasi-computer centers complete with high-speed Internet access. The UFW had caught the terrorists before by following the paths of their carefree emails. The cells had to be using a more unconventional way to communicate now. What was it?

Random website activity was monitored through visitation, length of visits, and origin of visits. Reports and statistics spewed from printers in each and every room, and the newly added task force members contacted their supervisors whenever they noticed something of interest. The Anti-Terrorism Task Force went to work investigating every lead that was brought to them.

The hackers had a short window of time to prove effective. The terrorist cells were expected to make contact with each other as soon as their members began to exhibit symptoms of SP4. The idea was that the government could intercept these attempts to make contact, and a swift plan of action could put an end to this merciless group once and for all.

The men and women who'd been recruited for this computer research knew little about the ultimate goals of their work, but they all felt the same passion in knowing that their efforts could help.

The anxiety grew in the deepest pit of his stomach as Shane paced the floor of the task force headquarters. With each step he walked, he could feel the time ticking away. Each second that didn't produce a solid Internet lead frustrated him even more. With the resources of every web report and every website tracking method, he thought for sure something would've broken by now.

Working with diligence, the staff increased in number by the minute. New computer specialists were hired on as clearance investigations were completed. Computers were operated around the clock as the task force filtered through hundreds of leads. However, the compiled pertinent information yielded little more than a string of concealed pornographic web sites and popular on-line catalogs.

Something had to give. At some point, these cells had to be called together in an attempt at an emergency meeting. They would need to activate their cells in order to get help for their own sick and dying. The death of any of their members would represent the failure of their cause. Their arrogance would not let this happen. Shane was sure of it.

He tried to remain patient, although he was well aware that time was one luxury he didn't have. On all fronts, time had proven to be the most valuable amenity necessary to preserve life. He excused himself from the task force headquarters and started back to his office to check into the latest CDC reports, hoping that the events of the past twenty-four hours had acted on their side.

Reports lay waiting on his desk. Someone had been in to organize the papers for him, or so it seemed. Could this be Cheryl's handiwork? Recalling that she was still on leave with her daughter, he made a mental note to call her. His heart broke for her and for her little girl.

Twirling around in his chair to face the wall, he read the top report on the stack of papers. The CDC logo in the page header extended a ray of hope to Shane that maybe this document contained some good news. The unfortunate reality hit with power as he read through the four short paragraphs.

"Tell me something I don't know." He spoke aloud to the empty room. This is what the CDC had to say? SP4 had shown signs of adverse reaction to the smallpox vaccine. Everyone already knew that. He read more from the report.

The vaccine has been shown to strengthen the effects of the virus.

Frustration overwhelmed him. Was this as far as they'd gotten? This information had been reported days ago.

"Well, well," a pleasant voice rang out from the doorway. "I see you're about as excited with that report as I am."

Even before he had swung his body around all the way, Shane turned to face the door. His expression spoke for him.

"Happy to see me?" Cheryl spoke in a weary voice. Weeks past her regular trim, her blonde bangs hung over her eyes. "I'm sorry to have been gone for so long. I still can't be back full time just yet, but I thought a few hours a day would be helpful. It sure will help with the bills. Plus, I can use the distraction." She waited for her boss to respond, but his delay prompted her to continue. "I hope you aren't angry that I stole a peek at that top page. I was just trying to get your things organized. I didn't mean to intrude."

Shane stopped her from apologizing. "It's fine, Cheryl."

"I know, but people talk ... at the hospital, I mean." She waited for a second, desiring to regain her composure. "Hannah's sick again. I'm sure you already know. But it's not just the AIDS. She has smallpox. She has SP4." Tears streamed from her eyes.

With a gentle hand on her arm, Shane guided his secretary and friend to an overstuffed armchair. As she took a seat, he did his best to console her.

"Our top scientists are working every day, hour and minute to figure this thing out. We beat smallpox years ago, and we'll beat SP4. You have to believe this, Cheryl."

"I know," Cheryl said between sniffles. Crying choked off her voice.

Shane struggled to find words, any words, to say. In a gesture of support, he reached out and touched Cheryl on the shoulder.

Standing, she pulled herself together.

"Thank you, sir. I'm so sorry for all of this. I know I'm the least of your worries right now, and rightfully so." She wiped her eyes with the back of her hands and took a deep breath. "I was just released from the hospital myself. Hannah and my sister are still there. I came by to square away a work schedule. I can only work a little each day. But I'd still like to put in some time, if that's okay with you." She hoped for Shane's support.

"That sounds fine." Shane's voice cracked. "Hannah and your sister are still at the hospital? Is your sister sick, too?"

Gathering the strength to respond, Cheryl fought her tears so she could speak.

"Well, I'm not sure. See, after Hannah was diagnosed with SP4, the doctors made me and Kendra stay overnight for observation. I'm fine, at least so far. But Kendra developed a high fever, and now they want to keep her. They won't let her go until her fever goes down." Cheryl looked into Shane's eyes and let out a weak laugh of irony. "I'm praying with all my heart that Kendra picked up a bad flu bug in Florida. As awful as that sounds, it would be better than the alternative. But, I guess only time will tell, right?"

"But, you're okay, right?"

"Weirdest thing—" Cheryl shrugged her shoulders. "So far I haven't shown one sign of getting sick, and I've been around Hannah more than anyone else. The doctors want me to come back this afternoon for more tests, but they said they couldn't rationalize keeping me if I didn't even have a fever. I'm still not allowed to see Hannah, though. They said it's too risky. They don't know what too risky is. Keeping me from my daughter against my will is too risky for their own well being." She managed a small laugh. With a wink, she went on her way.

Shane sat in the same armchair where Cheryl had been sitting only moments earlier. Why hadn't she presented with any signs of illness following the Orlando Celebrate Freedom? According to the latest reports, this region had posted the highest number of SP4 victims to date, with New York and Washington, D.C. following. He prayed that she wouldn't be next. Someone needed to keep up the strength for that little girl.

Propelling himself forward, he used his hands to push against his thighs and stood. He moved with slow steps to his desk. Fishing around in a bottom drawer, he took part in his new ritual of taking aspirin. After swallowing three caplets with one gulp of water, he tossed the bottle back into its place. As soon as this whole mess was straightened out, he'd visit the White House physician for an exam.

-29-

With her hands clasped around the tote bag on her lap, Cheryl listened to the familiar clanging of the Metro Rail. She was on her way back to the hospital to bring some things for Hannah. Even though they'd eventually have to be destroyed, they would make her happy now. The bag bulged with a stuffed dog and several comic books.

Churning through the tote, she spotted the mail she'd tossed in at the last minute. A letter from her mother caught her eye. This was probably better left unopened until she was situated at the hospital.

Seeing that letter reminded her that she'd never mailed the note she'd written to Joel. She rolled the envelopes into a cylinder and tapped herself on the head as if to assign punishment for her forgetfulness. All of the time and effort she'd put into writing the letter was pointless now, as it sat on the side table in Kendra's hospital room, a place Cheryl wasn't permitted to enter. She could always call him.

Between her own tests and waiting for news about her family, she expected to have plenty of downtime at the hospital. That might be a good time to call. She fumbled through her bag to see if she'd remembered her cell phone. The glowing of the display panel brought about a sigh of relief. She cut the power to conserve her battery.

The doctors had planned to run a series of blood and viral tests on Cheryl, in addition to a physical exam. Already having been tested once, she questioned why she had to come back, but they were adamant. Why had they seemed so surprised that she hadn't shown any symptoms of the virus herself? Had all the known patient contacts become sick? Was she an exception?

As she waited in her room for the nurses to guide her through the tests, she separated Hannah's things from her bag. She would ask the nurse to take them to her daughter. After scanning the letter from her mother, she decided she couldn't concentrate on reading. Seeing no reason to concern her family with unsubstantiated information, she was hesitant to write back. The better choice would be to wait until she had more definite news to share. Rubbing the smooth face of the cell phone with her thumb, she contemplated making a phone call to her mother, but decided against the thought. Perhaps a call to Joel would be a good way to pass some time.

From the bottom of her tote she retrieved a small address book. She'd printed Joel's information with the tiny pencil she kept tucked inside. Names and addresses represented temporary labels, but loved ones lasted forever. This was the theory that Cheryl lived by. She refused to use ink in her address book. This was a sign of bad luck to her ... bad karma. As she flipped through the pages, she noticed the occasional scribbled out penned names and numbers and remembered why she'd adopted this belief. Before her phone was powered up and ready for dialing, the door opened. Cheryl turned off the mobile and allowed it to slide back into her canvas tote.

"How are you feeling today?" Dr. Watters had requested Cheryl as her patient, since she had such an established history with the family. She knew Cheryl would be most comfortable with her administering these tests.

"Fine. Same as I did yesterday."

"Any signs of fever or nausea?" Dr. Watters pressed her cool hand against Cheryl's forehead and cheeks.

"Nope, none." Cheryl replied with conviction.

Making small scribbles on the chart that rested on her knees, Dr. Watters kept her focus on Cheryl. When she knew she couldn't stall any longer, she folded her hands on her lap, on top of the charts.

She made direct eye contact with her patient.

"I'm not going to lie to you." The doctor looked down as if she was following a script on her clipboard. "Kendra has moved into another phase of illness over the past several hours. Her fever has gotten worse, and she's developed nausea. She's also experiencing severe stomach cramping. We've not yet received word back from the CDC regarding the virus sample that we sent down, but I'm afraid there's a good chance her results will be the same as Hannah's." Dr. Watters waited for a reaction from Cheryl.

Numb and without expression, Cheryl sat paralyzed. She reached for a blanket and wrapped it around her shoulders. Fighting the urge to cry, she attempted to continue her discussion with the doctor.

"So, you think Kendra has smallpox, too? Does she have the rash?" She remained in complete control.

"Not yet, but the progress of the virus is moving right in line with that of the smallpox cases that we've been monitoring to date. If she is diagnosed with SP4, I would guess that we'd begin to see signs of the rash within twenty-four hours." Dr. Watters paused again to see if Cheryl had any questions. After continued silence, she went on. "But I do have some positive news. It has to do with Hannah."

Cheryl's moist eyes lit up at the mention of the word positive in connection with her daughter's health. "Hannah? Is she doing better?" The inflection of her voice climbed.

"Well, her condition hasn't improved, but it hasn't gotten any worse over the last twenty-four hours, either." Dr. Watters dropped Cheryl's chart on the bed and used her hands to complement her words as she spoke. "You see, she still has a fever, and she's experiencing stomach cramps and nausea. She has some remaining pustules from her facial rash, but—this is the intriguing part —this rash should've escalated into a full-body rash by now. However, this hasn't happened. The rash hasn't moved passed the first stage in appearance. This is unexpected, especially for SP4. With this strain, the stages of the virus have been moving faster. Also, her temperature has stopped climbing, allowing her body to stabilize."

"Are you sure she has smallpox?" Cheryl grasped at the minis-cule chance that the initial diagnosis had been incorrect. "Maybe this whole thing was a part of her current condition." Cheryl hated to say AIDS. "Maybe her body is fighting to keep it under control."

"Well, that's not it. If we hadn't already received a positive test confirming the virus, I would've been inclined to believe your theory as a possibility. However, she has a positive diagnosis for smallpox. She has the virus." Dr. Watters was sure of her diagno-sis. "But she's reacting to this in a different manner than any other patient we've heard about so far. I want you to keep praying, Cheryl. If anyone deserves a miracle, it's your daughter."

Cheryl spoke up as the doctor was almost to the door.

"Dr. Watters, is Kendra going to be all right?"

"We're doing everything we can. I promise."

Cheryl took a deep breath and looked down at the floor. Dr. Watters had obviously sidestepped the issue of Kendra's condi-tion. Closing her eyes, she began to pray.

Moments later, she reached into her bag and retrieved her cell phone. She dialed Joel's number. After two long rings, Cheryl considered hanging up, when she heard a sound on the other end. She could see Joel's blue eyes and bright smile as if he were stand-ing right in front of her.

"Hi, Joel." Cheryl wondered if he'd recognize her voice. "This is Cheryl Williams. How are you doing? Are you busy?"

"No, never too busy for you. I'm on a break between classes and work. Did you get my letter?"

"Yeah, and everything is happening so fast here that I thought it would be easiest to call you in return. I hope that's okay."

"Of course it's okay. I'm happy to hear from you. So tell me about this everything that's happening so fast. You didn't go off and get married or anything crazy, did you?" Joel hoped to bring a smile to his friend's face.

Cheryl's cheeks filled with color, and she let out a faint gig-gle in response to his joke. She tried to divert her attention from her daughter and focus on the conversation. "No, nothing that crazy. Well, I guess I could start from when we left Orlando. Do you have a few hours?"

"For you, I have all day." Joel leaned back in his desk chair and kicked his feet up on the stack of textbooks and medical journal reports that were spread out in front of him. A pen dropped from his hand as he swung around in his chair, leaving his back to face his desktop. His jovial expression changed as Cheryl began to speak.

* * *

Shane waited in the restroom until he felt safe to come out. His lunch hadn't agreed with him, and he felt somewhat embarrassed at the abrupt manner in which he'd exited the task force meeting. The vomiting was accompanied by painful stomach convulsions, and he perspired profusely in response to the inelegant activity.

Leaning over the sink in an effort to hold himself in a standing position, Shane used his free hand to wipe his face with a damp towel. Quivering exhales of air followed intentional, deep inhaled breaths. Finding it difficult to open his eyes after blinking, Shane got the impression he might need to call it a day. This thought, as attractive as it was, was simply unacceptable. An ordinary case of the stomach flu wasn't enough to take him away from his work.

Upon his returning to the meeting, Shane could feel the group staring at him. He looked down to check the front of his shirt.

"Thanks for waiting, everyone." Shane fumbled with the papers in his hands. "I know you've all been working very hard, following leads from all ends of the spectrum. This work might seem tedious at times, but may I remind you that work very similar in tactic was what led us to identify, track, and seize a large group of terrorists only months ago. I know we can do this again. Let's place ourselves in *their* mindset. We need to feel their desperation and determine what their next moves might be. I have some information I think you'll find interesting." Shane passed the copies of the latest tip sheet to his colleagues. Once everyone had the page in front of him, he spoke again.

"In the past, we were successful in catching the terrorists by following their Internet activity. I believe it's safe to say they won't attempt to locate each other by email again. We don't expect they'll have a public web site available for viewing, nor will they use personal email addresses to access their messages." Shane paused in order to catch the reactions from around the table. "This doesn't mean we have to give up. In fact, this is a positive. We can focus our efforts in another direction."

"Mr. President?" Several voices began at once.

"Does this mean we're going to abort the Internet investigation in order to pursue other avenues?" One committee member asked the question for everyone in the room.

"No, not at all." Shane wasn't surprised by that assumption. "We're going to continue the Internet investigation. However, now we're taking a different approach. A young man who's been working on this project has pointed out that the terrorists could be using an existing web presence as their vehicle for communication. For instance, they could be traveling through an existing web site to a page that's posted for their own text messaging. This man is a web site administrator for a graphics design company in Virginia. He's been studying the methods of tracking reports for a while. When our people contacted him, he was more than happy to give us a hand. Mark's been working with our Norfolk team for the past eight hours."

Shane moved around the table to refill his water glass. While attempting to hide his shaking hands, he downed the water and went for some more.

"The focus of our investigation is now in studying back door entrances into other web sites. Through the web tracking reports, we've found that some web visits are so quick in nature that they're given the term *click through* to describe a hit to a web site that came from somewhere else. In other words, if I'm correct in the terminology, the visitors are not making these particular sites their destinations. Instead, they're clicking through another link from somewhere else and ending up on a particular page, only to click through to yet another page. Imagine a portal that takes a person from one place to another without anyone noticing. This is what we're talking about. The distinct possibility exists that these terrorists are now being instructed to visit random sites which have been set up to allow for links to other sites, which will lead them to their final destinations – their contact pages."

Sipping more cold water kept Shane from losing it all together. He allowed several droplets to rest on his lips before he licked them away and took another gulp.

"So, our men and women are now busy looking for web sites that have recorded abnormally high numbers of click through visits over the past few days. When these sites are identified, then we'll investigate them to see if we can find any links that wouldn't have been obvious methods of Internet flow or transportation. Next, we need to find out where these take us. Our hackers will investigate anything that seems questionable." Giving himself time to catch his breath, he paused for questions. "If there are no questions, then let's get back to work. I've appointed Mark as a team leader on this project, and he's working in close contact with our Norfolk operatives. Any questions from your men and women in the field should be directed straight to him through our Norfolk team. Keep me posted."

Shane left the room with one thought in mind—he needed sleep. Locking the door behind him, he kicked back in his office. Wishing to relax for a mere thirty minutes, he stretched out on the couch. The nervous energy in his body forced his heart into an irregular beat, keeping him from accomplishing any quality rest.

Like the rebound of a pinball, he moved from the couch to his desk. Nothing new jumped out at him from the reports he read. Still, he repeated the words aloud, hoping to see something that he'd missed before.

* * *

Silence lingered in the phone line like stagnant water in a rain gutter. Joel's shock met the words that escaped from Cheryl's mouth.

She recited the sentences with clarity, as if they were the lines of a Broadway play. By enunciating every word with clear purpose, she described in detail what had been going on.

Although Joel wasn't surprised by the news, his heart sank with each statement that Cheryl made. Not wanting to interrupt, he waited for her to pause.

"Cheryl darlin', I'm so sorry. I had no idea you were going through this, but somehow it'll be okay. You believe that, right?"

"I do, Joel, but sometimes it sure is hard." Her voice cracked. She wiped the tears from her eyes with her right hand and gripped the phone with her left. "I want to be strong for Kendra and for Hannah, but I don't know what to say or do. The doctors are doing all they can, but SP4 is throwing them for a loop. I have confidence that they'll figure this whole thing out one day, but it may just be too late to save the people that I love." Cheryl's crying turned into sobbing.

Joel wished he were there to comfort her. He wanted only to hold her head to his shoulder and to make her feel that everything would be all right.

"Cheryl, let me ask you something. How do you feel about me coming to visit for a few days? You've been released from the hospital, right?"

"You want to come here? Yes, I've been released." Cheryl was caught off guard by his request. Who wanted to visit D.C. right then?

"Yeah, I'd like to come there. Why are you surprised? I don't mean to intrude..."

"Oh, no, you wouldn't be intruding at all. I'm just shocked that you'd want to come to a city where a new form of a deadly disease is running rampant. That's all."

"Well, to tell you the truth, D.C. isn't the only city where this disease is spreading, my dear. In fact, Orlando has had so many cases that my medical school has temporarily suspended classes. They've turned the hospital into a containment center. It's all pretty wild. I've been doing research on smallpox and other similar viruses, because I wanted to help at the hospital, but they've trimmed the staff down to the doctors and nurses who've been assigned to the treatment team. I guess they want to limit the number of people who are exposed, especially since they've classified the virus as a mutation. So, about this visit—" Joel changed the subject and waited for an answer.

"Why not? I guess I could use some company." Cheryl knew Joel was glad to hear her change of tone. "I have to warn you, though, my mood swings have given a new definition to the word emotional. Be prepared."

"I'm looking forward to it," Joel confirmed.

Cheryl looked up and noticed the doorknob turning. "I'll get in touch with you after they finish these tests. Hopefully they won't try to keep me here, too. That would put a damper on your trip."

Joel laughed. "Don't worry, I won't let them hold you captive. Keep your chin up. If you haven't gotten sick by now, my guess is that you'll be fine. Talk to you soon."

Dr. Watters entered through the open door, followed by two nurses and a second doctor.

"Hi, Cheryl, we're here to conduct the tests we talked about. This shouldn't take long."

"Okay, let's get started." Rolling up her sleeve to expose her veins, Cheryl tried to think of something other than the needles as the nurse approached. Funny how this used to be the scariest part of going to the doctor. Who cared about the needles now? These days, waiting for the results was more terrifying.

"Before I forget to ask, can someone take this stuff to Hannah?" Cheryl lifted the pile of comic books that were positioned next to the stuffed dog.

Dr. Watters motioned to one of the nurses.

"How's Hannah doing? Is there any way I can see her?" Cheryl knew her request was a long shot, but still worth asking.

"Actually, Cheryl, she's doing quite well, considering the circumstances. I can't explain what's happening, but her condition is stabilizing. If she were my daughter, I'd be encouraged."

"And Kendra, how is she?" Cheryl was half afraid to hear the answer.

"Well, Kendra's advancing in line with the expected progression of the virus. We're all working every day to find a way to treat this, Cheryl. Don't give up on us. She's a lot better off than the patients who were diagnosed with this virus a week ago. That's how quickly we're learning about SP4. In the meantime, you just keep your faith. Your prayers have been working so far."

***

Shane's spinning head created a skewed picture of his reflection in the mirror. This couldn't be happening. No way was he getting sick. He had so much to do and so little time to do it. With the cool rag that hung from his right hand, he wiped his head. To stabilize his balance, his kept left hand glued to the sink.

What time was it, anyway? Only hours earlier, he'd held his latest meeting with the task force, and now he found it difficult to determine the time of day. However, he could easily identify the deterioration of his health. Without even taking his temperature he could tell that his fever was worse. His muscles ached, and his nausea and stomach cramping had become more severe.

Shane knew these were symptoms of SP4. He hadn't been denying the fact that he was susceptible to the virus. His knowledge of the effects of SP4 on vaccinated individuals made him aware of the probable severity of his condition. However, he also knew that he had work to do.

He'd begun his job as President of the United States with one clear objective shining through the dense forest of other priorities. He vowed to bring an end to the terror in the world. The senseless killings and ruthless violence had to stop, and he swore he'd do whatever it took to make this happen. He knew if he gave up now, he'd fail his mission.

However, Shane's drive to succeed didn't shadow his judgment. He was also aware that if he were infected, he'd be a danger to those around him. The recent letter he'd received from the CDC gave him all of the information he needed. His belief had been confirmed. The disease was most often contagious once it reached the outbreak of the rash. To date, Shane couldn't find any sign of the rash on his body. Staring at his face in the mirror, he half expected to see the red splotches appear right in front of him.

The phone rang in the other room. Had it rung at all over the past hour, or did these latest three distinct rings represent the only call to his office in that time period? He felt disconnected from the hour of the day and from the room that held him inside. Tossing the washcloth in the sink, he hung a towel loosely around his neck. The ringing stopped as he approached his desk, so he peeked at the Caller ID system. The unidentified number surprised him. Most incoming calls to his office were traceable.

The silence of the halls implied that the hour was late. He was surprised that no one had come to retrieve him when he hadn't appeared for the end of the day meeting.

The ringing began again. This time a familiar number flashed on the screen, and Shane answered.

"Hello, sweetheart." His wife was understanding of his work, but she was bound to be frustrated at how little she'd seen of him over the past week. "I'm sorry. I guess the time got away from me. You know how it's been lately. I expect to be working through the night. I think we're getting close. I might creep in later, but don't wait up. If it's too late, I'll just stay here. I love you."

Twenty years of a trusting marriage made it painful for Shane to keep his worries from his wife. Should he be diagnosed with SP4, he knew his chances of kicking the disease were questionable. He didn't want to place his family in the same danger. Even if he wasn't considered to be contagious yet, he didn't want to take any chances. Once he'd finished what he set out to do, he would go the hospital for treatment. Those terrorists wouldn't win this one, not on his watch.

The time on the clock read twelve-thirty. He'd be back to work in less than six hours. After making sure he had a fresh change of clothes in his office closet, he made himself comfortable on the couch.

Wednesday, September 20th

-30-

Scurrying about the house, Cheryl cleaned and prepared for Joel's arrival. The early morning hours offered the only opportunity for her to take care of the house. An Internet airfare purchase had made Joel's last minute trip possible. The timing worked well for both of them. Joel's plane wasn't due in until noon, but she still hurried through her list of chores. She'd been given the word that she could visit with Hannah that morning, as long as her condition hadn't gotten worse. Dr. Watters seemed confident that this wouldn't be the case.

Changing her clothes four times before deciding on an outfit, Cheryl spun around in front of the mirror to confirm her selection. The khaki pants and sleeveless sweater complimented her long, thin body. Most everything looked good on her, but she wanted today's outfit to be perfect. She blushed for being so fussy. This was no big deal. In a fluid motion, she slipped on her clogs, grabbed Hannah's bag and moved toward the door. Before stepping out, she dropped the bag and retreated to the phone. She was connected to Abbie's voicemail.

"Hi Abbie, it's Cheryl. I'm heading out to the hospital. I should be there by eight-thirty. With the doctor's approval, I'll be allowed to go in. I'll call you as soon as I know for sure. I know she'll be thrilled to see you."

While walking to the Metro station, Cheryl pondered the proper way to greet Joel when she saw him. A hug? A handshake?

Had she agreed to a one-on-one visit too soon? After all, she hadn't known him for very long. Her time spent with him had been limited to her visit in Orlando, one phone conversation and a letter. She laughed out loud for a few seconds, realizing that, in spite of her worries, she liked the spontaneous side of herself, a side she hadn't allowed to surface in a long time.

Any spontaneity she once possessed had been left behind with the combination of her failed marriage and the deterioration of Hannah's health. This was ironic, though, because one would think that a person involved in a life with an uncertain future would live for the moment.

Hannah was a great blessing, but her diagnosis of AIDS had also introduced an element of uncertainty into Cheryl's world. Each day had to be taken as it came, because the unknown that lurked in the future made planning difficult, yet Cheryl had chosen a path of arranged exactness in her life, as if her rituals and routines could decide the fate of the days to come. A paradox existed within the walls of the sheltered world that she'd created. Even with all of her calculated efforts and careful planning, she couldn't predict the future. However, she had faith that the unexpected did not always bring negativity and sorrow.

Nothing could mask the smile on Cheryl's face. The opportunity to visit her daughter and the arrival of Joel were two solid reasons for her happiness. She only wished that some positive news would come to her regarding Kendra's condition.

At times, Cheryl almost felt guilty for not having gotten sick too. Why was she the one to have escaped this illness? What was different about her? She prayed a few silent words for her sister and opened her eyes to find Dr. Watters walking in her direction. The illuminated expression on the doctor's face gave Cheryl a reason to feel positive.

***

Like the morning paper being thrown on his porch, the reports landed on Shane's desk. These documents took on a new life from earlier editions. The notes were a collage of thoughts that had been pieced together by civilian recruits and task force members. Each notation made sense in its own way, but few of them worked together to form a comprehensive theory. However, each idea warranted a review. As he read through all five pages, Shane highlighted the points that intrigued him.

An impressive theme emerged from some of the ideas. Several task force members believed that the link between the terrorist cells and the Internet could involve the web site from the chemical plant that had supplied the potassium perchlorate to the Lonitesci factory. Since this product was contaminated, this was a natural path to explore. That made sense.

Were the terrorists even aware that the government had suspicions about the potassium perchlorate company? Even if they suspected that the task force had investigated this theory, research had shown that the company was not thought to have been directly involved in the contamination. If the terrorists thought the investigation of the company had been stopped, they might feel safe using the chemical plant's web site for their purposes.

The task force believed that the order for the potassium perchlorate had been intercepted by a third party during its electronic transmission. Trial attempts to place similar orders had been staged from private civilian internet access and had shown evidence of electronic travel to an invisible page after the order request had been made. Prior to the order confirmation form, another split second of a blank screen had suggested a similar electronic leap at this point in the ordering process. This invisible page was believed to have been sent to a terrorist contact who intercepted the Lonitesci order and arranged for its contamination. The only inconsistency was that each time this invisible page was detected it appeared to be traveling to different destinations. Whoever was behind this was doing a solid job of covering his tracks.

These most recent speculations intrigued Shane. Even if the terrorists didn't have internal connections to the chemical plant, they could be using the company's web site as an entry to their own page. This could be a long shot, but it was worth investigating.

Shane called Alan.

"Hi, Alan, I have some thoughts to run by you. Can you come to my office?"

"No problem, I'll be there in a few minutes."

The knock at the door came before Shane had the opportunity to drop the aspirin bottle back into his desk drawer. Having just swallowed three tablets, he was still gulping water when Alan entered. He lifted the nearly empty pill bottle and tossed it back in its place.

"Are you feeling okay, Shane?"

"Oh, I've been better, but I'm sure I'll be fine." Shane's voice lacked confidence.

"Why don't you go see your doctor? Maybe he can give you something."

"No, I'm okay. I think we're getting somewhere with this, and I just want to focus until we're done. When we're through, I'll go to the doctor, I promise."

"Okay, sir. What did you want to talk about? The notes we received this morning?"

"Yes. Several of those ideas sounded reasonable, but the part that got me thinking was the stuff about the chemical plant. I don't expect our answer will be simple to find, but I think these theories warrant some serious thought about where to begin. What do you think?"

"I agree. In fact, I'd been doing some thinking along the same lines. I'd like to bring this up in our task force meeting this afternoon. If we can get the team thinking about this, we might get somewhere."

"Okay. Get everyone working on that angle, Alan. Keep me informed of any progress."

"Will do, sir. Now get some rest. I'll contact you as soon as we find something."

With limp shoulders and a throbbing head, Shane remained in his chair as Alan left the room. No escort to the door for his friend today. With the palm of his left hand, he rubbed his eye. He massaged his fingers across his face, as if the stimulation would jolt him into a more alert state. The late morning felt like midnight. The past few days had blurred together in Shane's mind, and the hours meant little more to him than the time between taking doses of aspirin.

Shane knew his concentration was being broken with each wave of nausea and stomach cramping that ripped through his body. All the while, his headaches kept him in a constant state of discomfort. He moved from his desk to the couch, a ritual he'd developed over the past few days. He lay down to rest for a few minutes. The phone rang two hours later and woke him. Missing the call, he went to the restroom to assess his condition.

The light over the sink seemed brighter than usual. The mirror revealed a vision of a haggard man. The fluorescent illumination marred the clarity of his image. He blinked once, allowing time for his sensitive pupils to adjust to the light. Focusing took some effort, but the lenses in his eyes finally produced a clear picture of his reflection. After staring for longer than necessary, he dropped his chin to his chest. No mistake could be made about the red pustules on his cheek. Unable to delay the inevitable any longer, he called for his doctor.

Drawing little attention to the car, the driver pulled around to the back entrance of the White House. Dressed in protective clothing, a mask, and gloves, he waited for his passenger. After a minute, he caught a glance of movement from the rear right side.

Shane removed the handheld oxygen mask from his face long enough to thank the driver for picking him up. He insisted that the Secret Service Agent ride up front, as far away as possible.

Pulling his hat down over his eyes, he wrapped himself in a blanket that he'd brought along. Even his head was covered as he stepped out of the car and was escorted into his new quarters.

Once in his room, he looked around at the technology center that had been set up at his request. The bedside table held a laptop computer and a fax machine. Connected to a caller ID box, a phone waited to take calls that were forwarded from his office.

A selection of files and notes were arranged in a neat pile on a second table.

"Does it meet your standards?" Alan emerged in the doorway without Shane noticing. "You should have everything you need. If you think of anything else, just call."

"Are you supposed to be here?" Shane was concerned for his friend's well-being.

"Maybe not, but you leave those decisions to me. Besides, did you really expect me not to stick around to make sure you were comfortable? After your call this morning, I didn't have much of a choice. I wanted to see you so I could tell you in person that you will get through this. I also wanted to make sure you knew that your task force won't let you down. We'll meet our objective, and you'll *witness* the outcome. Now, you take care of yourself. Listen to your doctor and get better. I'll be in constant contact."

Holding the oxygen mask over his face, Shane nodded his thanks. The mask was cumbersome, but breathing on his own had become increasingly difficult over the past twenty-four hours. He watched as his friend disappeared behind the closed door. Looking around his room, he wondered if he would ever work from inside his White House office again.

-31-

Listening to her mother's excitement made Hannah smile.

"Mom, I might only be ten, but I can tell that you like this guy."

"Of course I like him, he's my friend. You like your friends, don't you?" Cheryl tried to avoid the obvious forthcoming explanation.

Hannah smiled and said nothing as her mother's cheeks turned pink. "You look funny in that oxygen mask, Mom." A knock on the door interrupted the conversation.

"Come in," Cheryl sang out. As Abbie entered, Cheryl jumped up and greeted her with a hug. "Most of her scabs have fallen off, but we're still not supposed to touch her," Cheryl whispered. "I see you were given the same stylish mask that I've been wearing." They all laughed.

"How are you sweetie? I've missed you." Abbie took a seat across from the bed.

"I'm fine, Abbie, a lot better than before. I think I'll be ready to go home soon, right Mom?"

"Well, we need to wait for Dr. Watters to give us an answer on that, but you are doing much better."

"Wait for Doctor Watters to answer what?" The doctor had appeared in the doorway just seconds before.

"Hannah was saying that she felt well enough to go home. I told her we should see what you had to say about that. So, what do you think?" Cheryl asked with pleading eyes.

"I know you'd take great care of Hannah if we let her go home. However, we still need to follow her progress closely," the doctor explained. "I know she's feeling well right now, but we shouldn't jump the gun. I think I'd like to keep her around for a little while longer."

"Well, I can't blame you for wanting me around," Hannah chimed in. The room filled with laughter.

"Is all of this cheering for me?" a voice asked from the hall.

Cheryl craned her neck to find Joel standing in the doorway.

"This must be the most popular room in the building," he noted.

"Hey, how was your flight?" Cheryl made her way to the hall to greet her friend.

At the sight of her mother's new acquaintance, Hannah exchanged looks with Abbie. Raising her eyebrows, she nodded her approval.

"Okay, everyone, I'll be back in about an hour to see how Hannah's doing," Dr. Watters announced. She winked at her patient and headed to the door. As she slid past Cheryl and Joel, she spoke again.

"Cheryl, could you meet me downstairs in a few minutes? I have some details to go over with you."

"Of course, Dr. Watters. I'll be there in a few minutes."

"I can wait here," Joel said. He didn't want to get in the way. "Or, maybe I'll head to the cafeteria. Are you hungry? I could bring something back for you." He looked to Cheryl for direction.

"No, thanks, I'm not hungry, Joel. Plus, I thought we could grab some lunch in town. That would be more exciting for you than eating in the hospital cafeteria." She giggled and grazed the bend of Joel's elbow with her soft touch. "Hey, why don't you come with me and Dr. Watters? I could use your help in deciphering the terminology she might use when she talks to me about Hannah. Sometimes it's difficult to comprehend, so you might just come in handy. What do you say?"

"I say it sounds like a plan. I'd like to hear about Hannah's condition anyway. This way, maybe I could ask some questions, too, if that's okay with you."

"Of course it's okay," Cheryl said. "Hannah, I'll be right

back." She returned to the hall and replaced her hand on Joel's arm, ready to escort him downstairs. She knew the way to the conference room.

Both Joel and Cheryl took their seats in front of the desk in the doctor's secondary office. Dr. Watters spoke one-word answers into the phone as she offered an apologetic look to her guests. She glanced at her watch and motioned that she'd only be another minute. They waited with patience for her to finish her phone call.

In less than a minute, Dr. Watters hung up the phone. She crossed her hands and rested them on the desk in front of her. Waiting for Cheryl to introduce her friend, she hesitated before speaking.

"I'm sorry," Cheryl said, embarrassed. "This is my friend, Joel. He's a medical student at the University of Florida Medical Center. He's taken a special interest in the recent outbreak of SP4, so I've asked him to attend this meeting. Is that okay?"

"Sure." Dr. Watters welcomed the presence of Cheryl's interested friend.

"I not only have a special interest in SP4," Joel interjected. "I also have a special interest in Hannah's case."

Dr. Watters smiled and began. "Hannah's lucky to have love and support on her side. So far, it seems to be working in her favor." She paused to draw a file from a cabinet to the right of her desk. "I have some good news to share with you. We're seeing improvements in Hannah's condition." She paused. The look on Joel's face made it clear that he was as baffled by this conclusion as she was. "The virus still exists in her body, but the signs of its growth have disappeared. Something seems to have stopped it in its path—a *roadblock* of sorts."

"Well, this is wonderful, isn't it?" Cheryl looked to Joel for agreement.

"Yes, it's encouraging," Dr. Watters answered. "However, we're still stumped about how this happened. She's shown signs of recovery much more quickly than any other victims have experienced. This doesn't make sense. We need to move forward with optimistic caution. We need to find out why this virus has regressed when this is uncharacteristic of its behavior. It's important that we determine what's caused the virus to stop progressing in order to ensure that it won't be prompted to carry on again."

"Well, I do feel encouraged," Cheryl said.

"I do, too," said the doctor. "But we have to keep testing Hannah until we figure this out. Therefore, she'll have to stay with us for a while."

"I understand. But I can still visit, right?" Cheryl asked. "She's not contagious, is she?"

"All of the pustules have scabbed, and most of the scabs have fallen off. Once the scabs are all gone, she won't be contagious at all. In the meantime, keep wearing your gloves and masks, and don't touch her."

"And Kendra?" Cheryl posed this question in a soft voice, so as not to ruin the moment by its answer. "I know this meeting's about Hannah, but is there any chance that Kendra could experience the same kind of *roadblock*?"

"I wish I could say yes, Cheryl. Well, I guess I can say there's always a chance, since we can't explain how it happened in Hannah's body in the first place. But to date, the virus in Kendra's body hasn't shown any signs of slowing." Dr. Watters took a second to soak in Cheryl's reaction. "But, if this happened in Hannah's body, then we should all keep praying that Kendra will have the same outcome."

Waiting to speak until the lump in her throat allowed the passage of words, Cheryl fought her urge to cry. "Has this roadblock occurred in any other SP4 patients?"

This was the question Dr. Watters had prayed would not be posed. She waited a few seconds before commenting, giving Cheryl a hint to what the answer would be.

"I'm sorry, Cheryl, but we haven't seen any sign of this reaction to the virus in any other SP4 victims." She could tell that her response confirmed Cheryl's fear. "In fact, that was the CDC on the phone when you came into my office. I was just confirming this information so I could be sure. But we can still hope that whatever we learn from Hannah's condition will help us to treat other patients, including Kendra. Don't give up yet. We've only just begun."

"Can I at least see her?" Cheryl was aware of the answer before she even asked the question.

"No, Cheryl. I'm sorry. We just can't take that risk," the doctor explained. "I know you've been lucky, and you haven't gotten sick, but we can't take any chances. Hannah needs you. You can't risk anything that would take you away from your daughter."

Cheryl nodded. With her head hung low, she gasped as a waterfall of tears began to flow down her cheeks. In quick breaths, she inhaled through her mouth as she sobbed.

She allowed Joel to pull her tight to his side, and she let her body fall until it rested with surprising comfort against his.

Dr. Watters showed compassion and excused herself from the room.

***

Using his bed pillows to prop himself up, Shane concentrated on making the most of his new office headquarters. Against the doctor's wishes, he'd had his equipment set up inside the confines of his oxygen tent. How could he get any work done if everything was beyond his reach? He was serious about finishing what he set out to do, even if it had to be done from a hospital room.

A faint ringing alerted him to yet another fax being printed. Reading the daily reports from the CDC made him cringe. Ongoing research had led to no breakthroughs regarding SP4 treatment. The words were almost painful to digest. He skipped to a news alert in the middle of the page.

Reading the message, a smile of relief appeared on his face.

A ten-year-old girl in Washington, DC has proven to be the first

SP4 victim to experience signs of recovery. This young lady presented with escalated symptoms of the virus when she was admitted to the Georgetown University Hospital only three days ago ...

From the personal description and the dates that were noted, Shane knew this report was about Hannah Williams. A surge of happiness raced through him at the thought that Cheryl was finally involved in a positive turn of events regarding the health of her daughter. No one deserved this more. The information about Hannah was by far the most exciting news in the memo. What a refreshing start to the day.

Placing the fax on a pile of others, he rested his head on the pillows behind him. He closed his eyes and inhaled long, intentional breaths from the pure oxygen that lingered in his enclosure.

Shane had felt similar frustration once before. He'd grown tired from the countless leads that had taken the UFW nowhere in the search for the terrorist cells in the world. The members of the United States Anti-Terrorism Task Force had spent each day chasing scraps of information to no avail. The cooperation of the members of the UFW had multiplied the avenues of opportunity in the search, and yet nothing had panned out.

His mood had been the same as it was now. Why couldn't they find these guys? Shane knew they weren't far away from him, or from anyone for that matter. Years ago, DaKish's personal computer had provided a well-drawn map to the locations of his formerly undisclosed *business partners.* They'd caught a break three years ago, and Shane knew they'd get another break this time. There was some fighting left in this war, but it was far from over.

Adrenaline from remembering the last victory gave Shane the strength to continue on in his present day battle. If they could do it before, then they could do it again. He was sure that this time the terrorists would be more careful to conceal their whereabouts, but these cowards were dwindling in number and would get sloppy in their state of poor health. They didn't plan to infect themselves with SP4. Shane knew this would be his ace-in-the-hole.

SP4 was blind to the distinction between terrorists and the rest of the free world. This virus did not discriminate, and the smallpox vaccine only made it more devastating to its victims. A few months earlier, the terrorists were left with reduced forces, and their egos would not let their few remaining members die. They knew that with their extinction, their cause would be left unfulfilled. They would have to seek help. To these men, failure was not an option.

Shane lifted his hand to reach for the stack of reports from the White House. The list of Internet leads appeared to be endless. Somewhere in that pile there was an answer to this riddle. He would find it. Sifting through, he separated out the notes that supported the theory of the involvement of the Chinese chemical plant. This stack included a hefty handful of leads. Getting comfortable, he motivated himself to read. A new thought occurred to him. Thankful for the invention of tables on wheels, he pulled the phone closer to his bed with ease.

An answer came in seconds after Shane dialed Alan's line.

"Jackson here."

"Alan, hey, how's everything going?"

"Well, hello. How are you feeling, Shane?"

"I'm hanging in there. The accommodations are nice." Shane chuckled. "I've had plenty of time for reading, so I have some questions for you."

"Fire away."

"Well, first, have we explored the patient status of the Chinese hospitals around the geographical area of the chemical plant?"

"We're checking that out, but we haven't found much." Alan hoped to have a better answer for the next question.

"My thoughts are this: China didn't participate in Celebrate Freedom. Therefore, they shouldn't have any known cases of SP4 anywhere within their country. The spreading of SP4 could eventually get there, but it would be a while before it could travel that far. Also, if they do have any cases, I would expect they'd be traditional smallpox, since SP4 came about from mixing the virus with potassium perchlorate, and most defined the mutation through the detonation of the fireworks. If China's posting any cases of smallpox, then this may prove that the origin of this outbreak could've been in their country, as we believe, in the chemical plant. What are your thoughts?"

"That makes perfect sense." Alan agreed with enthusiasm. "I'll see what we can find out from the World Health Organization. However, China's not the most cooperative country when it comes to sharing information, especially with us. I'd hope that in the midst of a health crisis their attitudes would change. If this all originated from a group of terrorist-connected employees, then the Chinese Health Organization shouldn't feel that they have anything to hide. I'll be in touch as soon as we dig something up. In the meantime, you get some rest."

"Will do. Please, call me as soon as you find anything. I'm going to keep reading these Internet theories that your teams have put together. Some of them are quite interesting. I'll talk with you soon, Alan."

Getting back to work, Alan kept the phone in his hand. He made one call to the World Health Organization and another to the task force member who was in charge of the civilian recruit research efforts. The pieces of the puzzle were coming together.

Shane read the pages that rested on his lap. His attention span was shorter than it had been hours ago, so he had to read some lines two or three times to comprehend their true messages. He focused and continued his efforts. Flipping through the pages, he searched for a specific report, the one from Mark. The end was nearing. He could feel it. He liked the ideas he'd read from this young man before, and he'd been looking forward to seeing more from him. About two-thirds of the way through the stack, he spotted a page that was titled with his name.

Mark had supplied an outline for his report, taking its reader through the steps that he proposed a terrorist would have to follow in order to reach communication with their organization. His steps were numbered in order from one to five. Shane read them aloud, from the first to the last.

-32-

In the doorway of Hannah's room, Cheryl threw her arm around Abbie's shoulders.

"Thanks for staying with Hannah while we met with Dr. Watters. We'll give you a call later."

"Of course. It was no problem. I'll be back at some point tomorrow afternoon. Stay positive, Cheryl. This sounds like a true miracle."

As she entered the room, Dr. Watters observed the celebratory nature of Hannah's surroundings. While making her way to the bedside, she rehearsed her words in silence. How would she explain this to a ten-year-old? She did her best to offer Hannah as much detail as she could comprehend.

The use of the word *roadblock* brought a smile to Hannah's face. The news of her condition jump-started her with energy. She liked what Dr. Watters had to say. In her experience with doctors, a typical conversation usually ended with the information that her health was worse. For the first time since she could remember, she was being told that she was getting better. Her renewed sense of hope shone in her eyes.

Cheryl felt the happiness that charged her daughter's emotions. With this development, her own strength returned. However, she did her best to avoid Hannah's questions about Kendra. She hoped Hannah would become too preoccupied with her own good news to inquire about her aunt. She'd raised her daughter to be more compassionate and caring than that. In this instance, she wished perhaps this wasn't the case.

"How's Aunt Kendra doing?" Hannah looked to each of the visitors in her room.

Aware that Cheryl didn't have the strength to address this question, Dr. Watters offered an answer.

"She's plugging along, sweetie." The vague response prompted another, more specific, question from the little girl.

"Does she have a roadblock, too?"

"Well, so far we haven't noticed one. But, she didn't get sick until after you, so maybe she's headed in that direction." Dr. Watters tried not to sigh with relief when she realized Hannah had halted her line of questioning.

"Honey, we have to go now. Visiting hours are over. I'll be back first thing in the morning. Is there anything special you want me to bring for you?" Cheryl took the moment to change the subject.

"A pizza would be nice." Hannah raised one eyebrow and spoke through a giggle. It was worth a shot.

"Well, I'll see what I can do." Cheryl replied with a grin. Lifting her palm to her lips, she blew a kiss in Hannah's direction. She couldn't wait to be able to make contact with her daughter again. "I'll see you in the morning."

"Bye, kiddo." Joel winked at Hannah. "I'll stay on your mom about that pizza." Laughing, he escorted Cheryl from the room.

"So, what's on the agenda now?" Joel asked. He swung his bag over his shoulder and lifted Cheryl's tote from her slender arm. He situated her canvas carrier on the same shoulder as his own bag.

"Well, I've invited my brother-in-law to the house for dinner. He owns a restaurant, and he's a fabulous cook. I hope that's okay with you." Cheryl looked to Joel for a hint of approval of the added company.

"That sounds great to me. Do we need to get anything from the store?"

"No, I think we have everything we need. I hope you like seafood. I think he's going to make seafood pasta."

"That sounds wonderful. So, where do we go now?" Joel peered to the left and the right of the hospital exit. Throwing his arms in the air, he crossed each hand in a different direction.

"Oh, this way." Cheryl moved Joel's right hand until it pointed in the same direction as the left. She led the way to the Metro station. "To the Metro. It's not far. I hope your bag isn't too heavy. How did you get to the hospital? Cab?"

Joel nodded. "The bag's fine. Plus, I'm certain I can use the exercise."

Before he could continue, Cheryl broke in with an apology.

"Joel, I'm so sorry! I just remembered we never ate lunch. I told you we'd eat in town, but, after our meeting with Dr. Watters I was a little out of it. I'm such a terrible hostess. You must be starving." Cheryl's face burned with embarrassment.

"Please, don't worry. I'm fine. I'm a big boy. If I was hungry, I could've grabbed something at the hospital. Plus, I was happy to have been with you for that meeting. That's what I'm going to be doing for a living one day, you know."

"You're sweet." With a gentle stumbling motion, Cheryl purposely bumped into Joel's side. "I'm glad you're here."

Nudging him to the right, she eased him in the direction of the Metro station. She waited while he fed his money into the machine before she shuffled him forward through the gate. Once they were seated on the train, she realized how tired she was. At the risk of appearing rude, she let out a short yawn and rubbed her eyes.

"You must be exhausted," Joel said, watching her actions.

"Oh, I'm fine. I've just had a lot on my mind. I'm looking forward to dinner, though."

"Cheryl, do you have a computer with Internet access at home?"

"Actually, I do. Why do you ask?"

"I'd collected some interesting reports about smallpox from the Internet. After that meeting with Dr. Watters, I was wishing I'd brought my notebooks with me. But, if you wouldn't mind, I could find the information again from your computer. I think it might be something your doctors could be interested in. You never know; it could help them in determining why this virus has been blocked in Hannah's system, but not in Kendra's."

"Of course you can use the computer. I'd be interested in

reading any information you can find. I understand so little about what's happening to my daughter and my sister. I know there are a lot of people in the world who are feeling just like me."

Their conversation lasted until Joel and Cheryl had arrived at the town home.

Gerry had already gotten started with dinner. The smell of garlic floating through the air welcomed Cheryl and Joel at the door.

"Hey Cheryl." Gerry greeted her with a hug. "I let myself in. I hope that's okay. I had Kendra's keys on me."

"Of course it's okay. Gerry, this is my friend, Joel. Joel, this is my brother-in-law, Gerry."

Joel reached out and shook Gerry's hand. "It's great to meet you. Anything I can do to help?"

"I think I've got it under control, Joel. But you could pour some wine, if you'd like. It's open on the counter. I hope you enjoy shiraz."

"That sounds great to me."

"Hey, Joel, why don't you come with me and I'll get you started on the computer?" By closing the cabinet doors, Cheryl interrupted his search for wine glasses. "I'll take care of the wine. I need to talk to Gerry for a minute anyway."

"No problem. Which way to the computer?"

Cheryl escorted Joel to the living room where a computer sat on a wooden desk. She took a seat and made the Internet connection.

"All right, the computer's all yours. Here's the browser. Do your thing. I'll get us some wine."

* * *

The tests from the hospitals in China had proven positive for smallpox cases. The news inspired Shane. Due to a lack of cooperation from the Chinese Health Organization, the number of cases hadn't been confirmed, but they had been reported. Finally, the Internet research was taking shape.

Within the past hour, the Virginia Beach based computer tech had been moved from his Norfolk based office to Washington, D.C. His five-step theory had proven so interesting that Alan had demanded he be moved closer to the scene.

Wishing to be walked through the steps of Mark's outline, Shane was anxious for him to call. He waited in position to work, with his laptop computer to his immediate right and his phone on the bed to his left. His request for additional phone lines had been met with little resistance, and, in return, he promised to rest often. Although he attempted to uphold his end of the bargain, he'd been delivering less than satisfactory results.

"Yes?" Shane spoke with as few words as necessary. More words meant deeper breaths, and this was easier said than done.

"Mr. President?" A boyish excitement garnished the voice on the opposite end of the line. "I was told to contact you at this number. My name is Mark."

"Yes, Mark. I was waiting for your call. Excuse me one moment." Shane took a long breath from his oxygen supply. "Mark, thanks for calling. I'd like for you to walk me through your five-step outline. Do you think you've found a link to a communications hub for the terrorists? Please, start from the beginning. I have a computer in front of me, and I'll be following your instructions." Aware that the work would require both hands, Shane made use of the earpiece that connected to his phone. The lightweight of the cord was enough to irritate the inflamed rash on his neck and cheeks.

"Okay, sir, follow my lead." Mark spoke rehearsed words with a methodical approach. His excitement was clouded by the seriousness of the moment. "First, let's go to the web site." He waited a few seconds, until he heard Shane's muffled confirmation that he was there. "Now, look to the bottom left corner, where a visitor can send a request for an order."

"Okay, I've got it. Now what?" Shane was eager to see where the sum total of these steps would take him.

"Click on the link where the site directs its users to place an order," Mark instructed. "Pay attention to the subtle *redirect* that occurs at this point. What you'll see is a quick flash of a blank screen with a blurred word at the top. If you pay close attention, you'll be able to read the word *re-routing*, but it'll be quick. Let me know when you've seen that."

Shane witnessed the redirect, just as Mark had explained. After the quick flash of the white screen, he appeared to have settled on a normal ordering form for the chemical plant.

"Where does the redirect take us, Mark? I'm staring at a harmless order form. I don't understand why we're here if we've been re-routed."

"At this point, you'll need to stop and listen to where I'm going with this. We can't risk your computer sending identification to that site and exposing you. Since I haven't personally set up your system, I don't want to place you at risk like that. The identity of my computer's been concealed, so I can move about as an incognito traveler. You stay put, okay?"

"Okay." Shane was reluctant to hold off, but he valued Mark's opinion.

"I'm going to place an order for random chemistry class products. There, done. Now, my page is redirected again, back to what I believe is the true site of this chemical plant. Now, I move to another Internet connection and place an order for potassium perchlorate," Mark paused when he heard Shane's voice.

"Wait a second ... you have more than one connection, and they can't track that?"

"No, sir," Mark explained. "I have several wireless connections working on different systems. Plus, I've set up all of my operations so that they shouldn't be traced. Anyway, now the order for the potassium perchlorate appears to stay within the web world of our first redirected page. The two pages are obviously different, which tells me that the Lonitesci company was also directed to a dummy page after they placed their order for the potassium perchlorate. In my opinion, the information from this order is being recorded somewhere and then probably being sent back to

the Chinese company after its final submission. It's like someone is proofreading all of the orders ... ya know? An outside set
of eyes is checking them as they come through. Are you following me so far?"

"I'm with you, Mark. Go on." Shane followed from a distance behind Mark. This seemed a little extreme. Where was he
going with this?

"Okay, I'm gonna sidestep giving final approval for this order.
Instead, I've found my way down to the bottom of the page where
a small symbol appears. In my opinion, the symbol is more noticeable than I expected it to be. It's a picture of fireworks exploding.
I think it's obvious for a reason. Like, maybe these guys thought
we'd think it was too obvious to give it any further thought.
Anyway, I'm one step ahead of them."

The adrenaline rush that Mark got from solving this puzzle
reminded Shane of the energy he felt when he accomplished goals
of his own.

"The link, when I press on it, takes me to one last page." Mark
talked faster as he moved downward through his list of steps. "This
page is a form used to pay for the order. It's a typical credit card
form, however, it's not identified as a secure page, which is what
made me suspicious. I haven't been successful in moving anywhere from this page, though. This is where my trail stops. I just
need to find my way to what's next. I'm confident that it goes
somewhere out of the ordinary. It's not normal web practice for
a typical on-line sale, so it's clearly a decoy page of some sort. I
need to find where the hidden link is from here, but I know we're
on to something."

"I think you're a very smart man, Mark. I do have one question, though. If the terrorists used the chemical order form to
intercept the Lonitesci order, why would they still have this page
link in operation? Why wouldn't they have gotten rid of it?"

"That's a fine question. My guess is that it was an easy way for
them to stay in touch, especially in light of their unexpected turn
of events. Also, they might have thought we'd notice any other
recent activity on the Internet, you know, messing with someone

else's web site. This thing was already set up and running, and we hadn't noticed it before. There could be a variety of reasons why they decided to use this, but I'm confident it's how they're communicating."

"I want you to stay in contact with me and with General Jackson, Mark. Please let us know as soon as you find the next step. I'm confident you'll figure this out. Thank you for your time."

Shane returned the phone to his left side. Disappointed that he wasn't able to follow the trail with a more firsthand experience, he disconnected his laptop from the Internet. He respected Mark's awareness of the safety issues that were involved, and he was anxious to hear from him again soon.

Earlier, Shane had left a call with his wife on an uneasy note, so he took the free moment to try to reach her. He knew she was upset because he'd hidden his health condition from her. There was no reason for her to worry. She would see that one day. He was aware that the most upsetting part of this whole thing was that she wasn't allowed to visit him. Plus, how was she explaining all of this to the kids? God bless her for being so amazing.

He talked with her until his breathing became too labored. Then he powered down the phone and placed it on his bedside table next to his computer.

Closing his eyes, he gave in to much needed rest. The medication for his pain made him even more tired than his weakened condition could've accomplished on its own. He was asleep before his phone rang. Deep slumber kept him from answering.

***

His sandal-clad feet padded over the stained carpet in the airport. Alexei drew little attention to himself. He remained silent while the ticket agent studied his boarding pass. His thumb ached from its tight grip on the shoulder strap of his laptop computer.

Her eyes locked on his facial expression, as she looked from the photo ID to his features multiple times.

"Thank you Mr. Stephalotivis." She returned his identification card. "Enjoy your flight."

The three-hour flight flew by, as it had been one of several for Alexei over the past two days. While he waited in line at U.S. Customs, his heart skipped several beats.

The past week had sent Alexei and Sharona into a tailspin. His original plan of committing suicide had been changed, because his wife had not fallen ill. After learning that she'd appeared at the celebration against his wishes, he was certain she would've shown symptoms by now. Why did she disobey him, anyway? This was unlike his wife, as were many of her most recent actions. He was shocked by her willingness to participate in his plan to leave their home.

After abandoning his country, Alexei expected he'd become a marked individual. His guilt over leaving his nation overwhelmed him, but not enough for him to stay. His colleagues had decided their own destinies when they sold out to the terrorists. No matter how he'd weighed the situation, he always wound up staring at the plain truth. The government of the Russian Federation had allowed their insecurities and paranoia to cloud their judgment. They knew that what had been done in the past was wrong, yet they'd chosen to ignore it. Now, the events of the present had made it impossible to ignore the past any longer.

Gathering his bags from the table, Alexei watched the customs officer stamp his passport and wave him through to the next line. He contemplated making another attempt at contacting Shane, but decided against the idea—at least for the moment.

After two screwdrivers and as many hours later, Alexei checked his watch. One drink an hour had left him with little attention from the bartender, yet he wasn't prepared to weaken his state of awareness by consuming more alcohol. Peeling his thighs from the vinyl-cushioned stool, he made his way to the cabstand outside. Quick instructions directed the driver where to go.

Opening the door revealed a modest but comfortable efficiency. The couch had been pulled out into a bed, and clean towels rested on an armchair. The refrigerator housed bottled water and two deli wrapped sandwiches. An envelope on the counter held four American twenty-dollar bills, a godsend to Alexei. His friends had taken even better care of him than he'd expected. Praying that Sharona was finding her room without any problems, he hoped that her accommodations were as comfortable. Sighing, he peered through the window to the dark street outside. Desiring the safety of privacy, he closed the blinds.

His cell phone had been turned off for the past twenty-four hours. He plugged the signal-scrambling device into the base and tried the number one more time. His disappointment at the lack of an answer drew him closer to the conclusion that something was wrong. Shane should've been available at least one of the times he'd tried to call over the past two days.

As much as he desired to investigate the situation, he grew tired at the thought. His fever had intensified over the past day, and he knew that his hours without medical care were numbered. He only hoped to track down his friend before he was interrupted by his deteriorating health or by an uninvited visit from a Russian colleague. Either way, the outcome would be the same.

***

"Cheryl, do you have a printer connected to this computer?" Joel looked around to the side of the desk.

"Voila." Cheryl opened a drawer from the bottom right, exposing an ink jet printer. "Here we are. Print away, young man."

Joel resumed his business at the computer as Cheryl returned to the kitchen to check on Gerry.

"How's dinner coming? Anything I can do to help?" She poured herself another glass of wine and waved the half empty bottle at her brother-in-law.

"You'd better drink up, or you might not get another glass," she teased.

"Don't worry. There's more where that came from."

Cheryl sauntered back to the living room, only to find Joel's glass full as well.

"What is it with you men? Are you trying to get me drunk?" Cheryl looked at Joel for an answer. The wine sure helped her to let her guard down. Sometimes she needed a little nudge in that direction.

"That's the plan." Joel responded with a wink. As he leaned back from the computer, the printer hummed with life. Lifting the glass to his lips, he drew in a long taste of the red wine. When he replaced his goblet on the far corner of the desk, it was almost empty.

"Now that's more like it." Cheryl was satisfied with Joel's progress. She filled the wine back to its appropriate three quarter mark. "What are you printing? Anything interesting?" She took one page from the paper tray. Her brow wrinkled into a baffled expression.

"I think you might be interested in this," Joel said. "But let's head to the kitchen. It smells like Gerry's ready for us. This will be a good dinner topic." He took the paper from Cheryl's hand and paired it with its partner from the printer tray.

The table was set with attractive fiesta ware dishes and colored water glasses. The seafood pasta delivered a scented trail of garlic and onion toward the living room, enticing Cheryl to hurry to the table. She took her seat at the head and motioned for Gerry to sit to her right. Joel fell into the chair on her left.

"If you don't mind, men, let's bow our heads."

All three diners took a moment of silence and meditation. Afterwards, the men looked up for Cheryl's approval to dig in. When their eyes met, she lifted her wine glass to offer a toast.

"Cheers, to good friends and even better family." She tipped her glass into Joel's and Gerry's. "May God bless us and everyone in our lives." So as not to distract Gerry from savoring his desperately needed escape, she kept her words brief. With the first bite melting in her mouth, she proclaimed her approval of the dish.

"Gerry, you've done it again, not that I'm at all surprised. This is wonderful."

"Oh, yes, I have to agree," Joel chimed in. "This is one of the best meals I've ever eaten." He sipped his wine and went back to his plate for a second bite.

When the entree was almost finished, Cheryl turned to her houseguest with a question.

"Where's that stuff you printed from the computer? You said you were going to tell us about it. I'll make some coffee, if anyone's interested."

Filled from dinner and too tired to drink more wine, both men seemed interested in fresh coffee. Cheryl denied their attempts to help to clear the dishes, so they relaxed and waited for her return.

Without trying to conceal his pleasure in watching her, Joel admired her graceful movements from the sink to the dishwasher to the coffee maker, cleaning dishes and grinding coffee beans in one motion. She was even more beautiful than he'd remembered.

"She's great, isn't she?" Gerry took the opportunity to secure some man-to-man conversation with Joel. "She's the only sister I have, you know. You better treat her right." His joke was wrapped in a serious tone.

"Don't you worry. I would only offer the best to her, if she'd take it." Joel responded with sincerity. Before he could continue, Cheryl returned to the table. Joel knew she was aware that she'd walked in on an obvious discussion about her.

"What did I miss?" She expected a hasty change of subject. Guys just weren't good at that. She chuckled at their display of awkward silence.

"The coffee will be ready in a few minutes. Dessert, anyone?"

Gerry's eyes lit up at the thought. "What do you have?" He was surprised by the suggestion of dessert, since he hadn't thought to bring anything.

"Oh, just a little something I whipped up this morning, before

I left for the hospital." Cheryl enhanced her answer with a confident flip of her hair. "I have homemade brownies and vanilla ice cream. It's nothing extravagant, not like our dinner, but it sure will curb that sugar craving."

"That sounds perfect," Joel said. "But first, have a seat. I want to show you what I found on the Internet." He retrieved his papers from their resting place on the empty chair beside him. "This is a report from a medical journal that I found while I was researching smallpox at med school."

Cheryl took a glimpse at the first printed page as Joel handed it to her. After a quick scan, she passed it to Gerry. She watched as Gerry returned the page to Joel. Together, they waited for Joel's explanation of the information.

"This is a research article from the Medical Tribune. The report is based on a study done by a well-known doctor and researcher from California. Frankly, I follow this guy's work on a regular basis. He always seems to find the most exhilarating information, because he believes in pursuing the unlikely and the unexpected, more so than most researchers." Joel stopped to finish what was left of his wine.

Cheryl headed to the kitchen for the coffee.

"Stop there, for one second. I'll be right back." She didn't waste any time getting to the kitchen. Whatever this was, it sounded good. She returned with a tray of eclectic coffee mugs, cream and sugar. After placing the tray in the center of the table, she handed each of the men a mug and a spoon. Taking the last of the utensils for herself, she mixed French vanilla creamer with her coffee. As she clinked the spoon back and forth on the sides of her mug, she offered the creamer to Joel. Now she was ready to listen.

Joel poured while he spoke.

"Anyway, this report is all about smallpox and how it possesses similarities to the AIDS virus." After glancing down to stir his coffee, he looked up to catch the reactions of his companions. He passed the creamer to Gerry, who covered his coffee and politely refused. Joel placed the small carton on the tray and went on with his discussion. "Read the highlighted parts of this report.

I have copies for both of you."

Anxious for them to finish reading, Joel awaited the reactions from Cheryl and Gerry. Intrigue and confusion consumed the facial expressions of both parties.

Cheryl processed what she could from the passages, preparing to pose the first question.

"Joel, what does this mean? You think you can help with Hannah's AIDS treatment?"

Joel smiled at his correct prediction of the first inquiry.

"Well, maybe, but I'm looking at this from the complete opposite end of the spectrum. In fact, I think this information could be a breakthrough in learning how to treat SP4. Hannah may provide the perfect case study to convince the medical world of the possibilities of this theory."

"What's that?" Cheryl's surprise left her with few words.

"Let me explain the parts that struck me. If I'm interpreting this correctly, I believe that this research proves that there are significant similarities between smallpox and AIDS. This was actually HIV research, but their results found that smallpox attacks cells in a similar manner to HIV. The doctor who wrote this article believed that a better understanding of the method of infection could help to defeat HIV, maybe leading to a vaccine. However, this doctor looks at the similarities from a unique angle. He looks at the common way that the two viruses move through the body." Realizing he'd lost Cheryl, he backed up. "Bear with me. I know this seems far fetched."

"I'm following you, Joel. I think. I'm just trying to understand. Tell me how this could help Hannah."

"I know it's a long shot, but this is how I see it helping Hannah. The information explains that both HIV and myxoma poxvirus, which is similar to smallpox, attach themselves to the CCR5 or CCR4 chemokines. These are structures on the surface of the immune cells. When the virus attaches, it allows for penetration of the cells and triggers infection throughout the body. Since they've found HIV to work much like smallpox, it's very likely that smallpox also invades cells by attaching to chemokines.

They're using this information to develop a vaccine for HIV or to produce new HIV drugs designed to block the chemokine receptors from allowing HIV to enter the cells. Currently, the HIV drugs try to block the virus from replicating itself." Speaking so fast made Joel's mouth dry and chalky. He swallowed the last few droplets from his water glass.

"I think this sounds fascinating. But I'm still missing the connection to how it can help Hannah beat SP4. I'm sorry, Joel. I just don't understand what you're saying." Cheryl stood to clear the dessert plates.

"Wait. Sit down for a second." Joel led Cheryl back down into her seat. He glanced at Gerry, who sat quietly processing the information. "The article says that if HIV and smallpox are both linked to the CCR5 chemokine, then resistance to HIV may actually be traced to a mutation of smallpox. Some people are genetically resistant to HIV because their bodies don't make the CCR5 receptor. Without the receptor, the virus is unable to enter the cells and infect them. The part that keeps ringing in my ears, is that if we can stop the virus from getting to the receptors, we may be able to stop the virus from entering the body all together. Maybe Hannah has started to get better because her receptors are already full from another virus. Therefore, SP4 wouldn't have the vehicle it needs to move through the body and gather the strength to replicate. And maybe the right combination of her AIDS medications could help other SP4 patients, too. Who knows, this could lead to discovering a vaccine for SP4. It's all speculative, but worth some investigation. The doctors at the hospital could take this to the next level, I'm sure." Joel's eyes gleamed with confidence.

Thursday, September 21st

-33-

Even in his state of illness, Alexei's slumber had been broken. A combination of nerves and a high fever had kept him awake. The branches of a somewhat neglected ficas plant stretched with determination toward the window in his room. A tiny ray of light seeped through the narrow gap in the vertical blinds and awakened him. The mild brightness of early morning daybreak felt like a spotlight to Alexei. Squinting as he made his way to the window, he did his best to straighten the blinds. What time was it, anyway?

He'd set his watch to Eastern Standard Time on his arrival in Washington, but he still felt disorientated. Would he ever catch up on his sleep? The trip had drained him. Alexei blamed his fatigue on the change in time zones, but deep inside, he knew his deteriorating health was responsible for the way he felt.

A quick shower gave him a temporary sense of renewed energy. Moving about the apartment, he threw his things into his duffel bag. Wrinkled pants and shirts showed his lack of concern for neatness. Time was the only thing that mattered. Before abandoning his temporary home, he checked his voice mail.

A message from the evening before waited from Sharona. After hearing her voice, he was glad that he'd checked. Longing to hear her tender words once more before he erased them, he replayed the message.

"Dearest Alexei, I hoped to find you awake. But I do not know what time it is where you are, or what time it is where I am. I have some difficulty getting in touch with you today to make plans for the morning. So I need a change in plan. I will meet you tomorrow in evening, at a new location." The voice softened. "I will call again when I am close."

She really wasn't coming that morning? Wasn't she frightened to be away from him? Alexei dialed a pre-set phone number, only to find that Sharona's phone had been turned off. There was no point in leaving a message. He'd wait to hear from her.

He tossed his bag back on a chair in the corner of the room. Alexei molded a new Washington Wizards cap to fit his head. The souvenir from the airport had come in handy for his day in the Northern Virginia city. The pressed blue jeans and long sleeved t-shirt he wore allowed him to fit right into the world outside his door. Sliding his cell phone into the front pocket of his baggy jeans, he pushed the key into his rear pocket. The door snapped to a close behind him.

For seven-fifteen in the morning, Old Town Alexandria was bustling with activity. Alexei stumbled to his right to avoid bumping into a nanny pushing a stroller past him. The beep of a car horn warned him to stay on the sidewalk.

Could he walk the distance to the coffee shop? His cramping stomach made his decision easy. He turned back in the direction of his apartment. The short walk had already left him breathless. Although he'd just gotten up for the day, he couldn't wait to rest.

Back inside, Alexei dialed another number. After the first two rings, he suspected the call was being forwarded to another line. He heard a weak voice answer.

"McAlister here."

* * *

Anxious to get to the hospital, Cheryl hurried Joel along. She'd urged Gerry to join them, but he'd declined. She knew that visiting the hospital was too hard for him unless he could see his wife. Cheryl had promised to call him as soon as Joel had presented his theory to Dr. Watters. The Metro couldn't move fast enough.

"Come on train, let's get moving." She spoke out loud, craning her neck to see how far along they'd gotten. "I hope Dr. Watters is ready to see us when we get there."

"I bet she will be," Joel answered. "We're lucky she was able to make time for us this morning. She probably wanted to talk with you about Hannah, anyway. I'm confident she'll be interested in what we have to show her."

"With what *you* have to show her," Cheryl interjected. "I'm just as excited as anyone about your theory, but I can't even begin to claim that I truly understand any of it."

"Don't you worry, I'll make sure you understand every word." Joel drew Cheryl closer to his side. Surprised by the natural comfort he felt when he was with her, he squeezed a little tighter.

The doors of the Metro had barely parted when Cheryl charged through, tugging Joel behind her. "Come on. We're almost there."

"I'm coming. You shouldn't have fed me so much brownie delight last night. You know you forced me to eat that." His grin confessed his embellishment.

Like a child lugging her favorite doll around, Cheryl pulled Joel along. No time could be wasted, not even for joking.

As soon as she entered the hospital, Cheryl saw a group of doctors heading in her direction. Leading the group of three men and two women was Dr. Watters.

"Well, good morning, Cheryl. How are you this morning? Joel, nice to see you again."

"Hi, Dr. Watters." Cheryl motioned to Joel at her side. "Whenever you have time, we'd like to meet with you about the information Joel has." Intimidation caused her to stammer. She'd never have the confidence to speak to a whole group of doctors. She hoped Joel wasn't nervous.

"We're ready whenever you are," Dr. Watters answered. "If you don't mind, I'd like to have some of my colleagues sit in on our meeting. They're all doing research on SP4, and I felt it would be beneficial to have them join us. Of course, as long as that's okay with you, Joel..."

"No problem. The more the merrier." Joel was anxious to share the information he'd found, but nervous just the same. After all, he was sure he would be viewed as an overzealous medical student in the eyes of his present company.

"We're headed to the conference room now. I think we're all anxious to get started." She tapped Joel on the back. "Come on, you're the man of the hour."

Encouraging Cheryl and Joel to follow, she led the way to the room.

Dr. Watters motioned for Joel to take a seat at the head of the table, and she pulled out the chair next to him for Cheryl. The doctors filed in afterwards, taking their respective seats one by one.

As he stood to pass around copies of the information he'd brought, the jittering in Joel's stomach disappeared. The momentum of the pages circulating around the table altered his physical state to enthusiastic anxiety. His blue eyes twinkled as they locked in on Cheryl's expression of support. For luck, he winked in her direction.

"Folks, I thank you for your attention this morning. I know that many of you already know Ms. Cheryl Williams and her daughter Hannah. My name is Joel Birmingham, and I'm a friend of Cheryl's. I'm a medical student at the University of Florida, and I've taken a personal interest in researching SP4." Joel sipped the cold water from the glass in front of him. He hoped the perspiration he felt forming on his forehead wasn't noticeable to the rest of the group.

"If you'll take a glance at the information which I've passed around, I'll begin." Joel waited while the papers crackled. "I think the first step in understanding why I brought this to you is to understand what triggered my memory about this research that I'd heard about in a medical school lecture." He paused, allowing the medical professionals time to read and to process the information. Wiping his forehead with his hand, he took another sip of his water. The glass had not quite met the table when he began to speak again.

"This report was published in 1999 by a well known doctor in San Francisco, California. The original interpretations that were set forth by his team focused on a viral disease similar to smallpox that reacted with cells in the body much like HIV. Their initial thoughts were that if they could show enough similarities between myxoma poxvirus and HIV, then maybe they could develop more effective drugs for the treatment of AIDS. The research revealed that this smallpox-like virus was found to move through the body by attaching itself to chemokine receptors, much like HIV is known to attack the body. This new direction of development, if all things panned out, would focus on finding drugs which would block the chemokine receptors and prevent HIV from entering the cells, instead of focusing solely on trying to stop HIV from replicating itself." Joel's heart plunged as he noticed the looks of confusion and sheer disinterest from around the table.

"Well, Joel, I do appreciate these insights which you've brought to us regarding the AIDS research. We're all aware of how important treatments are for this deadly disease." Dr. Watters' delicate letdown started out with an unintentional condescending tone. She tilted her head and squinted her eyes as if it pained her to address Joel. "But I think we can all agree that our primary matter at hand is how to contain, treat, and eradicate SP4 from our society. Unless this information somehow led you to a probable solution for this..." She stressed the obvious urgency for Joel to get to his point.

"I'm headed in that direction." Joel felt his heart pound as he launched his main idea. "When I first read this report, my initial reaction was the same as yours. *This is a new angle for us to approach AIDS treatment.* That's why I put this research on a personal shelf, and I hadn't thought about it since. We all know that our country is filled with capable AIDS researchers, and if there was an opportunity for developing a new treatment in 1999, then I'm sure it's been tested. In fact, it wasn't until Hannah was introduced into my life that I even remembered having read this research years ago." Joel made eye contact with each person in the room. "And, it wasn't until I sat with Dr. Watters yesterday that I even made this connection ... one I think could be a catalyst for a breakthrough in medical research."

"All right, Joel, please, go on then." Dr. Watters' tone changed, encouraging him to continue.

A rustling erupted in the back of the room as the most established of the five doctors chose to re-read his information.

"Dr. Watters referred to Hannah's status with regards to SP4 as *atypical* with respect to other known SP4 patients. She said that the virus had come on strong, probably even stronger than in other patients because of Hannah's already weakened immune system. Yet, to everyone's surprise, it's progression halted. She even referred to this phenomena as a *roadblock*, isn't that correct?" He looked to Dr. Watters for confirmation.

"Yes, that's correct, Joel," Dr. Watters offered her input.

"Well, that's what struck me first ... the roadblock. The virus must have entered Hannah's body, because she presented with all of the obvious symptoms. But, at some point SP4 was stopped dead in its tracks, as if it just couldn't go any farther. Perhaps the virus couldn't move throughout the body because its *taxi* was already full. Perhaps the chemokine receptors were already overloaded by the AIDS virus, therefore stopping the SP4 virus in its path. It can't move throughout the body if it can't attach to these cells, and it can't attach to these cells if the sites are full. Therefore, maybe we should focus on a treatment for SP4 that mirrors these experimental treatments for AIDS ... the medication that this research is talking about. If we try a medicine that will block the virus from attaching to the receptors, we might get somewhere. It's just an idea, but it might work."

Sweating as if he was center stage, preparing to shoot game-winning free throws, Joel's dry mouth puckered. In one gulp, he drank the last of his water. He wiped the perspiration from his forehead once more. The mumbling within the room grew to a louder rumble. He decided to plow forward while he was on a roll.

"I have one more thing," he added. "I also found it interesting that Cheryl *didn't* get sick with SP4 when her daughter and her sister, who were exposed in exactly the same way, *did* get sick. This medical research report which I've passed to all of you also touches on the fact that if the pox-like viruses and HIV are related in the way they attack the body, then there may be an explanation for those people who are naturally immune to AIDS. For example, the article states that some people are genetically resistant to HIV, because their bodies don't make the CCR5 chemokine receptor, and that without the receptor, the virus is unable to enter the cells and infect them."

"Aren't we getting a little ahead of ourselves?" Dr. Watters tried to remain objective.

"Maybe, but I think this is important, too." Joel wasn't even going to consider stopping. "The research also suggests that this genetic mutation could be the result of a plague of smallpox which occurred over seven hundred years ago. If people can be immune to HIV, then couldn't they also be immune to SP4, especially if the two viruses move through the body in the same manner? I believe that if we test Cheryl for the CCR5 chemokine receptor, the test will show that these receptors are nonexistent in her body. Therefore, it's my belief that Cheryl hasn't been infected with SP4, because it can't enter her body. It doesn't have a vehicle to do so."

An excited energy mixed with the humming of conversation in the conference room. Under the table, Cheryl squeezed Joel's leg. An overload of emotion streamed down her face before she could verbally agree to Dr. Watters' request for more tests.

"Joel?" Cheryl competed for his attention with the rest of the individuals in the room. A warm feeling overcame her as she watched his head turn at her immediate calling.

"Yes, Cheryl?"

His genuine concern was admirable, but Cheryl could tell the doctors were anxious for him to continue with his thoughts. She'd make it quick.

"Do you think this could help Kendra, too?" Anticipation of

his answer excited Cheryl and terrified her at the same time.

"If I'm even half-way right about this, I think we can help Hannah, Kendra, and the rest of the world." He helped her from her seat to a standing position and wrapped his arms around her.

His touch was deliberate and true, of this Cheryl felt confident. She felt her worries and her fears disappear, absorbed by his strength.

"Now, you go with Dr. Watters and show them all that we know what we're talking about." He touched her forehead with his lips. While pressing his cheek against her cool skin, he realized that his head felt warm. His nerves had gotten the best of him after all. Or at least he hoped that was it.

* * *

Alexei spoke with prepared words. "Shane, it is I, your friend and colleague, Alexei Gousev."

"Alexei, my heavens, where are you?" Shane struggled for the breath to speak. He didn't want to lose his strength before he had a chance to catch up with his friend. "I've wondered about you ... where you were ... how you were doing ..." He stopped to breathe from a handheld oxygen supply.

"Did you get my letter? Did you understand my plight?" Alexei was fearful that he may have placed himself in danger by confiding in Shane.

"I did receive your letter, and I have so many questions for you. I know it takes a brave man to discuss such confidential information with respect to his country, Alexei."

"I do not blame my country." Alexei spoke with conviction. "My country and those who lead it did what was necessary. They have done what it took for all of us to survive. My country is not to blame for their actions, however ugly they seem. I need for you to hear this."

"I understand, Alexei, and I do hear you," Shane replied. "My comment is only that I have respect for you. I respect your bravery, and I care about your well-being. Where are you?"

"I am here, in Washington."

Shane's body stiffened. His heart raced at the thought of Alexei traveling all the way to the United States in the midst of such danger. What was his motive for this? "You're here ... in the city? What brings you here, Alexei? Please, be careful, the people here are not well. This virus has taken its toll. I myself am sick."

"I am aware of the state of the health of your people." Alexei didn't sound surprised by Shane's news. "Russians are sick, too. My country is fighting this disease, with as little success as I suspect your people are having."

"What makes you say that? Little success?" Shane dug for information from Alexei.

"If your doctors were able to treat this mutation of smallpox, then I do not believe you would be where you are." Alexei expanded on his previous comment. "I come not to question the capabilities of your medical professionals. I am here to help, to answer questions. I come in truth and in honor. I knew you would have questions, and I wanted to give you answers before I have to go. I've stopped here on my way to a more definite destination."

"Go where? Where are you going?" Alexei's plans intrigued Shane.

"I must leave soon. I am waiting only for my dear Sharona to join me. She is on her way as we speak. We are not safe here, or anywhere that my former colleagues may look for us. I do not blame my country, but I cannot stay there, either. Money is their driving force, their vice. They will do whatever is necessary to get paid money, and I cannot live knowing what they chose to do. However, when they realize I have left, they will not want me to live at all."

For a moment, Shane felt the pain that he heard in Alexei's voice. Reason took over, as he remembered who he was with respect to the man on the other end of the phone line. He was still the President of the United States, an evil country in the eyes of many Russians.

"Alexei, where are you now? How did you know I was sick?"

"I cannot talk now, I must rest, for I am not well myself," he said. "I will be at the steps of the Jefferson Memorial this evening. If you should want to, feel free to send a trusted colleague to meet me at seven o'clock. I will answer questions, if this person can prove that he was sent by you. Tell him to approach me from behind and to greet me by saying 'Hello, Dmitri.' After we speak, I must go. I do hope the best for you."

The phone line went dead.

Alexei slumped over on the bed, holding his abdomen and trying to extinguish the pain from the cramping. His fever had climbed, causing him to feel light headed. He closed his eyes and waited for the evening to come.

* * *

In regular rhythms, Shane breathed the oxygen that surrounded him. With each deep breath, he hoped to feel that his lungs had been filled, but they never were. The air supply lasted for less time with each inhalation. Staring at the pustules that lined his arms, he felt the urgency to work harder. He was curious to hear about any progress that had been made on the computer research. But first, he needed to set up a meeting with Alexei. He pressed a preset number on the phone, and Alan answered before the end of the first ring.

-34-

With the anxiety of an expectant mother waiting to see the color of her pregnancy test, Cheryl waited for her lab results. Still confused by the details of Joel's medical theory, she saw the big picture with a clear vision. If the theory was correct, then help for Hannah and Kendra was a possibility. On so many levels, she wanted this to work. As she prayed for him to be proven right, she squeezed her eyes closed.

"Cheryl, do you want to come with me for a minute?" Without making a noise, Dr. Watters had approached. She saw Cheryl jump as she spoke. "Sorry, dear, I didn't mean to startle you."

Cheryl seemed pleased by the surprise. "Oh, no problem. Where are we going?"

"We're heading to check the results of your test." The doctor's smile spread across her face. "I thought you and Joel would like to be present to hear what our friends in the lab had to say. Joel has already been notified and directed to meet us up there. Ready?"

"As ready as I'll ever be." Cheryl bounced into a standing position.

While she walked, she recited the silent words of one last prayer. On the way to the elevators, she debated asking about Kendra. Her curiosity won over her emotional side. "Dr. Watters, how's Kendra? Have you told her what we're doing? Did you tell her that I've been asking about her?"

"She's aware that you've been here, and she knows that you're always asking about her," Dr. Watters confirmed. "However, I haven't told her about the most recent developments. As much as I feel positive about what we're doing, I don't want to create any false hope until I'm sure we have a plan. I don't think that would be fair to your sister."

"I understand," Cheryl agreed. "I just wish she knew that things could be looking up for her. You know what they say ... a positive attitude is the best medicine. I've witnessed that firsthand with Hannah over the years."

Dr. Watters put her arm around Cheryl's petite shoulders and squeezed her in a friendly gesture.

"Let's see what the lab has to say, Cheryl. If all goes well, I'll pay a visit to Kendra."

Satisfied with the plan, Cheryl pressed the elevator call button. As the doors opened on their floor, Cheryl saw Joel in the lobby area.

"I was hoping it would be you." Joel escorted Cheryl from the elevator. "I didn't want to go in without you." He reached out for her hand and pulled her toward him. Together, they followed Dr. Watters.

"Okay, we're all here." Dr. Watters knew Cheryl was anxious for the results. So was she. "I don't see any reason to wait. Let's see the report." Pulling a single page from a file, Dr. Watters read, "The preliminary tests were done using a typical blood sample as a reference and Cheryl's blood as the test subject. The results show that Cheryl's blood is negative for CCR5 chemokine receptors."

Cheryl watched Joel throw his head back and let out an audible gasp. Uncertain if this was the answer she was supposed to want, she took his reaction as a positive sign and let out a squeal of laughter. She looked to Dr. Watters for a more definite assessment of the results.

"I do believe you may be on to something, Mr. Birmingham." Dr. Watters offered Joel a congratulatory look. "But, please, let's keep this all in perspective. This may prove that Cheryl may not be susceptible to AIDS, but we still have a lot of comparative analysis work to do to determine its connection to SP4 ... if there is one." She was cautious by nature. She'd seen too many people hurt by their hopes over the years, but this did feel right. "And do we have Kendra's results?" She dug back into the file for the final piece of paper. "Kendra's blood work is positive for the presence of the receptors."

Dr. Watters exhaled her deep breath. "Well guys, I feel good, so far. We need to further test both Kendra and Cheryl. In the meantime, I think we should work on some variations of Hannah's AIDS meds. Maybe that will help her to get stronger faster. I'll go and check on her and make that adjustment to her chart."

"And, Kendra? Can you do anything for her, yet?" Cheryl held her breath as she waited for the doctor to answer.

"I'm not sure right at the moment." Not having the answers people prayed for was painful. "But if this virus is moving through the body in the way your friend has proposed, we may begin some *experimental* treatments right away ... given her consent, of course." She stopped talking long enough to shake Joel's hand. "Joel, please stay in contact. Cheryl, I'll let you know as soon as we decide anything regarding Hannah or Kendra."

"Thank you, Dr. Watters." Cheryl's words shook with excitement. How refreshing it was not to be quaking with tears. "We'll walk with you to Hannah's room. If you need to find us later, I would check there first."

"Okay, that sounds good. I'll tell you what. Why don't you head on to Hannah's room, and I'll meet you there," Dr. Watters said. "If I move fast, I can secure a substantial amount of research help, and we could use the support. The first call I'm going to make is to the Centers for Disease Control. See you in a few minutes."

***

The morning whirlwind of activity left Shane exhausted. With limited cognitive hours available each day, he had to make an effort to stay awake long enough to speak with Alan. This was too important to wait.

"Hey Alan, how are things?"

"Shane?" Alan called into the phone. "I can hardly hear you. Are you doing okay?"

"I'm well, Alan. It must be this phone," Shane lied. "I'm just a bit tired is all. I need to speak with you for a minute, do you have some time?"

"Of course, sir."

"I've been contacted by our friend, Gousev. He's here ... in Washington."

"Gousev is here? What's he doing here? He contacted you?" Alan asked all three questions in succession, without waiting for Shane's answers.

"Yes, he's here, but I'm not sure what the motivation is for his visit." Shane paused. The ease of living was often taken for granted. Shane realized this as he struggled to breathe. "He says that he's stopped here on his way to a more *definite destination*. He claims that he contacted me to help answer any questions I might have regarding the behavior of his colleagues. He's left his country, and he's made it clear that he's not going back." Shane paused again to catch his breath. "Well, I do have some questions for him, Alan, as you well know. Most important are the questions we have about the actions of the Russians. Why did they give vaccinations before the celebration? Were they involved with the terrorists? If so, do they know how to find the cells? We're sitting here with our hands tied, and they could have the information we need to stop this."

"I believe I'm aware of all of your questions," Alan said. "If you want, I can contact Gousev and ask for the answers. Does he know the state of your health?"

"Yes, somehow he does know," Shane said. "I don't know how to contact him, but I can tell you where to find him. He's offered to meet my representative at the Jefferson Memorial at seven o'clock. I have some instructions for you to follow."

As Shane expected, Alan agreed to meet with Alexei. The two men worked together to make a list of questions for him to ask. For the most part, both men agreed that their main objective was to extract any information that could lead them to the existing terrorist cells.

"Alan, one more thing," Shane began. "When have you last checked on the progress with the Internet tracking?"

"Earlier this morning. I had phone updates with every member of our recruit team. Mark had been up most of the night working away. He must be close to something. He's like a bloodhound on a trail."

"Well please keep me posted with their progress, especially his." Shane slipped an ice chip in his mouth. His words became muffled. "I have a good feeling about where he's headed."

"I'll call you as soon as I hear something, Shane. I promise. Now, please, get some rest. We need you back and healthy again soon."

A moment of awkward silence interrupted the conversation. Shane waited before he spoke again. Would he ever be back again, healthy? Shane couldn't condemn Alan for his positive thinking and encouragement, but he preferred not to think about the future.

"Well, at least I know things are running fine in my absence." Shane complimented his colleague. "I'll talk with you soon."

Shane situated the oxygen tube in his nostrils and pulled his white hospital blanket up to hide his pox-marked complexion. In an attempt to recharge his energy for some computer activity later that afternoon, he closed his eyes to rest.

Hours felt like minutes later, as Shane was awakened by the ringing of his phone. When he opened his eyes, he saw a masked and gloved nurse standing next to his bed, adjusting his I.V.

"Nurse, what time is it?"

"Five-twenty in the evening, sir."

Shane grabbed for the phone. "Please, excuse me." He waited as the nurse closed the door behind her, and he answered his phone. He knew it would be Alan.

"Shane, it's me." Alan began talking in a quick pace. "I have Mark here with me. We're going put you on speakerphone, if that's okay with you. I think you'll be interested to hear what he's discovered."

"Let's do it," Shane said. "How far have we gotten?"

"We're just about there," Mark answered. His voice sounded distant, evidence that the speaker system had been activated. "I think I've found the final link to the terrorists' communication hub."

Shane's eyes grew large and round. He waited only a few seconds before he responded. "You're sure? What makes you believe you've found it? Where does it go?"

"Well," Mark said, "I've followed the path through the final portal. I found it on the page where I was last stuck—the mock payment form for the chemical plant web site."

"Yeah, I'm with you," Shane said.

"I moved all over that page, and I couldn't find any exit besides the obvious, which closed me out of the page, and the site, all together." Mark took a deep breath. He prepared to do some talking. "But then, my own state of exhaustion actually helped me to find the link. I was tired, and my hand was getting lazy. When I placed the mouse over the *cancel order* button and held it down for what turns out to be three seconds, I was sent through a link to another page. You'd never know it was there if you weren't trying hard to find it. It's even well hidden in the coding. Anyway, this page is an obvious posting of instruction and information for the terrorists."

"What does it say? What are the instructions?" Shane was anxious for the answers.

"This is the most interesting part," Alan said, chiming in. "The instructions are not for the terrorists, but for another, a third party. The viewers of the page are sending information to a third party who's reading the notes that are posted. The terrorists are asking for help. They're sick ... very sick, and they're asking for their contact to bring them supplies ... money is the most common request. Apparently they've realized that the vaccinations didn't protect them. They think money is the answer to everything." Or, maybe they have something else planned. Alan kept this thought to himself.

"So what are they asking this contact to do? Where are they

asking him to go? Could we get anything from this?" Shane was seated with perfect posture. His cramping and muscle aches seemed to mysteriously disappear.

"Yes, we were able to extract quite a bit of information before the server bumped us off," Mark said. "I'm sure I was identified as an unauthorized user. These guys have gotten pretty sophisticated with their Internet capabilities." He let out a chuckle at his surprise regarding their impressive operations. "Anyway, here's the crazy part. If I'm not mistaken, the message asked loud and clear for this third party to meet the senders of the messages at the Jefferson Memorial, here in Washington, at eight o'clock tonight."

Shane tore the oxygen tube from his face and threw it to the floor. His weakened strength rebounded into action, as if he'd been given the powers of a super hero. "Mark, when was this message sent? Can you tell?"

"As far as I can see, I'm almost certain it was sent toward the latter part of the evening last night," he answered.

"Mark, thank you for your hard work. It will not go unappreciated." Shane spoke in his most official tone. "Will you please remove me from the speaker phone? Alan, stay on the line."

"Done. I'm here," Alan replied. "Don't worry. We're on it." He knew what to do next.

-35-

Narrow slits of light struck Kendra's eyes when Dr. Watters entered her room.

"Hello, Doctor." She attempted to speak, but very little came out. Her condition had deteriorated over the past twenty-four hours, and she expected this visit from her doctor to be a sympathetic farewell. Having made peace with her life, she accepted this. The gift of time over the past few days had left her feeling ready to go, should that be her destiny. Her only regret was that she couldn't see her family one last time. Her memory painted a picture of Gerry holding her.

She'd spent all of her time over the last few days thinking of what she would say, should she be given the opportunity to say good-bye. Now, she hoped to use the doctor as her voice.

"I want to say good-bye." Kendra's words trailed off.

Until now, the light from the window had been sealed off. The brightness caused pain for Kendra's sensitive eyes. She squinted, trying to focus on Dr. Watters' face through the glare of sunshine that was streaming through the now open curtain. For a moment, she thought she could see a smile. It was not just a smile of empathy, but a happy expression. Surely her medication was playing tricks with her mind.

She drew in as deep a breath as she could handle and made one last attempt at a conversation with her doctor. "Please, tell Gerry I'm sorry," she mumbled. In the manner of a maze-like game, the tears rolled down her cheeks in a zigzag pattern, moving through her pox-marked complexion like skiers maneuvering a mogul covered mountain. She couldn't say anymore, because her crying choked off her words.

"Kendra," Dr. Watters tried to get her attention. "Kendra, do you hear me? You don't have to say good-bye. I'm here with good news. I think I may have something that can help you, if you're willing to let us try some new treatments with you. Nothing we'll do can make your condition any worse, but it very well may improve your health. Do I have your permission?" Dr. Watters hoped Kendra was aware enough to understand.

Her expression was confused, but her mind was clear. Although she comprehended the words one hundred percent, her reaction reflected a mix of emotions ... hope and surprise. "Of course, I'll try anything." She spoke in clear, concise words. "When can we start?"

"We can get started right away, Kendra."

"Dr. Watters?" Kendra tried to stop her from leaving the room. "Will this help Hannah, too?"

"It already has. You may have your family to thank for all of this," the doctor explained. "Their love, faith, and support is what brought this to reality. Now, you rest. I'll be back soon." Dr. Watters left the room. She had a lot to do in such little time, but her excitement to get moving chased any feelings of exhaustion from her mind and body.

***

He could see them coming, all of them. They came from all angles and monopolized the steps of the well-known monument. They were laughing at him, mocking him and the country he represented. He knew his men were nearby, but he couldn't reach them in time. Their phones weren't working. The moment played itself out as if it were a poorly written suspense film. He was the only good guy left to dwell on what he had done, or what he had failed to do. They ran around him, dancing. They were celebrating. Then the smoke, the red sky, and the darkness came.

Shane shuddered and jolted himself into a state of awareness.

His heartbeat rivaled the speed of an Olympic racer. Beads of sweat rolled from his forehead, and his already irritated skin burned. His back and legs felt the same painful aggravation. It was only a nightmare. He'd gotten used to bad dreams, but the extreme anxiety, which had begun earlier that morning, had borne itself a playwright during his last bout of restless sleep.

He waited with patience for the word from Alan. He knew that this meeting could lead them to the last of the terrorists, once and for all. Looking at the clock, he wished it were twelve hours later, when he would know the results of the day's activities.

The phone rang. It couldn't be over already. "Hello, McAlister," Shane answered. His soft voice was acknowledged by his trusted colleague.

"Shane?" Alan responded. "We have all of our men ready to go. Everything we've found points to this meeting at the memorial. I never suspected Alexei would've had such a connection to this. The Internet messages make it clear that their third party companion has been in on this activity for a while."

"I'm not sure what to make of this either, Alan. I always thought Alexei might have something to hide, but this? Was the identity clear?"

"I believe so. We're still sorting through the Internet chatter. We'll know soon enough who we're looking for. We're ready. Rendezvous should be in exactly one hour and thirty minutes. We know to take present parties into custody. I just wanted to let you know that we've identified thirteen Internet origins, which have traveled our suspected route of web activity over the past twenty-four hours. The even better news is that these same thirteen addresses have been identified to have traveled this route multiple times over the past three days. I think we've identified all that's left out there. We have Special Forces preparing to pay visits to each of these locations within the next two hours. We've got 'em now, sir ... we've got 'em."

"Alan—" Shane pushed to continue his side of the conversation.

"Yes, sir?"

"If I don't get to speak with you afterwards ... good job." Shane's hand fell to his side, as he saluted his general from the privacy of his hospital room.

"I'll call when we've completed our mission." Alan fought hard against his emotions and refused to say good-bye. "I'll speak with you then."

Shane allowed his eyes to close and prayed for an end to his nightmares. He felt the corners of his mouth curl up to form a smile as he drifted off into another period of slumber.

***

The thick denim of his jeans felt hot and heavy on his feverish skin as he moved from the Metro. He'd chosen the baggy pants to avoid this problem, but it didn't matter what he wore now. Life wasn't fair. Or was it?

Alexei followed his mapped-out route to the Jefferson Memorial. In previous visits, he'd never realized the beauty of this city. So much to see and feel existed in this capital. Signs were supposed to point him in the direction of 15th Street, SW. Where were they? His mind wandered, almost causing him to head down the wrong street. He'd been waiting for this day, but his nerves kept him from thinking clearly.

Finding a bench, he took a seat. With his shirtsleeve, he wiped the sweat from his forehead. The cool fall air felt refreshing but also brought chills to his feverish body. Studying his reflection in the mirror that morning had confirmed that visible signs of his illness had not yet appeared. He was relieved, because he didn't want to be stopped from boarding his plane later that evening. Even though he looked okay, his appearance was not a true representation of how he felt.

Without realizing it, he gnawed away at his fingernails. It was amazing what anxiety could make a person do. Struggling to find an activity to help pass the time, he searched for anything that would keep him from standing out in the crowd. Thinking became his pastime, and he wondered if Shane would choose to send someone to meet him. He expected the American contact by seven o'clock. That would give him one hour before his final meeting.

Chuckling to himself, he recognized the irony of the situation. His father was watching him, of this he was certain. Did he like what he saw? Alexei felt that he did, and that was all that mattered. This was as close as he could come to pleasing *everyone* ... something his father tried to do, but failed at. That attempt had cost his father his life, and he'd pleased no one, not even himself, in the process. Alexei felt relief in knowing that his attempt at success would at least bear fruit. He was doing what everyone wanted. They should all be pleased.

Checking his watch began as a habit and became an obsession. He now knew what it meant to have too much time on his hands. Walking closer to the monument to take in a little American history, Alexei read the mounted plaque, "... dedicated to the third President and writer of the Declaration of Independence ..."

He recited the passage. From the very beginning, freedom represented the alma mater of this country. How ironic was it that this location was his meeting place on this day? He bowed ever so slightly to the nineteen-foot bronze statue in front of him.

-36-

Staring at her feet, Sharona stepped from the airplane and moved out to the lobby. This was not her first time in America, but she felt nervous just the same. Clutching her only bag, she moved forward through the thick crowd of travelers. Alexei had not wanted her to draw attention to herself. This was easier said than done.

Moving her way around the slow walking passengers, she grasped her cell phone in her free hand. She had one call to make to confirm her plans. The time on the flight monitor read seven-fifteen. Sharona had forty-five minutes to get to her destination. At the curb outside, she hailed a taxi. Her instructions were clear.

"Jefferson Memorial," she said to the cab driver.

"No problem, ma'am." By habit, the driver reached out to take Sharona's bag.

"No. I can get it." Pulling the bag from the grasp of the driver's hand, she struggled to get it into the car.

She watched him shrug his shoulders, as he returned to the driver's seat. Sharona followed her luggage into the back of the cab and settled in for the ride. She dug into her purse for the American money she'd been given for her trip.

***

Alexei continued to read the words on the plaque in front of the monument, completely unaware of the activity around him. He shuffled to the right side of the steps of the memorial. Tossing a tissue in a waste can, he looked around for another bench where he could rest. He chose only benches that were unoccupied, wishing to draw as little attention to himself as possible. His nerves coupled with his fever made him shaky and lightheaded. He wished for a quiet room where he could relax. Rest was only hours away. The next hour would bring a new start, and it couldn't arrive fast enough.

FBI agents stationed throughout the mall and around the monument listened through sophisticated equipment as the agent in charge dispatched orders. CIA operatives were plainclothes officers, filling in around the marked stations. The agent in charge spoke into his radio. "I see company for our contact approaching from the west."

A parade of camouflaged movement throughout the area followed the comment.

"The companion has settled near the steps of the Memorial. He's dressed in blue jeans and a black hooded sweatshirt. His hood is up ... his head, down. Copy?" The responses gave the agent in charge confirmation that the contact had been identified. "The time is seven thirty-seven. Twenty-three minutes until show time."

From the command vehicle, Alan listened to the activity proceeding as planned. He switched frequencies and confirmed that everything was under way in New Jersey, Florida, and Boston, as well. His men were moving forward in Russia, waking their targets out of their deep slumber in the early morning hours. The effort was well under way.

The bag weighed Sharona down as she walked from the cab to the Jefferson Memorial. She looked around, feeling vulnerable in the wide-open setting. He'd told her ten minutes. This would only take ten minutes, and it would all be over. In ten minutes, they'd be on their way again, and she could put this behind her. Clammy with perspiration, her hands slipped from the heavy bag's handle.

The agents watched as two more contacts were identified to them.

"They must have sent multiple representatives due to their diminished health," the commander observed. "They're getting sloppy. Whatever you do, keep your gloves on. They're probably contagious."

"What'll we do with them when we get them?" an assistant to the commander asked. "I mean, it's a legitimate question. If they're so sick, will we take them to the hospital to keep them healthy until the trial?"

"As far as I'm concerned, they can all be thrown together in one hospital room," the agent in charge answered. "Our doctors are having a hard enough time treating our own people. These guys gave up their rights for treatment when they released SP4 into our world." He paused to reflect on what he'd said, but he felt no regrets. "Here we go, men. It's time to move."

Alexei stood and turned to look around. He felt a surge of activity, but he couldn't put his finger on its origin. His paranoia had painted pictures in the shadows more than once over the past few days. Still, he could feel *something*. Crowds of people walked by, but no one seemed interested in what he was doing. He settled into his seat on the bench again, realizing that Shane must've declined his offer to meet. He had one last contact to make. Then he'd be free to leave.

Sharona passed through the Memorial and moved to the backside of the steps. After having spotted Alexei from a distance, she'd succeeded at getting past him without his noticing her. Why was he so early? She'd told him eight-fifteen. She looked around again, nervously waiting for her contact to approach her.

A pair of men walked by, joking with one another. Alexei smiled at them. He didn't even notice the man on the left reach out for his arm until he'd already been forced into walking with them.

"What are you doing? Who are you?" Alexei resisted.

"Quiet," the first man said. His hood was up over his dark skin, so far that his face could barely be seen.

Alexei could make out the presence of red pustules protruding from the man's complexion. His heart stopped. Were these men sent by his government? Searching for Sharona, he tried to look behind him. He didn't want her to get caught in the middle of this. Should she arrive and find him trapped, he hoped she had enough sense to go directly to the airport and board their flight. His heart sank at the thought of her going on without him.

"Move," the commander said into his microphone. "The contacts are in transit."

Armed and ready for the word, the men moved through the paved area as if they were roaches scattering away from the light. Alexei was startled when he saw the men coming toward him. They were yelling for him and his escorts to drop to the ground. His confusion blended with the cramping in his stomach and the pounding of his head. He felt dizzy. The men on either side of him dragged him to the front and used him as a shield as they ran for cover.

Behind the memorial, Sharona thrust her bag in the direction of a third hooded individual. "I want my part of the money, now," she demanded. "You said my brother's money would be used to pay me. Here it is. I want my part. I risked my life to bring this, for his soul. For his debt that he owed to you. I did my part. I took over in your business where he left off, but it is over now. He can be in peace. But this money is mine. Arvidis would want me to have it."

"You'll get your money," he said. He didn't care what happened to her. His Middle Eastern ethnicity had taught him that woman were worthless. She'd served her purpose. He tried to make his way to a car that was parked at the street, when a uniformed agent stopped him.

"Stop where you are," the agent barked. "You've got nowhere to go, now."

Sharona turned to run, but two additional agents grabbed

her, one on each arm.

"Sharona Gousev?" the first agent asked. "You'll have to come with us."

The agents seized her and pushed her to the ground.

She sang out in words of another language. Aloud, she prayed to her God for help. Her legs fell limp, and she sank to the ground. All the while, the two agents stood over her with their guns pointed at her. Her prayers grew louder, and she dropped her head to the cement.

The men lifted her and took her away. They placed her bag in a protective covering and whisked it away.

Alexei struggled to free himself from his captors. He witnessed the man on his left retrieving a gun from his back pocket. In the direction of the FBI agents, the hooded man shot two rounds. A shot hit one of the agents on the arm, even as he tried to avoid the bullet.

Alexei drew from the little strength he had left in his body and reached out to knock the gun from the intruder's hand. In one move, he jolted his body loose from his tight grip. Another shot rang from his captor's gun. The bullet felt like a cool blade slicing through Alexei's chest. As he fell to the ground, he buckled over in pain. The voices around him merged into one sound. He fought to make out the faces of the crowd surrounding his body. His focus was on Sharona being carried away in the background.

The officers held her with strong hands. She looked in Alexei's direction. Certain she had made eye contact, she mouthed the only words she felt fitting to say. "I'm sorry."

Alexei wanted to believe those were the words she said. He struggled to keep his eyes open. Amidst the noise of the panicked street ... the sirens and the gunshots ... he closed his eyes for the last time. At last, he could sleep in peace.

***

With pride-coated enthusiasm, Dr. Watters spoke about the

report from the CDC research team. "Kendra's blood work has astonished the doctors on our team. Our comparison of her cells from only one day earlier has shown obvious improvement in her condition, enough to authorize offering this treatment option to other willing SP4 victims. Friends, we've been given the blessing of time." This concluded the doctor's announcement.

Cheryl sat with Joel and Gerry in the back of the room, leading the applause. Her tears spoke her gratitude loud and clear.

Holding her tight, Joel felt his own emotions taking charge.

Overwhelmed by his happiness, Gerry sat motionless. He'd been cleared to visit with Kendra later that afternoon.

The attendees filed out of the lecture hall, one at a time.

Epilogue

Ten Years Later

The senior class of Wakefield High School crowded around the grounds awaiting the beginning of their ceremony. Proud to be the class responsible for helping to plan this historic activity, they waited in silence out of respect for the serious tone of the event. Groups of organized individuals paraded in to fill the empty spaces behind the students.

The senior class advisor moved to the front of the stage and called the crowd to order. "Ladies and gentleman, we're ready to begin." She paused, while the few remaining voices in the audience subsided. "I welcome all of you to the ten-year anniversary of the burying of the Wakefield High School Time Capsule." A light applause filtered through the spectators. "We'll begin our ceremony with the raising of the capsule. This event will be executed to the music of the Wakefield High School marching band."

The instruments played a soft transition of the National Anthem, as the class officers lifted the canvas straps supporting the capsule. Once the structure was resting in its place, the advisor continued with the agenda of the day.

"I'd like to introduce General Alan Jackson, former Director of the Anti-Terrorism Task Force. He'll open the capsule and make an announcement regarding its relevance to this day." The teacher smiled to the guest speaker as he approached the podium.

"Thank you," Alan acknowledged. "I'm honored to be here on this day. I'm proud to relay the message of importance represented by the contents in this time capsule that was buried ten years ago." General Jackson spoke for several minutes to remind the youth in the crowd of the battles that the world had won in the war on terror. He cited newspaper articles that painted a picture of the country ten years past. He explained how the persistence and the cooperation of the whole country had overcome such a dark time. Alan recited the names of heroes who'd played integral roles in finding the criminals who were responsible for that attack.

From the side of the stage, a teenage boy watched and listened as the general spoke. Jake Lonitesci placed his hand over his heart as his father's name was announced. Feeling a strong arm drawing him close, he looked up with appreciation.

"Come on Jake," George whispered. "Let's get ready for the finale."

At the close of his speech, Alan requested the assistance of two students to gather the new items to be added to the capsule. He waited as they carried the mementos from the side of the stage. Alan explained the significance of each item as it was added to the collection. Among the items were notes of the number of democratic governments in the world as well as documentation of plans for a revised version of the UFW. When he made it to the final and most important object, he called another speaker to the floor.

"To discuss this final addition to the capsule, I ask you all to welcome Dr. Joel Birmingham to the stage."

Joel made his way from the front row where he'd been sitting next to Cheryl. Taking his place at the microphone, he began to speak in his naturally energetic tone. He displayed a framed certificate as he spoke.

"Good afternoon and welcome to a proud moment in American medical history. Today, we present to you a medical documentation that represents a most astounding find. Official confirmation has been made by the Centers for Disease Control and Prevention that a cure has been found for Acquired Immune Deficiency Syndrome ... AIDS."

The crowd broke into an applause that lasted for minutes. The roaring chased a flock of doves from their perches on the telephone wires above. The fluttering of their wings as they flew away caught the crowd's attention. Joel waited for the spectators to quiet.

"It's important to remember how this long overdue answer to a medical dilemma actually came about. Ten years ago, our world was inflicted by an outbreak of a deadly virus, SP4. This virus, a variation of smallpox, was inflicted on our nation by terrorists. In the midst of a sorrowful time, scientific links were discovered to connect SP4 to the well-known HIV virus. In an attempt to contain and control the SP4 outbreak, a double achievement occurred. The treatment that worked for SP4 came from a variation of the drug therapy that was used to treat AIDS. In the development of the SP4 medications, researchers discovered the cure for AIDS." Joel paused again. This time, he wasn't waiting for the crowd to quiet. He wanted to make certain that this point was digested by each soul in the audience.

"As I stand before you, I want to stress one fact. Had it not been for the cowardly act of those terrorists, we would not be here today. Without the mutated strain of smallpox, our theories may have never come together as they did. Some people say that everything happens for a reason. I believe the events leading to the cure for AIDS supports this statement. I thank you for coming. God bless."

Amidst the applause, Joel exited the stage and returned to the spot next to his wife. Accepting Cheryl's tight grip on his hand, he watched as Hannah wiggled her way through the aisle and squeezed in between them. She gave her mother a kiss on the cheek.

"Sorry I missed your speech, Joel," Hannah said. "My bio class ran a little over with the review for our exam tomorrow. But I'm prepared for the test."

"That's okay, sugar. I'm just happy you're here now. Your school work is more important anyway, especially if you're going to be applying to med schools in a couple years." He ruffled her hair. "Did you talk to your aunt?"

"Yeah, she stopped by the lecture hall. She said she had to

turn in a paper, but she should be here soon."

The thought of her sister in college brought a smile to Cheryl's face. Kendra was taking her classes a few at a time, but Cheryl knew her sister was determined to graduate. Kendra's determination had been known to pay off in the past.

The final speakers took their positions at the front of the crowd, but Shane had been standing for too long already. He'd seen what he came to see. Short, deliberate steps moved him from his place in the back of the audience toward the car that had been waiting for him. His slow pace was accentuated by a pronounced limp, a battle wound left from the war of his day. It had all been worth it in the end. Saluting Alan Jackson as he ducked into the passenger seat of the black Cadillac, he made a mental note to give his old friend a call while he was in town.

About the author

J.KELLY WRIGHT is employed as a Sales Manager for VistaGraphics, Inc.—a publishing and graphics company. Her current professional focus is in advertising and hospitality marketing. Additionally, she's completed a variety of free lance writing projects over the years. A graduate of The University of Pittsburgh, she grew up in Saltsburg, Pennsylvania. After spending summers at the beach during her college years, she relocated to Ocean City, Maryland, where she still resides.